A
Stolen
Kiss

A Victorian Era Novel

Books by M.A. Nichols

Regency Love Series

Flame and Ember

A True Gentleman

The Shameless Flirt

Honor and Redemption

Victorian Love Series

A Stolen Kiss

The Honorable Choice

Hearts Entwined

The Villainy Consultant Series

Geoffrey P. Ward's Guide to Villainy

Geoffrey P. Ward's Guide to Questing

Magic Slippers: A Novella

The Shadow Army Trilogy

Smoke and Shadow

Blood Magic

A Dark Destiny

Table of Contents

Chapter 1

London
Spring 1848

Not a single person was looking at Lily Kingsley. She knew this with absolute certainty, for her eyes were turning about the ballroom with more frequency than the dancers, and nary a person noticed her. Yet an anxious tickle along her spine warned her she was on display.

Ludicrous. No one was watching.

Pressing a hand to her stomach, Lily took in a calming breath and attempted to look as though nothing were amiss. And if everything went as planned, nothing would be.

"My dear, you look positively faint," said Mrs. Pratt, giving Lily a start.

Lily tried her utmost to infuse confidence into her smile. "I arrived in London a mere fortnight ago, yet I am already worn to threads."

Mrs. Pratt took Lily by the arm and gave her a motherly smile. "You must forgive your aunt for being overbearing. She never had the opportunity to present a daughter to society, and I suspect she adores having you in her care the Season. She mounted quite the battle when I petitioned to act as your chaperone for the evening."

"You have my thanks, Mrs. Pratt," said Lily with a grin. "It is nice to spend an evening with so many familiar faces from home. I know so little of my aunt's set, and it does me good to be among friends. Though I do apologize for the added burden as you have your hands quite full with the festivities. After all, I am of an age where a chaperone is becoming unnecessary."

"Nonsense, my dear," said Mrs. Pratt with a shake of her head. "You could never be a burden—except when you spout such rubbish. You speak as though you are an old maid, but you are far from it."

Lily knew better than to say such things; to even hint at her prospective spinsterhood brought naught but a flurry of denials and platitudes about the marital bliss she was certain to find. True, nine and twenty was not yet an old maid, but it was nowhere near the age of the other mademoiselles in attendance. Surely that should secure her a single evening to do as she wished.

And Lily knew precisely what that was.

Another flutter took hold of her, and Lily pressed a hand to her stomach once more, taking a quiet breath to calm the flurry of nerves. The mere thought of what was to come filled her with giddy delight, but the audacity of her plan was difficult to ignore, so Lily was stuck swinging between anticipation and dread.

The Pratts' ballroom was hardly more than a drawing room, though what it lacked in size it made up for in beauty. The parquet floor was laid out in an elaborate pattern and fastidiously polished to reflect the candlelight, and the walls were painted a soft green that reminded Lily of the fields surrounding her home; the rich color was quite striking next to the white plaster scrollwork adorning it. Truly, it was a lovely room, but at present, Lily was focused on its occupants.

Her eyes leapt from person to person, scouring the crowd for the gentleman who occupied her thoughts.

"Have you spied Mr. Farson?" Lily's throat tightened, strangling the words to a near squeak, but she fought through it.

"No, though I was told he would come and bid farewell before he leaves us for good. I do hope he will make an appearance." With a sigh, Mrs. Pratt shook her head. "I will miss having that dear boy in the neighborhood. To think of leaving this beautiful country for the wilds of Canada. And after such a brief sampling of all the Season has to offer. It's a shame he cannot delay his departure and spend a few more weeks here in London."

Hiding a smile behind her fan, Lily wondered how Mr. Farson would react to being called a "boy." Though younger than Lily by a couple of years, someone of his stature could hardly be called that.

Dropping her fan once more, Lily replied, "It was not as though he was given a choice in the matter. That inheritance was a gift from heaven. Not many younger sons have such a fine property and living dropped in their laps."

"Of course," said Mrs. Pratt, patting Lily's hand with a smile. "I would never begrudge him such a blessing, but it is difficult to see so many of your generation leaving Bristow. The world is changing too rapidly for my tastes, and I am becoming quite the curmudgeon."

Lily laughed as she was meant to and squeezed the sweet lady's arm, though it saddened her to feel how frail Mrs. Pratt had become over the years. She was by no means derelict, but time was changing her as well as their beloved country home.

"But you will say something when Mr. Farson arrives?" asked Lily, feeling quite proud that her tone remained moderate—even though she had to clear her throat before continuing. "It is quite fortuitous that he decided to visit London one final time, as I had not the opportunity to say farewell before I left Bristow."

Mrs. Pratt straightened and turned a thoughtful eye on Lily. "You are rather keen to see him."

The tone insinuated much, and Lily's face blazed bright red, her eyes darting away from Mrs. Pratt as she fumbled to salvage the conversation.

"Mr. Farson is a fine gentleman, but he is merely a childhood friend, and I wish to bid him farewell as it is unlikely that our paths will cross again in this life."

Those words were truthful enough that Lily felt only the smallest tinge of guilt at omitting the rest of it. The thought of anyone other than Mr. Farson discovering her plan was enough to set Lily's cheeks heating once more as her stomach twisted in knots. If only he had responded to her note, then she might be at ease. As it was, she was left to flounder in the dark.

Lily knew he had received her missive. Of that, she was certain. But where did he stand on her proposition? Certainly, it was odd to write to a gentleman and beg him to bestow her first kiss, but she hoped it was not a repulsive request. Convention claimed a man needed little enticement to agree to such tokens, but then again, young ladies rarely resorted to begging for one.

"Dear, you look a little peaked," said Mrs. Pratt, her brows drawing together. "Do you need to lie down? Your mother and aunt would never forgive me if your health took a turn while under my care."

Lily shook her head and ran a hand over her teal skirts. "No, Mrs. Pratt. I assure you I am well. Merely a little flustered. I have too much of my mother's temperament to be fully at ease in crowds."

Mrs. Pratt nodded. "And no doubt you prefer to be on the dance floor as well. I have never seen anyone who enjoys dancing as much as your mother. It is always a pleasure to see, for she is so light on her feet."

Smile frozen in place, Lily knew not how to respond to that gross misjudgment. Not about Mama, of course. Mrs. Simon Kingsley was notoriously fond of dancing and exceptionally light on her feet. But though Lily had inherited many of her parents' talents, dancing was not one of them—a fact that was common knowledge in Bristow.

Reaching for the dance card hanging from Lily's wrist, Mrs. Pratt glanced at the conspicuously empty spaces.

"Oh, dear," she murmured, glancing between the card and Lily. "I have monopolized you and not given the gentlemen ample space to claim dances."

Lily bit back a laugh; they both knew Mrs. Pratt's presence had naught to do with the absent dance partners even if the lady wished to pretend otherwise.

Mrs. Pratt raised a hand to someone across the ballroom, and Lily followed the lady's gaze and connected it with Mr. Pratt, who was conversing with a young (and likely eligible) gentleman; the older fellow nodded at his wife and motioned for his victim to follow. Lily's cheeks burned even brighter, and no amount of fanning set them to rights. Her eyes searched for an escape, though she knew there was no avoiding her fate.

"My dear Mrs. Pratt," said her husband as they drew closer. "I was speaking with Mr. Wimpole, and he was asking after our sweet Miss Kingsley."

Lily's mouth went dry. Poor Mr. Wimpole feigned a smile, but she knew this dance far better than the waltz; he was no more a willing participant than she. After all, it was a host's duty to ensure that all young ladies secured dance partners—by whatever means necessary.

Mr. Pratt went through the proper introductions, and the pair gave the appropriate bow and curtsy, though Lily could not think of what to say to the fellow. An apology for being conscripted into this farce was foremost on her thoughts, but it would not do to draw attention to their situation as the Pratts likely thought they were being quite subtle.

"That is a fetching gown, Miss Kingsley," said Mr. Wimpole.

Nodding, Lily glanced at the teal silk and ignored her heart as it dropped low in her chest. Not that she disliked the compliment, but it was a familiar refrain. The gentlemen felt obliged to give some bit of flattery, but honor dictated they speak the truth. So, her dress was lovely. Her coiffure was elegantly styled. Her jewelry was dazzling. But such descriptors were never applied to the lady herself.

With a few polite words, Mr. Wimpole led her onto the dance floor, and Lily wished the Pratts had chosen a more robust gentleman to press into service. Though she knew many young ladies found his lanky frame attractive, standing next to this stick of a man made her feel all the plumper.

They took their places facing each other, and Mr. Wimpole smiled at her, though it was more commiserating than warm.

"Do you live in London?" asked Lily, grasping the first topic that popped into her head.

"No, I hail from Derbyshire," came the quick reply.

Lily smiled. "That county boasts lovely countryside."

Mr. Wimpole gave her a responding grin. "I wholeheartedly agree. My heart will always belong to Derbyshire."

The first notes of the song began, calling the dancers to their places, and Lily tensed; this was a quadrille and a quick one at that. Others may enjoy such lively dances, but it required moves that only amplified Lily's gracelessness. Dancers slipped around each other, ducking under raised hands and passing through tight spaces that fit their average frames, whereas Lily nudged and squeezed her way through the steps, bumping into and colliding with anyone unfortunate enough to be nearby.

No one was watching her.

The others were too interested in their steps and partners to care about her, but knowing it was irrational did not keep Lily from feeling as though the others were watching and laughing at the great ape of a lady attempting to dance. Years of receiving comments about her ungainly size (both in good-natured jests and cruelly-minded mockery) had left Lily in no doubt that everyone noticed it and had some opinion on the matter.

"My family has visited the area several times, and I never tire of wandering the peaks," said Lily as she and Mr. Wimpole came together for a few steps.

With each pass, she continued to speak of her travels

through Derbyshire, giving her tongue free rein as Mr. Wimpole's smile grew more brittle; though he kept his eyes trained on her, his gaze became unfocused. It was an expression Lily knew well; his mind was elsewhere.

"...it was one of the most delicious things I have ever tasted," she said, her words coming at a quicker clip. "I described it to my family's cook, and she replicated it passably, but it couldn't compare to a proper Bakewell pudding."

Mr. Wimpole gave a vague nod as his eyes drifted to the other dancers.

"Have you traveled much?" she asked.

"Some, but I prefer to remain at home." He spoke readily enough, but his tone was as disinterested as his expression.

"I find new places thrilling," she said. "My parents are currently touring the Continent with my uncle and aunt, and I had thought to join them but decided to visit my Uncle Nicholas in London instead."

Even as she recognized that she ought to remain silent and leave Mr. Wimpole be, Lily's mouth continued to move, searching for the perfect subject that would engage him once more. The situation was not helped by the next dance, which was slow enough that they were forced to interact more often, and the conversational distance between the pair grew.

Her partner gave all the proper compliments and comments as their set came to its close but left with all possible haste, leaving Lily deflated. Though gentlemen likely felt they were being inconspicuous, she had seen enough of their retreating forms to be in no doubt as to her lack of enticements. Perhaps he would not have disappeared so hastily if she had found a better topic or flattered him.

Lily had no romantic interest in Mr. Wimpole, yet his rejection pained her. It was unbearable to be treated like nothing more than a chore to complete before he was free to do as he pleased; an unwanted price to pay to please the ball's host. Lily's breaths grew shallow as she clenched her jaw against the ridiculous tears prickling in her eyes; she would not add to the misery of the evening by crying. This was naught but a bit of foolish pride.

"There you are," said Mrs. Pratt, and Lily held in a cringe, reminding herself that she adored the lady.

If not for the hope of Mr. Farson's imminent arrival, Lily would've run for the nearest carriage.

"Mr. Wimpole seemed to enjoy himself," said Mrs. Pratt. There was such honesty in her eyes that Lily's heart warmed even further to the dear lady. Any unbiased observer would have seen how uninterested Mr. Wimpole had been, but Mrs. Pratt was nowhere near unbiased and couldn't countenance a young man finding Lily unacceptable.

Lily merely smiled in response, for any words would be a dishonest agreement or a truthful rejection, which would upset the kind-hearted lady.

"I do appreciate your assistance, Mrs. Pratt," said Lily, giving the most honest answer she could. "However, I am quite content to sit the next set out. I enjoy watching the dancing far more than doing so myself."

Mrs. Pratt took Lily's arm again and shook her head. "Nonsense. Every young lady longs to spend her evenings dancing with handsome gentlemen."

Yet another sign of Lily's shortcomings. No young lady would reject the opportunity to dance, and no young lady would petition a gentleman to bestow a kiss.

"In all honesty, I prefer to watch," she replied, but Mrs. Pratt opened her mouth to protest, so Lily shifted the conversation. "Have you spied Mr. Farson?"

"I do believe he arrived not long ago," said Mrs. Pratt.

Lily's heart squeezed in her chest. Her note had said to meet during the fourth quadrille, and it could be no coincidence that Mr. Farson had appeared at that precise time.

Writing that letter had taken all her courage, but Mr. Farson suited her needs too perfectly to let the moment slip by her. He was a friendly, approachable sort of man who would not bandy her audacious request about, nor was he close enough to her family to maintain ties once he left for Canada. If the evening proved an embarrassment, none but Mr. Farson would know, and Lily would never see him again.

Another such opportunity was unlikely to present itself, leaving her life devoid of that most basic experience. Every lady should know what it is like to be kissed. Shouldn't they?

Her pulse then thumped a rapid staccato that was at odds with the languid music filling the ballroom. Drawing in her lips, Lily bit down to keep them from trembling, though she could not tell if it was in anticipation or fear; both were equally present.

Mrs. Pratt raised a hand to call to her husband again. "There are some excellent bachelors in attendance who are clamoring to make your acquaintance. In fact, there is a business associate of Mr. Pratt's who is a perfect match for you. I do not see him at present, but I will have Mr. Pratt search for him."

"Do not trouble yourself," said Lily with a shake of her head as she grasped for any excuse to release herself from the next dance. "I feel a little faint at present."

Mrs. Pratt's eyes widened, and Lily hurried to calm her. "I am well enough, but I would like a few moments of quiet to gather my strength. Might I rest in your library?"

Patting Lily's hand, Mrs. Pratt nodded. "Of course, my dear. Let me have Mr. Pratt escort you—"

"I assure you that is unnecessary. I am well enough. Merely fatigued. I know my way and do not need assistance. And I would hate to pull him away from your guests."

Mrs. Pratt patted Lily's cheek. "You are a dear. I will never understand why you haven't been snatched up. Men are utter fools."

That wasn't the first time Lily had heard one of the matrons bemoan her lonely state, and she still had no response for such statements. So, she smiled and squeezed Mrs. Pratt's free hand before turning towards the ballroom doors.

Though she had assured Mrs. Pratt she was in fine health,

Lily felt a touch light-headed at the prospect of what was to come. She wove through the crowd, her eyes fixed on the doorway as her breath came in quick bursts. Lily banished the harried thoughts that whispered for her to retreat. Mr. Farson knew her intentions, and his precipitous timing was a silent acceptance of her offer; she would not abandon her plans now.

Once out of the ballroom and down the corridor, the lights faded. Only the occasional candle was lit along the way, casting the house in shadow, which appealed to Lily. It was easier to face the coming interlude while hidden in the darkness.

Silently twisting the door handle, Lily slipped into the library and found an armchair positioned in front of the dying fire. She snuck behind it and saw an elbow propped on the armrest and two sprawled legs.

Lily cleared her throat, and the gentleman jerked, getting to his feet. With the fire at his back, his features were silhouetted, but she recognized his broad shoulders and imposing physique. Though fashion demanded a trim waist on gentlemen, Lily had never admired that hourglass figure on a man, and no amount of tailoring would give Mr. Farson such a feminine shape.

"Good evening, Mr. Farson," said Lily, her eyes cast to the floor; it was a pointless exercise as his features were little more than vague outlines obscured in blackness, but she could not meet his gaze. Her cheeks reddened, her pulse fluttering like a hummingbird's wings.

The gentleman began to speak, but Lily continued. "I know my letter must have shocked you. I am quite shocked at myself for having written it…"

Lily's throat tightened, and she tried to clear it, but every muscle in her body tightened as though readying for a fight. Or to flee.

"Miss—"

"Please," she said, cutting him off once more. "I cannot imagine what you think of me for even asking, but I…"

Her words faltered as she struggled for the proper ones.

How could she give voice to the desperate feeling demanding she not surrender all her dreams? Facing a solitary life without husband or children was painful enough, but to have never experienced the heady delight of a kiss was unbearable. She could not change her marriage prospects, but she could do this.

"Clearly, you must understand, or you would not be here," said Lily in a rush. "However, I feel..." She paused. "No, I need to..."

Lily had experienced more than her fair share of awkward moments, but this was the pinnacle, and it was of her own creation. Unable to contain her nerves any further, she closed her eyes and clenched her fists.

"It is only a kiss." Though spoken aloud, the words were more for her benefit than his.

Leaping forward, Lily threw her arms around Mr. Farson's rigid form and collided with him, striking with more force than intended. Bringing her lips to his, she missed her target, and it took a second attempt before her aim was true.

Her heart seized at her ungainly movements; this wasn't the lovely experience she'd envisioned.

But then his arms came around her, pulling her flush to him, and the kiss became something more than a mere touch of lips.

Lily had imagined her first kiss many times over the years. Never once had she pictured enlisting a gentleman to give it to her. And never had she expected it to feel like this. Thoughts and nerves faded into the distance as she lost herself in the passion of his embrace. Though no expert on the matter, she was quite surprised—and pleasantly so—to sense his ardor grow. His arms drew tight around her, and his kiss held a touch of urgency, as though he could not get enough of it. Of her.

Tears filled her eyes as she reveled in the feeling of being wanted. Cherished. Though Lily knew this was nothing but a borrowed moment, the way he held her and touched her made her feel desirable. Beautiful even. Her heart expanded, filling her to capacity with utter bliss. It was so much more than she'd hoped for, and Lily could not imagine this moment ending and reverting to drab Miss Kingsley.

The kiss slowed, and Lily's hands rose to his chest when it ended. His lips hovered above hers, as though unwilling to part from her, his breath caressing her cheek. Her eyes opened and met his gaze.

"You are not Mr. Farson!" Lily stiffened, her breath hitching in her chest as her eyes widened. Frost swept through her, and she trembled at its icy touch.

The gentleman's arms did not release her, and his lips brushed hers as he asked, "Does it matter?"

Lily knew she should be shocked or horrified. Both in fact. At the very least, she should be concerned about embracing a stranger of unknown character. But those fretful sentiments melted away when faced with the desire gleaming in his eyes. Never had a man looked at her in such a manner, and Lily had not the strength to pull away.

Especially when he kissed her again.

Chapter 2

J ack Hatcher did not care for surprises. In his experience, they were nothing but a deviation from his carefully constructed plans. Structure and order were paramount to success—whether professional or personal—and any unanticipated alteration was rarely an improvement.

Except when it took the form of a beguiling lady throwing herself into his embrace. Perhaps an occasional surprise wasn't a terrible thing.

Ever since his arrival in Town, Jack's life had become a stream of parties, outings, and meetings of every variety. Such things were not an anomaly in his life, and Jack had learned to tolerate the thrust and stab of social politics, but the sheer volume during the Season was staggering. For all their pretension, society's functions were often as noisy, overcrowded, and energetic as any dockyard. And far less engaging.

A few minutes of solitude, and Jack could face the Pratts' ball once more. If not for the fellow's investments and connections, Jack would never have accepted the invitation tonight, but neither could he manage a whole evening without a respite.

Having that moment of solace interrupted had not improved Jack's mood. Nor had the lady's insistence on speaking over him. Twice.

"It is only a kiss," she whispered, after stuttering on about a letter and some other nonsense that he had no interest in deciphering.

Jack was not easily shocked, for that emotion was reserved for those too blind to see the way the world worked. People were predictable creatures, and so much of life followed clear paths that little could be deemed as truly shocking when one had the sense to pay attention. But never would he have assumed that the timid lady standing before him would do something so audacious as launching herself into his arms.

Her lips fumbled to find his, and if Jack had not been so thoroughly taken aback, he might have laughed at her clumsy attempts. But as he was about to step away, they connected, and Jack's well-ordered world upended itself. This was not his first kiss, and Jack had sampled such tokens from women far more adept than this strange lady, but something in her simple touch summoned a depth of feeling he had never experienced before.

Like some green lad, Jack stood frozen in place as his heart pounded against his ribcage. A brief bit of logic worked its way into his consciousness, telling him that she'd mistaken him for someone else and that the gentlemanly thing to do was to step away, but the press of her lips muffled those thoughts. She stood rigidly before him, but that did not mask the tremble that had taken hold of her. It called up an instinctive need Jack hadn't known was buried in his heart, driving all else from his mind as he pulled her into his arms.

The lady was taller and wider than most, but she fit perfectly in his embrace as though designed specifically for him. Jack had never felt an inkling of desire for such a large figure, but he could not argue with the rightness that emanated from her being there.

Feverish need pumped through Jack's veins, and reality faded from his mind as he lost himself in the flood of feelings coursing through him. The strength of the emotion startled him, but he could not back away from it—from her. The allure was too strong, and he was decidedly too weak. When reason took hold once more, Jack might regret his behavior, but now, he could hardly recall that anything else existed.

Only a faint glimmer of reason allowed him to slow the ardor consuming him. Though that deep-seated need begged him to surrender, Jack slowed the kiss, knowing he should end it now despite his desire to linger. The lady's hands rested against his chest, and he cursed all the layers of fabric that kept him from feeling her touch.

They stood together in silence, and the lady leaned against him as though unable to stand. Her eyes remained closed as he examined her features, and he was certain he did not know her. How had he overlooked such a lovely creature?

After her initial arrival, the lady had not met his gaze, and Jack longed to know the color of her eyes, but he was afraid to speak as any words might break the spell binding them together.

Was her hair as soft as it appeared? The room was dark enough that the brown looked nearly black, though the flickering firelight at his back caught a few red and gold highlights that gave her hair a russet hue. The flowers adorning it filled the air with their scent, leaving an indelible mark on his memory that would forever link that fragrance to this moment.

The lady's eyes opened, and they were as dark and warm as Jack had expected them to be, and she gazed at him with such contentment that Jack could not help smiling. But a heartbeat later, her eyes widened and the lady stiffened.

"You are not Mr. Farson!" Her voice was little more than a squeak.

Hearing another gentleman's name on her lips sent a flash of anger through Jack, as though someone had lit a gaslight in his chest.

Her fingers shook, and though her expression betrayed a fair amount of shock, it was the darkening of her cheeks that made Jack think the lady was mostly embarrassed. Granted, he did not favor her feeling either of those sentiments and wished she would soften in his arms once more, but Jack counted it a victory that she hadn't stepped away.

Whoever this Mr. Farson was, his lady was in no hurry to distance herself from Jack, which made that spark of anger dull to a gentle flame that warmed him through. Clearly, she did not find Mr. Farson enticing enough.

"Does it matter?" he asked. His lips brushed hers as he spoke, and he felt that whisper of a touch down to his toes.

The lady stared at him. Not up, but at, and Jack wondered why anyone ever thought a petite lady was desirable.

The firelight flickered in her eyes, drawing out hints of gold in the rich brown, and though she did not say her answer aloud, those expressive eyes spoke volumes. There were hints of chagrin and confusion, but still, the lady remained in Jack's embrace. He felt the barest niggle of pity for the poor fool, Mr. Farson. Clearly, the fellow was inept at wooing.

And though Jack might be called many things, he was no fool. Capturing her lips once more, he kissed her thoroughly. Soundly. Until he was certain that the lady could not recall Mr. Farson's name, let alone that it was he she'd intended to meet.

"Lily!"

Through the haze, Jack heard the name, but it left no impression until the interruption was repeated, and he recognized that it had come from across the room. In a flash, Jack's good sense returned to him, and sanity prevailed. The lady remained plastered to him, but Jack freed himself as she swayed like a drunken sailor before coming to her own senses.

"Lily, what have you done?" Mrs. Pratt asked, taking the young lady by the arm.

Wide-eyed, Jack stared at them. Mrs. Pratt glared in return, but his mystery lady would not meet his gaze. Her shoulders drooped, her chin quivered, and when her eyes met his for the briefest of moments, Jack saw a silent apology.

This had been no mere mistake or coincidence.

Having spent his youth in the navy, Jack had learned quite the array of colorful words and phrases, each of which streamed through his mind as he realized how pea-brained he was. He had heard of gentlemen being snared by conniving, grasping ladies, but never had he thought to willingly walk into the parson's mousetrap like some halfwit.

His teeth clicked together as his jaw snapped shut, his fists clenching at his sides. A burning fury snapped and sizzled in his heart, begging him to eviscerate the conniving lady who had caught him in this ruse, but then it turned inwards as Jack cursed himself for allowing her to bewitch him so.

Glowering at the ladies, Jack did not know what to expect of the two, but of one thing he was certain. Snared or not, he was not one to surrender, and they would come to understand why any gentleman with an ounce of sense never attempted to bend Jack Hatcher's will to his own.

·

"It is not what you think," said Lily, grasping Mrs. Pratt's arm.

"There is no other way to interpret what we just witnessed," said a lady from behind Mrs. Pratt. Lily jumped and turned to face the stranger, her stomach sinking at the sight of the lady's companion.

"It was shocking," said Mrs. Burke, with a gleeful smile that belied her statement.

"Quite," added the first lady with a nod as the pair stepped into the library.

If only someone would open a window and clear the stifling air. A cool evening breeze was just what her flushed skin needed. Perhaps then she could think.

"Ladies, please," said Mrs. Pratt. "I am certain there is some explanation."

Lily's head dropped, and she wrung her hands, wishing she could properly explain it all. The gentleman remained silent, though there was no mistaking the crackling energy radiating from him. Forcing herself to meet his eyes, she flinched at the fury she found there. Had she imagined the man who had held her so tenderly?

"Please allow me to explain," said Lily, though she knew not how to describe such shame.

"There is no explanation that can undo the damage that has been done," said Mrs. Burke with a sad shake of her head that was as false as the paste jewelry around her neck. "Unless there is a joyful announcement to make?"

The other lady nodded, her eyebrow arching.

Lily chanced another look at the gentleman, but he grew more sinister with each word the ladies spoke. Her stomach twisted itself into knots as she turned away from his glare.

Leaning forward, Mrs. Pratt whispered, "I am sorry, my dear. You were gone for nearly a half-hour, and when I came looking for you, Mrs. Burke and Mrs. Clogg were already there. No doubt looking for some scandal to stir up. I should have kept a closer watch—"

But Lily shook her head. There was a price to pay for this folly, but no one deserved to shoulder that burden but herself.

"No announcement is necessary," said Lily. "This was nothing but a misunderstanding."

Mrs. Clogg huffed. "That was quite a *misunderstanding*."

"You two looked quite intimate," added Mrs. Burke with an insinuating tone. Turning her gaze to the fellow, she added, "Are you not going to do your duty?"

"There is no duty to fulfill," said Lily. After everything that had occurred this evening, her heart felt wrung out, though it was thumping a rapid beat against her ribcage.

"Mr.—" Lily began, only to realize that she didn't know the fellow's name and had nothing to add to that appellation. And her pause admitted as much to everyone present. Mrs. Pratt gave a quiet groan.

Mrs. Clogg abandoned all pretense and grinned with a satisfied gleam in her eye. "You are not even acquainted?"

"I would say they are more than acquainted," replied Mrs. Burke.

"Please, you do not understand," said Lily. "This was nothing but a misunderstanding."

"Do you often throw yourself at strangers, Miss Kingsley?" asked Mrs. Burke, tapping her fan against her hand as she watched Lily through slitted eyes.

Mrs. Clogg leaned close to her companion and whispered with enough volume that everyone was privy to her words, "Some ladies have no other options, you know. The poor dear."

Lily pressed a hand to her stomach, as though that might calm the raging nausea that accompanied those toxic but true words.

"Ladies, please. Miss Kingsley is a good girl and does not deserve your censure!" said Mrs. Pratt. Wrapping an arm around Lily's shoulders, she stared down the others. "Sometimes love can blossom in an instant, and Mr. Hatcher and Miss Kingsley have developed a whirlwind romance. That is all. We should be congratulating them."

It would be easy to say yes. Saying that simple word would allow Lily to maintain some semblance of dignity. A yes would transform her from the sad, desperate near-spinster who had to connive her way into a brief romantic interlude into a lady so desirable that a gentleman had thrown aside caution to be with her. Her pride begged her to concede to Mrs. Pratt's fantasy.

As of now, Mr. Hatcher had not spoken a word. He stood there, silently watching the whole scene with obvious distaste. No gentleman in such a position would do anything but his duty, and Lily could easily force the issue, yet no matter how much her shame begged her to take the convenient escape, it could not outweigh the obligation she had to Mr. Hatcher. This was her folly and her price to pay.

"I assure you it was a mistake and not a romance," said Lily. Her voice was steady, for which she was eternally grateful, though she could not raise her gaze from the floor. "I mistook Mr. Hatcher for another. He is only guilty of being in the wrong place. The fault lies on my shoulders."

Mrs. Burke laughed. "You expect us to believe that you arranged an assignation with another gentleman?"

The derision in her tone was enough to bring tears to Lily's eyes. She tried to dispel them, but they continued to gather without bidding. Her lips pinched, and she fought against the wretched things. Why could she not maintain her composure? Why must her tears always betray the emotions gathering in her heart?

"Believe it or not, it is the truth." Though Lily fought to keep her voice calm, her words faltered.

"And where is your mystery beau, Miss Kingsley?" asked Mrs. Clogg. "If he intended to meet you, why has he not arrived?"

There had not been time enough to consider that question before, but now, Lily was forced to acknowledge that Mr. Farson had neither arrived nor sent word. He simply hadn't shown, saying with silence far more than a simple rejection. Facing that truth was painful enough on its own, but having to do so in front of those who found joy in her humiliation was more than Lily could bear. Chin trembling, she fought to keep the tears from growing, but the best she could do was fix her gaze on the floor so those carrion feeders could not see how thoroughly her heart was breaking.

"Even if we were to believe you," said Mrs. Burke, "that does not excuse Mr. Hatcher's part in this farce."

Hoping that her voice would not fail her, Lily said without hesitation, "It does not matter. I absolve Mr. Hatcher of any responsibility or duty towards me. He is blameless."

Lily had hardly placed a period at the end of that statement before Mr. Hatcher moved. With a speed that did little to soothe her injured pride, the fellow fled the room, stalking past the ladies without a moment's hesitation or backward glance.

Mrs. Burke and Mrs. Clogg followed in kind while Mrs. Pratt called after them, desperate to mend the tattered remains of Lily's reputation. But one could not beg for mercy from the merciless, and those harpies would never remain silent with such gossip to spread.

The strength seeped from Lily, and she sank into a nearby chair. Curling inward, she dropped her head into her hands, covering her face as though that would block her from the storm of self-recrimination.

She should never have come to London.

...

The pavement felt Jack's wrath with each pounding footstep as he stormed through the streets of London. Ignoring the questioning looks from passersby and the tremulous offers of assistance from servants as he arrived home, Jack climbed the stairs to his bedchamber, not pausing until the door was shut behind him. He yanked off his jacket and ripped his cravat from his throat. The deuced thing tangled in the shirt collar, and his frustration only mounted as he threw it aside.

Unable to sit still, Jack continued to walk, pacing the room as he cursed at himself in every combination and variation in his extensive repertoire. What a fool he'd been. An unmitigated fool! For all his purporting to be a man of sense and good judgment, he had willingly ensnared himself in the lady's trap. He cursed at himself for not stepping away when he'd had the chance.

What had happened to him?

With a defeated grunt, Jack threw himself onto the armchair facing his fire. Slouching, he leaned against his elbow, his gaze turning to the blazing fire without seeing the flames.

One does not merely stumble into such a compromising situation, and one does not lay a trap only to release the beast snared in it. Yet she had released him from any obligation.

His free hand tapped against the leather arm, and Jack mused about that bizarre twist. He had met debutantes and matrons who could outflank even the greatest military strategist when it came to the marriage battlefield. Jack's intractableness was well known, and tonight could merely be the first step in a complex campaign.

Jack Hatcher may be in trade, yet many an eligible lady had thrown herself in his path. The upper echelons of society may sneer when they spoke those two little words—in trade—but that did not preclude them from chasing after a wealthy husband from among the tradesmen. With enough money, they were willing to overlook such a *faux pas*.

Reaching for the basket beside his chair, Jack placed it on his lap and was frustrated to see only a pair of socks inside it. His hands itched to do some proper work, yet this would take only a few minutes to darn. It would have to do. Threading the needle and positioning the darning mushroom, Jack set to work. Though they required only a simple mend, he contented himself by adding a pattern into the stitching that he had learned in Africa.

Jack worked the needle through the fabric, and he could almost smell the salt air and feel the rocking of the ship. It had been years since he had stepped aboard a boat, yet every time he worked on the mending he was transported back to that time. While there were reasons aplenty to avoid such memories, this was one of the few that brought him peace. Doing his own sewing had been a necessity during his voyages, but now, Jack was loath to hand the task over to a servant as the methodical work had a way of focusing his thoughts.

Stitch after stitch, Jack puzzled over that evening, thinking through the ramifications of tonight's events. No doubt there would be rumors, but they were unlikely to hinder his negotiations. His business partner would know how to handle the Pratts; Silas had more tact with such delicate social politics. Though Mr. Pratt was not a significant investor himself, he was surprisingly influential. And if Silas's subtlety did not work, Jack would find a way to convince the gentleman to forgive this minor indiscretion. He would not allow some calculating young lady to ruin his business's future.

What would her next tactic be?

Jack mused over that, but when he pictured her in that mercenary light, he felt decidedly uneasy. His instincts had successfully led him through life, and they insisted the lady was not underhanded. There was something so genuine in her surprise and protestations that Jack struggled to hold onto his animosity. The best liars feigned innocence as well, but this felt like no act. Her fight for composure seemed earnest, and if he were to place money on it, he would bet that her trembles and faltering words were honest signs of embarrassment and shame.

And Mrs. Pratt had handed her a plausible explanation behind their compromising situation, yet the lady had rejected it, admitting the truth at great personal cost to her pride and reputation. If she was to be believed—and Jack's instincts were saying it was so—the lady had sacrificed her dignity and honor for him. That was admirable.

What was it about the lady that had so beguiled him? She was by no means an obvious beauty, but merely the thought of those warm eyes gazing into his and the feel of her in his embrace filled him with a desire to seek her out again.

It was absolute nonsense. Jack Hatcher had never been ensorcelled by even the greatest of beauties, and he was not about to surrender to Miss Kingsley.

Lily.

The name suited her.

Jack snorted at his ridiculousness. Viper was a better moniker. In his thirty-three years, Jack had seen much of the world and its machinations. He would not allow himself to be blinded or trapped by some lady, and if she forced the issue, she would soon discover why few stood against him.

Chapter 3

It was a sad day when a fellow couldn't get a moment's peace in his club, and Colin DeVere's day was decidedly sad. It was not the shabby coffee shop, which served as their meeting place, nor the weak coffee that had him in a dither. Nor the fact that his pilfered newspaper was so worn that its folds were fraying and the ink was fading. No, it was the sight of all those happy couples announcing their forthcoming nuptials that dampened Colin's spirits.

"What has you in such a foul mood, DeVere?" Kempthorne asked with that flippant laugh of his. Though Colin did not mind a good ribbing from his clubmate, his mood was far blacker than foul and in no state to suffer Kemp's jests.

The fellow dropped onto the adjacent armchair, and Colin ignored his persistent questions until Kemp leaned forward to see what held his attention. Shifting the newspaper so that the engagement announcements were no longer visible, Colin nodded towards another article.

"'*Water Shortages Continue in Southeast London*'?" Kemp read aloud as he frowned at Colin. "Whyever do you care about that?"

With a shrug, Colin folded the paper and tossed it aside.

"It wouldn't have anything to do with a certain gentleman

whose name we swore never to mention?" Kemp asked with an arched eyebrow. "I hear he is investing vast amounts in the Southend Waterworks Company."

Colin's teeth clenched together at the mention of *him*. Surely a gentleman's club should be a respite from the cares of daily life, yet he found none.

Then Massey looked up from his book to add, "There is more afoot than mere investments. I heard tell that last night *he* was found in a compromising situation with a lady at the Pratts' ball."

Kemp set down his cup. "The Pratts?"

"Mr. and Mrs. Barrington Pratt," said Massey with a vague wave. "They're here for the Season from some little town in Essex."

Kemp cocked his head to the side. "I am not familiar with them."

"I cannot think why you would be," said Massey, glancing back at his book. "Though well-off, they're not well-connected. I doubt your family travels in the same circles."

With a clink of china, Arnold called out from his corner. "Dash it all, get back to what you were saying. What is this about Hatcher?"

The other fellows in the area grumbled and hissed over Arnold's use of the name, and he quickly amended his statement.

"What were you saying about *that fellow*?" asked Arnold, leaning forward in his seat. "If he's no longer in the field of battle, then the rest of us might have a chance."

Massey chuckled into his coffee. "Yes, because all the matchmaking mamas are anxious for their daughters to wed reprobates with pockets to let."

The gentlemen let out a roar of solidarity, raising their cups to that.

Massey continued to look at his book as though he were not keenly aware of the ears awaiting every detail. "The most astonishing thing is that the lady in question was a not-so-young lady from a well-heeled family but not one of any consequence or connection, and certainly not a contender for the title of Mrs. Jonathan Hatcher."

Another round of groans accompanied Massey's use of *his* name.

"Settle down!" barked Arnold, his eyes locked on Massey.

But the fellow let the silence drag out as he feigned a greater interest in his coffee and book. Only when properly prevailed upon did he reveal the name of the lady involved, which elicited another raucous response.

Kemp looked at Colin. "When I settle down, I would prefer a lady who looks like a lady, but I suppose there is no accounting for taste."

"Not that it matters," added Massey, "for *the fellow* refuses to toe the line and left the poor lady in the lurch."

And that set off even more discussion, speculation, and a few colorful epitaphs cursing Jonathan Hatcher's honor. Not that *his* behavior surprised Colin in the slightest, for Hatch had not an honorable bone in his body. Not even when dealing with those he called friend.

In a flash, a plan formed in Colin's mind. It was simple, but that did not negate the impact it might have—if handled properly. Hatch had remained unchallenged for far too long and deserved a lesson in honor.

"That is quite the story, Massey, but not the whole of it," said Colin.

Silence fell as the gentlemen watched with rapt attention, and he held back a laugh. For all their mockery of ladies' wagging tongues, the gentlemen were no better when there was a story to be had.

"They say it was a touch more than an impassioned embrace," said Colin, sipping from his cup with a raise of his eyebrows. Those little words "they say" were such a pair. They were vague and tantalizing and held the speaker responsible for nothing the listeners may infer. Perhaps his words bordered on falsehood, but they were more implication than outright accusation, and that distinction allowed his honor to rest easy.

"Nonsense," said someone from behind Colin, though he didn't catch which gentleman had spoken. "I cannot believe that of Hat—" The fellow shifted his words before he finished that forbidden name. "—*him*. It is ungentlemanly."

Colin scoffed, dropping his cup onto the dish below. "His father may have been a poor country gentleman, but Jonathan Hatcher is nothing but an uncouth tradesman."

There was a rumble of agreement from the group, and Colin continued, "I have known him for many years, and I can attest to his utter lack of honor. He is a bounder of the worst sort."

With each word, Colin's muscles tensed, and that frisson of anger grew. Jonathan Hatcher was all that and worse. If not for Jack's lies and betrayal, Colin's life would be vastly different. As the others digested the gossip, Colin lost himself in thoughts of what-ifs and if-onlys.

...

With a few quick scratches of his pen, Jack worked through the figures in his ledger. Though he had never struggled with sums before, he found himself crossing out yet another incorrect entry. If he continued in this vein, he'd need to surrender the task to a clerk.

The door to his office opened, accompanied by the rattle of china. The newest of his clerks, Tims, balanced a tray laden with tea and cakes on one arm while nudging the door open with his other. But even once he made it inside and had the tray firmly in hand, the dishes trembled as the lad dropped his gaze away from Jack.

Tip-toeing across the room, Tims stood before the massive desk, his lips moving though no sound emerged. Jack glanced at him, and Tims blanched as though he expected to be eaten alive. It was true that Jack was peckish, but he far preferred the treats on the tray to some lanky lad. It had been a while since they had employed a new clerk, and Jack had forgotten how skittish they could be. Of course, the black atmosphere filling his office did not help the situation, but Jack was in no mood to reassure false fears.

With a dismissive wave, Jack motioned to a corner of the desk, and the clerk dropped the tray and scurried away.

But Tims paused at the doorway.

"Have you heard from Mr. Thomas?" asked Jack, scratching another figure into the ledger.

"No, sir," said Tims. He cleared his throat. "But there's a Mr. Nicholas Ashbrook to see you, sir. He said it was urgent. And of a personal nature."

"I am occupied."

Tims nodded, but he didn't move. "Begging your pardon, sir, but he insisted. Said he wouldn't leave until you spoke with him."

"Be that as it may, I am otherwise engaged."

But an older gentleman shoved past Tims, his expression almost dour and foreboding enough to impress Jack. However, his years at sea had taught him the difference between those capable of cruelty and those who feigned it, and this gentleman was all bluster.

"Mr. Jonathan Hatcher, I presume," said the fellow, staring down his nose at him. Rather than meeting the gentleman's gaze, Jack returned to his work.

"Are you so rude as to ignore me?" asked Mr. Ashbrook.

"Need I remind you that it was not I who barged in uninvited?" Jack asked with a few strokes of his pen.

"As is my right," said Mr. Ashbrook, punctuating his statement with the pound of his cane.

At that, Jack laid down his pen and settled into his chair to examine the fellow. But when he spoke no further, Mr. Ashbrook's complexion grew more apoplectic.

"You, sirrah, are a cad!" he said with another stamp of his cane.

This was not the first time he had heard such accusations

against his honor. There were far too many gentlemen who believed they could dabble in speculation and reap great rewards, only to discover they'd lost everything. Too many allowed entitlement to blind them to the truth, and in such cases, Jack made a ready scapegoat.

Or so they thought.

Jack gave him a quelling glare, and the irritation that had plagued him over the last few hours eased at the sight of Mr. Ashbrook's arrogance faltering. "I am not acquainted with you nor do I know which venture you are referring to, but you undertook the risks. If you chose to invest wildly, I am not responsible."

Mr. Ashbrook straightened again, though his bluster was decidedly deflated. "I am not speaking of business. I am speaking of my niece. You compromised her and then fled like a coward."

So, last night had been a ploy, and this was merely the next step in Miss Kingsley's elaborate plan. Holding in a sigh, Jack turned his gaze to his ledger. In normal circumstances, being proven correct was a joyful experience, but in this instance, his heart grew heavy.

"She is in my care while her parents are touring the Continent, and I will not allow you to destroy her reputation with impunity," said Mr. Ashbrook.

Jack huffed. "Is it to be pistols at dawn then? I warn you I am an excellent shot."

"Insolent blackguard," growled Mr. Ashbrook. "You would make a mockery of both her and my honor?"

Jack leveled another hard look at the fellow; he quailed, his complexion paling, but Mr. Ashbrook remained firm.

"It was a simple misunderstanding," said Jack. "Miss Kingsley mistook me for someone else. She fully absolved me of any duty in front of witnesses."

Mr. Ashbrook's mouth twisted into a frown. "She is a headstrong girl like her mother. Neither of them has the sense to understand what is best for them. You must do your duty."

"You would have a cad marry your niece?" asked Jack with a raised eyebrow.

"I would have the man who impugned her honor do right by her."

"It was she who kissed me. If her honor is impugned then her beau—who was the intended recipient of her amorous advances—should make it right."

Mr. Ashbrook stiffened, his eyes narrowing, and Jack met the fellow's gaze without hesitation. Mr. Ashbrook broke away first, turning away with a sharp frown. "I see there is no point in prevailing upon your honor—for you have none. Mistake or not, you had your fun with her and now refuse to behave as a gentleman ought."

"I am no gentleman," said Jack, crossing his arms. "A fact that your set is more than happy to remind me of when it suits them. Though they are willing to embrace me when I help them grow their coffers. Now, you will leave my office and never darken my door again, or I shall show you why most are not willing to speak to me as you have."

The fellow gave a good show of it. Truly, he did. Mr. Ashbrook looked as though he was of a mind to do battle with Jack, but he turned tail and fled, leaving Jack doubly disappointed. Neither Mr. Ashbrook nor Miss Kingsley was proving to be what they claimed.

Returning to his ledger, Jack grabbed the pen and rolled it between his fingers. His eyes followed the numbers, but they made no impression on his mind.

"I see your mood has not improved," said Silas, leaning against the door frame.

"It has been a trying day," said Jack, forcing himself to pay attention to the figures.

"And a trying night if what I hear is correct," said Silas.

"You are not going to lecture me as well, are you?" asked Jack, slamming his pen to the desk, and Silas dared to smirk at that and slide into the chair opposite.

Resting his elbows on the chair arms, Silas steepled his fingers and watched Jack with a hint of a smile. Having spent much of his life aboard ships, Silas Byrnes was as weather-beaten as one would expect of a former sailor, but there was a lightness in his eyes and a paternal air to him that belied the shrewd mind lurking beneath his greying hair.

Silas chuckled. "You are in a fine temper today."

"And you are not helping it," replied Jack, crossing his arms.

"I wasn't intending to help," said Silas. If not for the years of camaraderie they shared, Jack would be quite tempted to give the fellow a setdown that would send that smirk fleeing for cover.

"You are trying my patience."

"Growl all you like, Hatch, but I have no intention of leaving until I get a civil word from you," said Silas. "I rather like our staff at present and have no interest in finding new clerks because you scared off this lot."

Jack's expression pinched, his brows deeply furrowing. "I have never mistreated anyone in my employ, and I do not mean to change that."

Silas's own brows rose. "I am well aware of that. I simply wished to remind you of that fact, for you seem quite determined to forget it this morning."

Letting out a sigh, Jack scrubbed at his face. "As I previously stated, it has been a trying day.

Reclining in his armchair, he folded his arms and allowed his gaze to drift off into nothing. There were several long moments of silence before Jack finally asked, "What do you know of the Kingsleys and the Ashbrooks?"

With a thoughtful nod, Silas said, "We've had dealings with them in the past." When Jack gave him a surprised look, Silas added, "Mr. Ambrose Ashbrook owns Newland Mills in Lancashire. His brother-in-law, Mr. Simon Kingsley, is invested in it."

Jack cast his thoughts back and recalled that particular Mr.

Ashbrook. He'd reminded Jack of Silas in many ways. Both gentlemen were at ease with others and had a knack for the more social aspects of business, which was precisely why Jack left Silas to handle the public side; sailors and engineers were far more to his liking than politicians and investors.

Though not well acquainted with Mr. Ambrose Ashbrook, Jack knew the fellow's reputation. Not so much his social standing—which meant little to anyone other than society—but his business dealings. Those indicated a fellow's true nature far better than how he navigated a ballroom or treated his peers. Many a "gentleman" acted the part when it came to bowing and scraping at the altar of society, but when investments were involved, scruples became a fluid thing. Or non-existent altogether.

But not with Mr. Ashbrook. If Jack's sources were to be believed. And they were. Hatcher & Byrnes's shipping contract with Newland Mills was one of their least profitable, but working with a gentleman who truly deserved that appellation was worth the meager earnings.

Jack knew nothing of the fellow's brother-in-law, but knowing that the Kingsleys were closely aligned with Mr. Ambrose Ashbrook brought a modicum of relief. Though the Ashbrook he'd just met did little to recommend the family, Mr. Ambrose Ashbrook's connection gave Jack reason to think more kindly about his niece; perhaps she was as honest and forthright.

"I know Miss Lily Kingsley is not one of society's darlings, but she is generally respected," said Silas with an air too pointed to be anything but a direct jab at Jack's current situation.

"Then I suppose you've heard about last night's debacle," grumbled Jack. "It is empirical proof that I should never mingle. I blame you for abandoning me to my own devices."

However, even as he expressed that regret, thoughts of Miss Kingsley eroded any such sentiments. His fingers brushed against the leather arms of his chair, as though feeling her. The memory of her lips brought back the same warmth that had coursed through his veins the night prior. It was ridiculous. He was no lad to be so undone by a lady, but Jack could not deny she was alluring.

When he emerged from those thoughts, he found Silas watching him with eyes that held too much of a challenge to be ignored. Though Jack certainly tried.

"If you have something to say, then out with it," grumbled Jack.

"You will not offer for the young lady?"

Jack huffed and shook his head. "I would think that you, of all people, would understand how unappealing a marriage of duty is."

Silas's eyes narrowed, and he leaned forward, tapping the edge of Jack's desk with a pointed finger. "I, of all people, understand how important it is to do one's duty. My first marriage may not have been a happy one, but I have never regretted doing what I must. Its blessings far outweighed its burdens."

Jack huffed. "And it helped that you were at sea for most of it."

"Perhaps," said Silas with a begrudging nod. "But for all the frustration and pain it caused me, I would not undo it, for that would erase my children and grandchild, and I cannot imagine my life without them."

Silas's gaze grew unfocused for a moment as his thoughts turned inwards. "And you might say that without Deborah, I would not have met my dear Judith, who has given me more joy and happiness than any man deserves."

Crossing his arms, Jack tried to keep the impatience from his face. Silas had lectured many a time about the virtues of matrimony, and Jack was no more eager to enter that state than he had been the first time Silas had broached the subject; however, Silas's heartfelt words did not deserve such an apathetic reception.

"You needn't look so sour," said Silas, his brows lowering and his lips twisting into an expression that was at once exasperated and amused.

Forgive me, but you do like to wax poetic about my need
for a wife, and the topic is tedious."

Silas shrugged. "You need a wife."

"And you think some lady who threw herself into my arms
by mistake is the solution?" Jack didn't bother hiding the sar-
casm steeped in that statement.

Silas answered with another shrug and a smirk added for
good measure. "The situation has you at odds, which is your
conscience telling you what you should do. If you felt no guilt
over your part in it, you would not think twice about abandoning her. And you certainly would not be growling at the clerks
and scowling like a miser facing down a bill collector."

Jack caught himself before his expression darkened,
though he greatly desired to scowl, in part due to the smug way
Silas spoke, but also because the fellow was right. Life had
taught Jack prudence and caution, and for him to act rashly or
behave in a manner that roused his conscience was a rare thing.
Though there were plenty who attempted to inspire that emotion in him, he was not one to be easily swayed by the unin-
formed and narrow opinions of others. Yet he could not deny
that he was troubled by a niggling of guilt concerning Miss
Kingsley. If not for that, he could simply bid her *adieu* and continue his life without a second thought.

Perhaps.

"She was meeting a beau," said Jack, waving aside the er-
rant sentiment. "That fellow can repair her reputation in a
trice."

A single eyebrow crept up Silas's forehead. "And many a
silly beau has been frightened off by a sullied reputation. What
then?"

"Then he is not a lover worth having. Any fellow who allows
himself to be driven off by nothing but a bit of gossip is a coward."

Silas gave a decisive nod. "Too right. And I suppose if that
is the case with Miss Kingsley's gentleman, she will be better off
without him and all the others who will shun her as a result. It

was her mistake, and it is only right she bears the consequences alone."

Jack's chest burned at the unhappy picture Silas painted. His fingers tapped against the desk in a rapid staccato as shame took root in his heart and spread.

"You are goading me," he muttered.

"There would be nothing to goad if I were not in the right," said Silas, getting to his feet and giving him a final look so full of stern disapproval that Jack felt like a lad being dressed down by his father. There was no doubt that in this instance, he'd been found lacking, and that thought haunted Jack long after the gentleman strode out of the office.

Chapter 4

Twirling the stem of a leaf in her fingers, Lily examined the trees lining the pathway, feeling altogether grateful for the cover. Though the rain had cleared, clouds choked the skies, threatening yet another downpour. This spring was determined to be wet and miserable, and Lily hoped her parents were enjoying finer weather in Italy. And that her umbrella would be sturdy enough if the heavens opened once again.

The park was surprisingly busy for a day with such questionable weather, but it was the first rainless afternoon since Lily had arrived in London, and everyone was taking advantage of it.

"Only a fool would sit at home when the Park beckons," Aunt Louisa-Margaretta had declared as they mounted the carriage steps.

In truth, Lily was grateful for the time out of doors. The city air was by no means fresh, and this was one of the few patches that was not as clogged with the foul stench of humanity. It was not as pristine as the grounds around her home in Bristow, but the rain had cleared the perpetual fog clinging to the city, and Lily could pretend she was once again in the country.

They had taken the obligatory turn in the barouche, but

Aunt Louisa-Margaretta was quite determined to do more than the obligatory today. Scandal and gossip could be curtailed, and their resultant damage healed—with the right steps. However, Lily had not the skill for nor the interest in joining that delicate dance.

Watching her aunt and two cousins-in-law holding court, Lily wondered why they were so fractious about the situation. Her cousins had rallied around their mother-in-law to do all they could to repair the damage done, but neither they nor Aunt Louisa-Margaretta recognized that the others' detached treatment of Lily was precisely what it had been before that ill-fated kiss. The rumors about last night's debacle had done nothing to alter Lily's standing among them; she had been beneath their notice before and remained so now.

As it was, Lily was left to follow them about the park, strolling along the tree-lined pathways as the ladies called out to anyone with whom they could claim even the slightest acquaintance. The new arrivals always gave Lily the proper nods, bows, and curtsies, but then treated her with the same disinterest they always displayed.

Stepping apart from the group, Lily stared at the trees as she twirled the leaf in her fingers. No one noticed her growing distance, for which she was grateful. She could hardly stand another quarter of an hour listening to their jabbering. Scowling at herself, Lily sent out a silent apology for that uncharitable thought. Aunt Louisa-Margaretta and her cousins-in-law were doing what they thought best, and it was unkind of her to resent it.

Pretending to find the tree especially interesting, Lily turned her face away from the crowds and stared at the canopy of green to hide the blush spreading through her cheeks. What had she been thinking? Lily recalled all her reasons to kiss Mr. Farson, but they seemed ridiculous at present. This whole trip had been a mistake. She should be touring the Continent with her parents. Having accepted an invitation to travel with Uncle

Graham and Aunt Tabby, Mama and Papa had attempted to ca-
jole her into joining them, but London had been so alluring. A
final Season to bid farewell to her life as an eligible young lady.

Lily huffed at the ludicrous thought, for she had never been
"eligible." Unmarried, yes. Available, most certainly. But eligible denoted a level of desirability that Lily had never possessed.

Fluttering her eyelashes to stave off the tingle of tears, Lily
blinked as though nothing were amiss and dropped the leaf to
the ground. A covert glance around her, and she was certain no
one was noticing her.

Spinster. The word haunted her.

Like a clever predator, it shadowed her steps, drawing ever
closer until ready to pounce. It was an unwanted description of
an unwanted woman. Something impossible to ignore when the
world around her fixated on it. Lily was no fool; she'd known
her chances of marrying had never been great. How could she
find a partner for her life when it was nigh impossible to secure
a partner for a dance?

Yet still, she had hoped. It was a silly, unrealistic sentiment,
but Lily had clung to it. Somewhere, somehow a gentleman
would see her—the real her. Not the outer shell so many found
unappealing but the beauty of her heart and soul.

Of course, there were times when Lily dreamt of a gentleman falling madly in love the moment he laid eyes on her, but
even she knew that was too fantastical to happen. No, the gentleman would start as a friend or acquaintance, but as time
passed, that relationship would deepen and grow into the type
of love her parents shared.

But now, it was time to accept that she inspired no such
sentiment, no gentleman desired her, and she would be forever
Miss Kingsley. In Mr. Hatcher's arms, those wild imaginings
had become a reality, but when the passion faded, Mr. Hatcher
had fled as readily as any gentleman conscripted into service.

Lily's heart hung heavy in her chest. Though she had spent
many an hour wondering what it was that others found distaste-

ful about her, she was no closer to understanding it. In her family's eyes, she was beloved and precious, but so many others were intent on reminding her of her worthless state. Even Mr. Hatcher.

Wandering along the lane, Lily found herself delving deeper into those maudlin thoughts until they overwhelmed her. For once, she was heartily grateful that no one paid her any heed, for she was in no fit state for conversation.

.

There was something particularly calming about a stroll through nature. Jack preferred to do so at night when others were in for the evening and only the moon and stars were there for company; then his feet could march mindlessly along as he mused about the goings-on in his world without distraction. It was as though London were his alone.

However, there was nothing particularly calming about a stroll through Hyde Park in the afternoon. In his haste to find a bit of solace, Jack had set off for his next appointment on foot, hoping a few minutes alone in that verdant patch of earth would calm the tumult consuming his mind. But the lanes and roads were filled with people, coaches, and horses. Like a teeming anthill, they charged about their world with endless energy for their meaningless tasks.

No matter how he avoided attracting their attention, the toadies of Town invariably attempted to engage him in conversation. As they had nothing of import to occupy their time, they assumed all others were the same, but Jack refused to waste precious moments engaged in empty babble. With a nod of acknowledgment, Jack plowed ahead, never allowing his steps to lag; luckily, the upper class had not the determination to bother chasing a moving target and soon abandoned their quarry.

But one lady had the power to alter his course. As he turned onto a new path, he spied Miss Kingsley standing to one side.

His feet veered back, returning him to the straightaway before Jack realized he was beating a hasty retreat.

The last thing he needed was another scene. Not that he feared one; if the Kingsleys or Ashbrooks chose to push matters, it would not be he who felt the sting of embarrassment. However, he had no time to deal with such matters. His appointment with Mr. Bendimore was fast approaching, and Jack refused to arrive late. Following his detour, which took him down a parallel path, Jack continued and tried to ignore the sight of her green skirts flashing between the trees lining the avenue. But still, his steps slowed.

Jack did not recognize most in the party, but one of the older ladies, whom he thought to be Miss Kingsley's aunt, smiled at the young lady from time to time but remained ignorant of the growing distance between her niece and the rest. With a few steps, Miss Kingsley removed herself from the conversation and stared at the canopy above her. Shifting to observe her more fully while remaining unseen, Jack watched as she fought to hide away her heart. Miss Kingsley turned her face away from the others, but it was impossible to miss the tears in her eyes.

Jack's chest tightened.

Shaking his head, he went on his way, abandoning that distraction. Miss Kingsley had made her bed. It was her assignation with a gentleman that had brought her to the library last night. And her mistake had thrown her into Jack's arms. This was her doing, and it was not Jack's duty to alleviate her suffering.

But the whisper of guilt tickling his neck spoke of a different truth. Miss Kingsley may have initiated the first kiss, but the ill-fated second had been Jack's doing.

...

"That was an afternoon well spent," said Aunt Louisa-Margaretta as she took Lily by the arm while the others, chattering about some dinner or ball they were to attend.

Her aunt shook her head with a laugh, making the mass of blonde curls gathered on either side of her face bounce. Lily tried not to be jealous of the lady's gorgeous hair, but it was difficult when so many of the styles required such curled perfection while Lily's hair had an aversion to holding even the slightest wave. But then, Lily also wished she had her aunt's petite figure as well. Though well into her sixth decade, Aunt Louisa-Margaretta showed little sign of it apart from slight wrinkles at the corners of her eyes and mouth.

"We have made great strides in healing your reputation," said her aunt with a pat on Lily's forearm. "All may turn out right in the end, despite Mr. Hatcher's refusal to act like a gentleman."

Lily kept her own counsel, for there was nothing more to say on the matter. Listening to the sounds of their heels against the pavement, she merely nodded as her aunt expected and tried to keep her stomach from turning. The whole situation was mortifying and knowing Uncle Nicholas had confronted Mr. Hatcher over this mess was a painful punctuation to a most disagreeable interlude.

But Lily's face flushed at the memory of those blessed moments before Mrs. Pratt's interruption. If not for the scenes that had followed those enchanted kisses, that memory would remain a bright and pleasant thing to keep her company in the ensuing years—as she'd hoped it would be. But now, it was nothing but a fitting end to her attempts in the marriage arena.

Aunt Louisa-Margaretta prattled on as she did. Generally, Lily was happy to join in her effusive dialogue, but with all that had happened in the last day, she was worn through and had not the energy to feign interest.

"I had thought to stop by Bedford Market before returning home," said Lily as she caught sight of their carriage waiting at the end of the pathway. "It's not far from here, and it would be the perfect time to see it."

"I'm afraid we do not have the time," said Aunt Louisa-Margaretta. "We are expected at the Lamptons' for tea."

And that was precisely the reason why Lily wished to go to the market, though she would not say as much. Instead, she chose a more politic response. "They would not miss me, Aunt. And I am desperate to go to the market. I hear they have a beautiful selection of imports from all over the Empire."

The footmen stood at the ready as the ladies approached the barouche.

Aunt Louisa-Margaretta scrunched her nose. "Wouldn't you rather go to Bond Street? I can take you tomorrow if you are desperate to shop."

"It is not shopping, itself, but the marketplace that holds my interest. I wish to see the exotic wares they peddle," said Lily. "One of the footmen can serve as an escort, and I shan't be long. I promise."

"Do let her," said Cousin Selina, coming over to stand beside Lily in a show of support. "Mrs. Lampton will have no other guests Lily's age, and it must be difficult to spend her days socializing with strangers."

It took some convincing, but with Cousin Selina on her side, Lily was able to get her aunt to agree. She felt like a small child begging her nursemaid for a few more minutes of play before bedtime. Yet another reason to regret her decision to come to London. At nearly thirty, she should be allowed a bit more freedom than the young misses, but her aunt and uncle did not agree.

Giving her aunts and cousins-in-law a quick farewell, Lily set off in search of some peace as a footman trailed behind her. Of course, going to a crowded market was not an ideal place for such solace, but there was a degree of anonymity that came from joining the bustling throng. If she wished to speak, she might, but otherwise, Lily was free to keep to herself and merely observe all the activity around her.

Bedford Street was abuzz with people milling through the

shops. Though the market was a regular feature on the street, most stalls were little more than carts and barrows lined in front of the buildings. Filling the gaps between them were those who hawked their wares from baskets or boxes slung from their necks and street performers who sang, danced, juggled, or tumbled about. The thrum of commerce spilled out into the streets, clogging the roadway until a carriage wouldn't dare attempt the journey.

With a farthing, Lily acquired a small sack of cherries. Rolling the top of the brown paper down, she plucked one and popped it into her mouth. The fruit burst across her tongue, the sweet, sticky juices filling her taste buds with the first flavors of summer. Spitting the seeds onto the ground felt improper, but as others were doing so, Lily embraced the local custom as she strolled through the marketplace.

Most of the wares were of no interest to Lily. She had no need for pots or produce, but she enjoyed seeing the array of goods for purchase. Then a flash of bright colors drew her eye to a barrow arrayed with shawls, and Lily's breath caught. The display sat before a shop selling goods from the East, and Lily moved to get a better look. Her fingers brushed the feather-soft cotton, and she abandoned her cherries to pull the shawl free of the stack.

At first glance, it was a simple swath of fabric with no obvious decoration. The color—a bright cerise—was captivating enough on its own. However, another color was woven through it, giving the deep reddish-pink a hint of sapphire as though the shawl had a fine mist of blue covering it. She had seen shot cotton before, but the combination of colors and their vibrancy entranced her.

Truly, it was silly to feel such a strong pull for a little bit of fabric, but something in the color leaped out at her, seizing her attention in such a manner that Lily could not look away from it. She did not need another shawl, but she could not leave it behind, either. Especially when she fully opened it to discover that it was quite a bit larger than many others she owned. It was perfect for her larger frame, as though it had been made for her.

A short man with a pristine apron approached, his coin pouch jingling. "That does look lovely on you. Quite remarkable."

As Lily had every intention of purchasing the shawl, the proprietor's flattery and persuasion were wasted on her, but the fellow seemed determined to follow the usual steps of negotiation. He waxed poetic about the quality of the item and its rarity before Lily finally asked, "What is the price?"

Chapter 5

G iving a farewell nod, Jack stepped out of the teashop, grateful to be finished with that meeting. As importing tea was a vexing business, it was no surprise that his discussion with Mr. Bendimore had been equally irritating. High demand or not, he was ready to wash his hands of that commodity. The East Indian Trading Company's tactics in India and China were underhanded at best, and it was time to rid his company of that business. There was money aplenty to be made in other industries.

A couple of children approached him, their filthy hands reaching as they pleaded for any coins he had to spare, and Jack tossed a few pennies to each of them as he went on his way. But as his thoughts returned to the business at hand, a flash of a bright shawl caught his eye and drew him straight to Miss Kingsley.

What in the blazes was she doing there? Was he to get no respite from her? He had never noticed the lady before, yet she now haunted his steps. Of course, Jack refused to acknowledge that he wasn't wholly irritated by the idea. Any lightness of spirit he felt was purely due to the blessed relief of being finished with his meeting. Nothing more.

With the hustle and bustle around them, Miss Kingsley did

not notice that he was standing mere steps from her. But then, she appeared wholly occupied with a display of shawls. Clutching one, she began discussing prices with the shopkeeper, and Jack snorted at her ineptitude.

"It is lovely," she said, as though her posture and expression did not reveal how desperately she coveted the item. The lady had no sense when it came to bartering.

"Yes, it is," said the shopkeeper. "It was made from the finest Indian cotton by the best weavers that country has to offer. I fear that these are the only ones left of the shipment. Though it arrived only yesterday, most of them have been snatched up by eager customers."

Rolling his eyes at that tripe, Jack wondered why the fellow bothered inflating its value, for Miss Kingsley looked eager to part with her money. She had surrendered any power she had before the conversation had begun, and even now, she was retrieving coins from her purse before the price had been decided.

"For quality this fine," said the shopkeeper with a speculative nod at the shawl, "I can give it to you for seven shillings."

That exorbitant price was irritating enough to make Jack's blood boil, but what made his temper truly flare was that Miss Kingsley made only the slightest attempt at bargaining before dropping the coins into the shopkeeper's hand.

Stepping forward, Jack glowered at the fellow and snatched Miss Kingsley's money from his grasp.

"I beg your pardon, sir!" the thief blustered, though he quieted soon enough at the sight of Jack's dark scowl.

"Seven shillings for that frippery is outrageous," said Jack, dropping two coins in the man's palm. "Now, wrap the lady's purchase before I think better of giving you that much."

At least the shopkeeper had the good sense not to argue, for he scurried to do Jack's bidding without another word of complaint. Putting the crook in his place soothed a bit of his burning temper, but then he noticed Miss Kingsley staring at him with those luminous brown eyes of hers.

Good heavens. Mr. Hatcher was standing beside her. Though the day was far from warm, a hot flush swept over her as she stared at him, and Lily's eyes darted away from his and back again. The whole reason for enlisting Mr. Farson had been to avoid such interludes. His had been a convenient set of lips, and nothing more. But now, she was stuck with nerves strung taut and a desperate desire to flee to Canada herself so that she might avoid facing the gentleman she had accosted the previous night.

Breath coming in quick bursts, Lily's stomach rolled and buckled until she was afraid she might disgrace herself further by becoming quite sick in front of him. Mr. Hatcher stared at her, which did nothing to ease the tightening of her chest, and Lily knew she must say something—an apology at the very least.

Lily opened her mouth, but she did not know what to say. In all her lessons on decorum, none had addressed this situation, and it was beyond mortifying.

"I do apologize, Mr. Hatcher." Lily winced at the trite and awkward statement. Shaking her head at herself, she attempted a more intelligent statement. "With everything that has happened, I've not had the opportunity to tell you how very sorry I am that my mistake has caused you so much trouble."

The gentleman remained mute, which made Lily's mouth run away with her. If he would only say something or give any indication of what his feelings were on the matter, she might be able to rein in her tongue, but he simply watched her as she tripped and fumbled over her words.

"And of course, I feel wretched about my uncle's visit this morning. I give you my word that I did not mean for any of this to happen nor did I encourage him to hound you. What passed between us was merely a mistake, and I would never dream of holding you responsible for my reputation. There has been no harm done."

One of Mr. Hatcher's dark eyebrows rose, and she stumbled

over her words again. Though he had Mr. Farson's build, Mr. Hatcher's features were far more pleasing. She'd heard many a lady wax poetic over the eyes or smile of their love, but Lily thought a strong jawline particularly attractive, and Mr. Hatcher had that in spades. His looks were not overtly handsome, yet Lily struggled to maintain her composure around the fellow.

Mr. Hatcher finally deigned to speak, though it was not words Lily wished to hear. "Then your mystery beau has not been frightened away?"

Lily's cheeks blazed as bright as her newly acquired shawl, and she gave an inward groan. There were so many embarrassing confessions tied to that answer that she could not breathe. Perhaps she could settle on a partial truth.

"I have no beau, Mr. Hatcher," she said, retrieving her abandoned bag of cherries while fighting to keep her cheeks from looking like one of those fruits. "I was meeting an old friend who is emigrating and unlikely to return to our shores. It was to be a farewell."

There, that was not a lie. Mr. Hatcher may infer meanings as he pleased and need not know that the kiss was a farewell to her chances at courtship and marriage. Luckily, the shopkeeper returned with her package, leaving her free to escape.

"Do enjoy your shawl, miss," said the shopkeeper with a nod of his head, and Lily smiled, thanking him for his assistance.

"Ridiculous," grumbled Mr. Hatcher.

Lily blinked at the gentleman. "Pardon?"

·

Miss Kingsley was a most ridiculous creature. Jack could think of no better description than that. The shopkeeper had been robbing her blind, and yet she thanked him for it.

"You needn't terrorize the poor fellow," said Miss Kingsley.

Jack gave her a questioning raise of his brow.

"That scowl of yours could burn flesh, and the shopkeeper does not deserve such treatment, sir," she said while clutching her package.

"I cannot abide bullies or thieves."

"And he was neither."

His teeth ground under the pressure of his jaw, and Jack wondered why Miss Kingsley was determined to be so naive. But even as he thought to abandon her to her own devices, Jack continued to speak as if she had pulled the words from him.

"He was cheating you, Miss Kingsley. That shawl was worth exactly what I paid him and not a farthing more."

"But it was worth far more than that to me." As she spoke, Miss Kingsley squeezed the package and smiled as though it was the greatest of prizes and not a bit of spun cotton.

"So, you would allow yourself to be mistreated?"

Miss Kingsley cocked her head to the side, her brows drawing together. "I would hardly say I was mistreated. The fellow has a family and mouths to feed—not to mention those who are in his employ. A few shillings mean little to me and a world of difference to him and his staff."

Jack didn't know the shopkeeper's situation, but he doubted the man was hurting for money—and certainly not enough to justify the exorbitant sum he'd demanded from Miss Kingsley. Though some crude instinct wanted to set the lady straight concerning the ways of the world, Jack could not bring himself to snuff out that brightness shining through her. The lady stood there with the same dewy-eyed optimism and kindness that he had seen in many of the youngest sailors before the navy had beat it out of them.

Whatever doubts he'd harbored concerning Miss Kingsley's honesty evaporated like morning mist beneath a blazing sun. Anyone looking into the lady's sparkling eyes as she clutched that silly package with such pleasure could not doubt her sincerity.

Straightening her spine, Miss Kingsley turned to leave, but

Jack knew he had a duty to fulfill. Reaching over, Jack took the parcel from her and motioned for her to continue on her way. When she did not move as prompted, he sighed.

"I am to accompany you home," he said.

Miss Kingsley's brows drew together, and she stared at him as though he were a raving Bedlamite. "I thank you for your thoughtfulness, Mr. Hatcher, but I do not need your assistance. I have an escort."

"You mean your footman, who is keener on flirting with the grocer's daughter than doing his duty?" asked Jack, nodding at the young fellow who was currently chatting with a comely lass and completely unaware of anything his mistress was doing.

"I only brought him to appease my aunt," she said, reaching for her parcel, but Jack kept hold of it. "I am of an age where there is no need for constant escorts and chaperones." Then she blushed, and Jack thought it made Miss Kingsley look quite fetching, though he'd never thought red cheeks enticing before.

She stumbled over her words as she added, "Though after our interlude last night, I see how you might believe I need one."

"I was not worried about your reputation, Miss Kingsley, but rather, your safety. It is unwise to wander the streets of London on your own."

Miss Kingsley's brows rose. "This is hardly a dangerous section of the city, and my uncle's home is not far."

"Then it shouldn't take us long," said Jack, nodding for her to continue on her way as he shifted her package under his arm. Miss Kingsley's lips pinched together as she stared at him. Perhaps she hoped he would leave things be, but they would be standing here a long time if she thought him so easily thrown over.

Resignation played across her face before Miss Kingsley sighed and stepped forward, and Jack couldn't decide if he should be offended about her irritation or amused at the way she bristled when her feathers were ruffled; the lady was such an odd combination of timid and bold.

They walked along together, and Miss Kingsley offered up

a small sack of cherries, though she looked thoroughly displeased to do so. Jack huffed to himself, wondering what was to be done about a creature so determined to be used by others. No doubt, she had been sheltered from life's harsh realities and lived in a blissful state of ignorance as to how the world would mistreat her if she showed such kindness.

Regardless, Jack shook his head at her offering, and Miss Kingsley tucked the remnant cherries into her purse.

The lady walked stiffly beside him and seemed disinclined to speak, which Jack did not mind as he felt no need to converse. He was there to do his duty and escort the lady home. Without some assistance, Miss Kingsley was as likely to wander straight into the arms of trouble as naught, and it would cost Jack only a bit of his time to ensure she was safe.

Before long, Miss Kingsley's attention veered from him to the other stalls and shops. The pair strolled through the chaos of the marketplace, and Jack watched the lady as she stopped to admire the wares. Few were grand or elaborate. Mostly, they were little more than trinkets, yet her eyes shone as she examined each one, and Jack wondered how she would react to the array of genuine treasures that were to be found in the markets of the Far East and Indies. Compared to those he'd visited in his youth, the Bedford Market was nothing more than a breeding ground of cheap imitations.

But with her attention otherwise occupied, Jack had a moment to consider their predicament. The more time he spent with Miss Kingsley, the more convinced he was that she was as far from a mercenary as one could be. Giving a hard look at yet another seller who tried to gouge the lady, Jack said not a word but held the fellow's gaze until the man settled on a far more reasonable price for a string of glass beads.

Then there was the issue of her beau—or lack thereof. Instinct told him there was more to the tale than Miss Kingsley was admitting, but the details were of no matter to Jack. The fact was that Miss Kingsley had been caught in a compromising situation, her reputation was suffering because of it, and there was no one else willing or able to save her.

And the more Jack watched Miss Kingsley, the more his guilt grew at the thought of her bearing the brunt of society's displeasure. Not that he cared two jots for what others thought of him or her, but their cruelty would snuff out that brightness in her eyes and sweetness of temper.

.

Lily could all but hear Mr. Hatcher's thoughts churning in his head, though he spoke not a word. He was a silent sentinel at her side as she moved through the marketplace, and his eyes were fixed on her. It was intense and thoughtful in a manner that made Lily feel quite discomposed if she allowed herself to dwell on it.

Turning her attention to the world around her, she tried to lose herself in the joy of the marketplace. However, it was impossible with Mr. Hatcher's brooding demeanor. A marketplace was one of the noisiest places a person could be, yet his silence stood out among the cacophony until it was all she could hear.

The longer they walked, the more flustered Lily became. After what had passed between them, Lily was anxious to be rid of him and the reminder of her greatest folly. It was impossible to be composed when holding the arm of a stranger with whom she'd shared a romantic interlude. The whole thing was preposterous, embarrassing, and regrettable.

When she could not stand another moment, Lily turned them away from the market and pointed them home. The quicker she returned to her aunt and uncle's townhouse, the quicker she would be free of Mr. Hatcher.

The front door came into view, and Lily was grateful, quickening her pace.

"Thank you, Mr. Hatcher, for your escort," she said when they arrived, but the gentleman was undeterred by her dismissal and released her arm to open the door for her.

A footman appeared and took her jacket, bonnet, and gloves, and to her utter dismay, Mr. Hatcher handed his things over as well. The pair stood in the entryway, the gentleman as silent as ever while Lily stared at him, unsure of what more to say or do with her uninvited guest.

"Lily, is that you?" called Aunt Louisa-Margaretta, stepping from the parlor to peek at her niece, though the lady's eyes widened when she spied Lily's companion. "Mr. Hatcher?"

Coming forward, the lady gave him a curtsy. "What a pleasant surprise."

Mr. Hatcher gave a proper bow as Aunt Louisa-Margaretta's eyes darted between her niece and the gentleman.

"I did not think to see you two together," said her aunt with a furrowed brow, but the confusion lifted as a light gleamed in her eye. "Unless you have an announcement to make, perhaps?"

"Aunt!" Lily's cheeks blazed anew, her stomach twisting in unpleasant ways as she longed to flee to her bedchamber. But those anguished feelings were quickly replaced by shock when Mr. Hatcher finally spoke.

"Miss Kingsley and I are engaged."

Chapter 6

Lily gaped at the fellow, but her protestations were lost in the flurry of congratulations from her aunt. The lady babbled nonsense about the "joyous occasion," leaving Lily dumbfounded, for this occasion was anything but joyous. It felt as though the whole debacle was unfolding before her like a play; unable to speak or move, Lily was locked in place as the plot carried on without her.

Uncle Nicholas was sent for, and he only added to the revelries, slapping Mr. Hatcher on the shoulder as though he hadn't spent the morning railing against the "unscrupulous fellow." The party gathered in the parlor, her aunt drawing them to the sofa, and Lily had no choice but to comply like a marionette being led about by its strings. It wasn't until the gentlemen started speaking of announcements and wedding dates that Lily was able to grab hold of reality.

"But we are not engaged," she murmured, though no one paid any attention to her protestations. Lily's eyes darted between the other three, struggling to know what to say or do to derail this discussion. Her cheeks heated, her heartbeat racing as she tried again. But her words went unheeded once more, and the flustered, fluttery fear churning in her stomach began to burn.

"We are not engaged," she said more firmly, pulling her hands from her aunt's grasp.

"Nonsense," said Uncle Nicholas, beaming as though this were the best of news while patting Mr. Hatcher on the shoulder like they were old chums.

"I would prefer to get things settled as soon as possible," said Mr. Hatcher. "However, I understand that Mr. and Mrs. Kingsley are abroad at present—"

"Nonsense," repeated Uncle Nicholas. "Lily is in our care for the Season, and nothing would make her parents happier than to return home to find their daughter engaged to be married. You and my brother-in-law can decide on the marriage settlements when they return in a few weeks, but there is no need to hold the announcement."

"But we cannot plan the wedding without her mother," insisted Aunt Louisa-Margaretta, glancing over at Lily with a supportive look—as if that was Lily's greatest concern at present.

Lily's eyes widened, and a burble of laughter broke from her throat. Though her aunt and uncle did not notice, Mr. Hatcher's gaze moved to her, and there was a decidedly humorous glint in his eye. It was clear that he recognized her feelings on the matter and seemed to have no compunction about ignoring them.

"I assure you Mr. Hatcher and I are not engaged. The question was neither asked nor answered—"

"That is but a detail," said Uncle Nicholas, dismissing her with a casual wave of his hand.

"After your..." Aunt Louisa-Margaretta began the sentence, but her voice trailed away as she sought for the right word, "...*interlude* last night, there can be no question of an engagement. Especially not when the gentleman is so willing."

"And if the lady is not?" asked Lily, but the gentlemen had already begun speaking, drowning out her words as thoroughly as if she had not spoken them.

Aunt Louisa-Margaretta patted Lily's hands with a sweet but condescending smile before adding to the plans for Lily's future. The whole conversation was like a startled horse that had thrown its rider, speeding along unchecked as Lily gaped at the trio, wondering what in the world she could say to get it in hand.

"I do not wish to marry Mr. Hatcher." Lily's eyes moved between the three people, and it wasn't until her jaw started to pain her that she realized how tightly she was clenching her teeth. Unable to contain herself any longer, Lily got to her feet and raised her voice. "I will not marry him!"

The other conversation paused as the participants watched her. Lily's cheeks flamed red, and yet again, she cursed herself for concocting that "interlude." This whole situation was an unmitigated disaster.

Looking at the gentleman in question, Lily said, "I am grateful Mr. Hatcher desires to do his duty, but I do not wish to marry for such a meaningless reason. If there is a price to pay for my behavior last night, then I will pay it with my reputation—but not my hand in marriage."

"Don't be absurd, Lily," said Uncle Nicholas with another infuriating wave of his hand.

"Mr. Hatcher is an excellent match," added Aunt Louisa-Margaretta, coming to her feet beside Lily and wrapping an arm around her shoulders.

Uncle Nicholas nodded and continued, "Besides, it is the only choice in this situation, so there is no point in arguing."

Mr. Hatcher stood there in that silent, introspective manner of his as he watched her. Lily's cheeks flamed, and she wished she did not need to have this conversation in front of him, but she could not let things stand.

It was true that she fostered dreams of marriage and children, but binding herself to a man out of duty or obligation was the opposite of those fantasies. Lily had seen cold marriages from afar and had no interest in embracing a similar fate. The thought of agreeing to this sham sent a shiver along her spine and brought a tremble to her hands. Better an unhappy spinster than an unhappy bride.

"I do have a choice, Uncle. I may not care for my options, but there is always a choice, and I choose not to marry Mr. Hatcher."

Uncle opened his mouth to speak, but Aunt Louisa-Margaretta gave him a silencing look, and though the fellow looked put out, he remained quiet as his wife had prompted.

"I understand this may not be ideal, Lily, but it is the best solution," she said. Stepping closer to her niece, Aunt Louisa-Margaretta lowered her tone. "Unless you have a tendre for another gentleman. The fellow you'd intended to meet, perhaps?"

Lily's eyes darted away from her aunt's sympathetic gaze, and that accursed blush returned in force. Her instincts begged her to flee, and her feet itched to hide away in her bedchamber until this horrific Season finished.

Tripping over her words, Lily managed to say, "There is no one else."

"Perfect," said Uncle Nicholas as though that settled it, but Aunt Louisa-Margaretta gave him another look, and he restrained himself again.

"Then it was Mr. Hatcher you were meeting last night?" she asked.

Lily's mouth hung open in an ungainly gape, but she could not think of words with which to fill it. Of course, there were all sorts of unhelpful thoughts that cluttered her mind, but nothing of any value sprang to her lips, and Lily could only manage a simple shake of her head.

"I do not understand, dear," said Aunt Louisa-Margaretta, pulling Lily away from the gentlemen and lowering her voice. "I have not pushed matters because I knew you were very upset last night, but I must ask what you were doing in that library if not meeting a beau."

Lily's chin trembled as she fought for composure, but she had no explanation to give her aunt. It was as though the air had grown thin in the room, leaving Lily light-headed and wishing to escape the parlor. With a bit of quiet, the tightness in her chest might ease, and she would find some peace.

Her eyes moved to Mr. Hatcher and found him watching her with that look of his that said little and did nothing to help Lily's growing agitation.

.

Jack tucked his hands behind his back and watched the intriguing Miss Kingsley.

She had the good sense to rebut her uncle's idiotic claims as to her options and did so with an intelligence that made her all the more alluring. Though she quaked and shook, Miss Kingsley did not waver in her determination, and Jack found himself admiring her timid fortitude. The more she spoke, the more appealing she became.

Even though she was wrong.

Miss Kingsley did have other options, but marriage was the best. There was no beau, and thus no other offers. Marriage would secure her reputation and financial stability. And though the blessed state of matrimony had never enticed Jack before, he could see the merit of having a wife when it came to the social aspects of business. It would be mutually beneficial.

If Jack were a prideful man, he might be heartily offended at her refusal. But if he were being truthful with himself—and he tried to be—her reaction did sting the slightest bit.

From the way other ladies attempted to curry his favor, Jack knew he was considered a catch. He had a healthy income bolstered by a thriving company and varied investments. He was no wastrel or drunkard nor prone to violence. And he was by no means an unattractive fellow, as Miss Kingsley's passionate embrace could attest.

No doubt Miss Kingsley fostered fancies of some dashing young buck sweeping her off her feet, but it was only further testament that she needed guidance and protection. Jack did not know how every fortune hunter in the country hadn't beaten down her door, for she was a prime victim for such machinations. Jack had to marry her for her own good.

Mr. and Mrs. Ashbrook attempted to reason with the lady, but for all her timidity, she had a spine of steel and was not relenting. Standing there with her hands shaking, the lady held her ground, fighting point by point against her aunt and uncle's logic. And Jack liked her all the more for it.

But Miss Kingsley had a soft heart, and that was easily swayed with the right argument.

"You say you do not care if your reputation suffers," said Jack, taking a step forward. Miss Kingsley held his gaze and did not flinch or turn away as so many others were apt to do. "But what of the Pratts'?"

Miss Kingsley straightened, her hands falling to her side.

"Our scandal happened under their roof and while you were in their care," said Jack.

"People cannot hold the Pratts responsible for my actions," said Miss Kingsley, speaking as though she hoped it were true and knew it was not. Humanity was illogical, and rumormongers were more so. Only a halfwit would expect otherwise.

Jack did not bother refuting her claim; he merely raised his eyebrows at her in a silent challenge.

Mrs. Ashbrook came to her niece's side once more, taking Miss Kingsley's hand in hers. "You know they will. I entrusted you and your reputation to Mrs. Pratt. Their name is already being bandied about, and I fear this could hurt them as much as it will hurt you."

Miss Kingsley's gaze dropped to the floor, but as she stood there in silence, Jack watched a change come over her. Her slumped shoulders rose as she took several deep breaths, and when she finally met his eyes again, there was nothing of the frightened young miss.

Standing tall and proud, she held Jack's gaze and said, "Can we refrain from formally announcing the engagement at present? I wish to wait until my parents return."

"That would defeat the purpose of becoming engaged," said

Mr. Ashbrook.

"I am not saying we keep it secret," said Miss Kingsley. "I am simply asking that we do not put an announcement in the paper nor begin planning the wedding until my parents return home. As this is an issue of gossip, I see no reason why we cannot allow gossip to spread the news of our engagement."

Miss Kingsley's expression pinched as she spoke that final word, making it clear that his betrothed was an unwilling participant. Not that it mattered to Jack. He had plenty of experience in swaying the stubborn to his side, and in time, Miss Kingsley would come to accept their forthcoming marriage.

"As you see fit," said Jack with a sketch of a bow. "Until tomorrow, then."

"Tomorrow?" asked Mrs. Ashbrook.

"For a drive. It is expected of engaged couples." As loath as he was to waste his time on such a useless activity, there was no helping it.

Mrs. Ashbrook beamed and nodded, clutching her niece's arm as though this was everything Miss Kingsley had hoped for, and utterly ignorant of the simmering fire that burned in the young lady's gaze. It appeared that his future wife had a bit of a temper, and Jack hid his smile, though not well enough, for Miss Kingsley's eyes narrowed at him.

With a bow, Jack left, striding from the house with far more lightness of step than one would expect from a man engaged to a lady he hardly knew. But Jack never questioned his instincts, and they felt quite pleased with the outcome. Marrying Miss Kingsley had not been his intention, but it was one of those rare surprises that upended plans and landed him in far better circumstances. It was not often that such was the case, but Jack was not about to question his good fortune.

Chapter 7

L ily paced the parlor, her shoes striking the floor like pounding fists. With her jacket on, it was too warm for such frenzied movements, but she would not take it off. She must be ready to leave the moment Mr. Hatcher appeared, otherwise he might enter the townhouse. Her aunt and uncle may be forcing her to pass a few hours in Mr. Hatcher's company, but she needn't lengthen his visit.

To think that she had believed him dashing! Romantic even. Though their kisses had been tender, the fellow had a black heart beating in his chest. That calculating cad.

The only saving grace was that this ridiculous situation was only temporary. With time, the rumors would die and the Pratts' association with the whole debacle would be forgotten. Her parents would return, and they would never force her to wed Mr. Hatcher. In a few weeks' time, all would be forgotten, and Lily would break with her "betrothed."

That odious and infuriating man!

·

With a nudge of the reins, Jack guided the horse through the clogged street. This was absurd. Driving through London during the busiest time of day was an irritating way to pass the time, and attempting to visit any of the parks when the elite were out in droves was madness. But though he was battling the onslaught of carriages, carts, animals, and people, Jack wasn't terribly unhappy to see Miss Kingsley again.

Not Miss Kingsley. Lily. She was his fiancée, after all.

However, his stomach gave a slight quiver as he imagined facing her once more, and Jack couldn't account for that strange flutter of anxiety; Lily was not a fearsome foe.

Upon seeing her uncle's townhouse, Jack pulled to the side and tossed a coin to one of the street boys, who fetched the reins and held the horse still as Jack climbed the front steps. But before his knuckles touched wood, the door flew open and Lily was there, rushing down the stairs with the grim determination of a soldier doing his duty. She was practically climbing into the cabriolet before Jack could assist her.

"Good afternoon," he said, but the lady crossed her arms and gave the barest of nods.

Try as he might, Jack could not help but smile at her behavior; it was so righteous in its indignation and full of such dignified haughtiness, as though she were being led to her martyrdom. Today, he was graced not with the quelling, wilting miss that scarcely met his gaze. Today, it was the fiery Lily who faced down foes without flinching.

"I see you are a little piqued," said Jack, climbing into the seat beside her.

Lily's gaze jerked to him, her eyes narrowing. "You think this humorous?"

Nudging the carriage forward, Jack took them into the thick of things as he considered her statement; most people cowered and avoided confronting him, so seeing Lily in all her furious glory was rather entertaining.

"I suppose I do."

Lily's lips pinched together. "You are a cad, Mr. Hatcher. You bullied me into doing as you wish—"

It took the greatest restraint not to jerk on the reins when he heard that accusation, but Jack kept hold of his temper and managed not to crash the carriage as he defended his honor.

"I did not bully you," he replied with a dark scowl. "I did not threaten nor force you to accept."

"You announced our engagement without speaking a word of it to me, and then you manipulated me into accepting it."

Jack snorted and shook his head. He should leave it be. It was not as though he cared what others thought of him, but an itch of unease wrapped around his spine, and Jack felt compelled to respond.

"Call it manipulation if you like, but I merely made you see that it was in your best interest to accept my suit. Is it underhanded for me to cast an undesirable option in a favorable light?"

"You used the Pratts' reputation to force my hand," said Lily.

He nodded. "I saw a weakness in your resolve and exploited it, but you refused to see that more than yourself might suffer because of this scandal."

Lily gaped at him. "And you admit that without a hint of remorse?"

"Why should I be riddled with remorse?" asked Jack with a shrug. "It was the best choice."

"It is not your right to decide what is best for me."

"It is when you are being unreasonable."

Crossing her arms tight across her chest, Lily glowered. "And disagreeing with you is 'being unreasonable?'"

The lady was not interested in a level-headed discussion on the topic, so Jack kept his own counsel and let Lily stew in her anger. She did not remain silent for long.

"I cannot fathom why you insist on this engagement when you made it clear that you had no interest in furthering an acquaintance with me, Mr. Hatcher. You practically ran away that night and then tossed my uncle from your office when he pressed the issue."

Jack scowled once more. "I did not run away, and I have my reasons for changing my mind."

"And they are?"

"Of no concern, as the decision has been made," said Jack, steering the carriage around a particularly large cart that commandeered half the road. "And it is ridiculous for you to call me Mr. Hatcher, Lily."

"I did not give you leave to address me so informally," came the curt reply.

"You did when you agreed to our engagement."

Though the lady gave a huff of indignation, she voiced no further objection.

"My friends call me Hatch," said Jack, glancing over at his fiancée.

Lily grumbled something under her breath, and with the sound of the clogged street around them, it was impossible to say for certain what the words were, but Jack felt her disgruntled meaning well enough.

...

Fate was a cruel temptress. It was she who brought Miss Aubrey into Colin's life, tempting him with her sweetness and beauty, and it was she who kept him from claiming Miss Aubrey's love for his own. Strolling along the city street, Colin had only a vague notion as to his destination. Eyes fixed on the pavement before him, he cast his thoughts to that most gorgeous of creatures.

Though every rational thought told him it was futile to hold onto the hope of securing her hand, Colin could not give her up. If he were a better man, he would do so immediately and leave her free to pursue a gentleman who would provide her the life she deserved, but those few, precious moments they were able to steal away together during the odd ball or party were too precious to forego.

The Unnecessaries. That was the name his club had taken upon themselves, and it was a teasing veneer that hid an ugly truth. He and the other gentlemen of that illustrious group were the accursed third, fourth, or even fifth sons in the family—too low to ever hope for any inheritance of their own, and thus left to their own financial devices and ruin.

How was a fellow to secure a wife and family of his own when his situation was so dire? It was yet another manifestation of fate's cruelty. Colin DeVere had been raised with all the trappings of wealth but without any hope of securing it for himself. His allowance may cover his spartan bachelor lifestyle, but Colin could never hope to support his dear Miss Aubrey on such a pittance.

Of course, her dowry would do much to support them, but only those with money were considered suitable for ladies with fortunes of their own. Her father would be a fool to allow a vagabond like Colin to pay court to his daughter.

Ignoring the push of people around him, Colin halted in his tracks, head hung low. It was pointless to agonize over the situation; he must simply accept that Miss Aubrey was beyond his grasp. Yet even the thought of abandoning her wrenched his heart in his chest, the pain spreading through the whole of his being.

Miss Aubrey.

With a resigned breath, Colin straightened and continued on his way. And it was then that his eyes rested on a particular gentleman sitting atop a fine cabriolet not fifteen feet away. The pressure in his chest built, and his despair dissolved beneath the spark of fury that burned through him.

A gentleman keeps his word. That was the most basic tenet of their class. All Colin needed was an income. A position. If Hatch had only done as he'd promised, then Colin would be a successful man of business by now—someone worthy to court Miss Aubrey. Fate may have placed Miss Aubrey beyond Colin's reach, but the impassable gulf keeping them apart was the work of Jonathan Hatcher.

With a controlled snap of the reins, Hatch steered the carriage through the traffic, and the pressure in Colin's chest grew, pressing against his ribs until they felt liable to snap. For a quick moment, he saw himself at the helm, squiring Miss Aubrey around town, and the muscles in his arms strained as he clenched his fists.

When Hatch's carriage moved forward, Colin's feet followed. Traffic was heavy enough that the pair were easy to trail.

Colin did not recognize the plump lady sitting beside the blackguard, but he guessed her identity and assumed Hatch was now in the midst of an uncomfortable situation. Miss Kingsley scowled something fierce at her escort, and Colin hoped the lady was giving Hatch a thorough dressing down. No man deserved it more than he.

However, as he watched the play between the pair, Colin came to a realization that had him gaping. First, that they were engaged; appearing in public unaccompanied so shortly after scandal had linked their names together could mean only that. But more importantly, Hatch admired his betrothed.

Though passersby might believe the entirely hostile picture the two painted, they did not know Hatch. Years may have passed since they'd served together in His Majesty's Royal Navy, but Colin had known Lieutenant Hatcher well, and he was not one to bend to another's whims. Especially society's.

But more than that, Hatch watched Miss Kingsley in a manner that betrayed his interest. It was not the love-addled longing that was stamped on Colin's face whenever Miss Aubrey graced his presence, but it was clear that more lay beneath Hatch's reserve. It was not infatuation as of yet, but the fellow cared for Miss Kingsley.

How unfortunate for Hatch that the lady did not share his interest, for no one looking at her could mistake Miss Kingsley for a willing participant in their outing.

Collin was no fool. Though he had nourished and spread the gossip concerning Hatch's ungentlemanly behavior towards Miss Kingsley, Collin had never anticipated any repercussions beyond bruising the fellow's reputation and frightening off Hatch's more scrupulous investors. But as he followed the carriage along, that original plan shifted and altered, becoming something far grander.

Perhaps it was not the most honorable course of action, but the dark, angry part of Collin's soul that cried out for vengeance would not allow him to ignore this opportunity. For once, Collin would have the whip hand over Hatch, and he was not about to surrender his one chance to use it.

...

"You are quite forthright for a lady," said Mr. Hatcher. No matter what the cad said, Lily refused to use anything but his proper address—even if she could not stop him from taking that liberty with her.

"That statement reveals more about you and the simpering ladies with whom you surround yourself than it does about me, sir," said Lily, turning to watch the passing streetscape. "I know many who would not bow and scrape to a fellow who had forced their hand in such a devious manner. You may not believe me, but ladies do not care for being bullied and badgered. You would not wish to meet my Aunt Mary in a temper. Or my Aunt Tabby, for that matter."

Every word she'd spoken was true, but Lily knew that such an illustrious description did not normally apply to herself. Something about Mr. Hatcher loosened her tongue, and with the fury of this situation spurring her on, Lily could not remain silent.

"Why are you so opposed to our engagement?"

Mr. Hatcher's question startled Lily, for his motives were far more questionable. "Why am I so opposed to irrevocably binding myself to a stranger for the rest of my life? I think that question answers itself, sir."

"You were quick enough to throw yourself into my arms."

That verbal parry landed with precision force, striking a killing blow. Lily's heart constricted in her chest, and she turned her face away from Mr. Hatcher, refusing to allow him to see the tremble of her chin.

Desperate. That was a terrible word far too many ladies embraced. As years passed and their prospects dwindled, they settled on unacceptable bridegrooms or resorted to underhanded methods to force a gentleman to the altar. Trapping a husband hadn't been Lily's intention, but others would assume it was.

Poor Lily Kingsley. The unwanted young lady who resorted to throwing herself into the arms of a stranger to steal a few minutes of a fantasy that would never be hers. Clearly, Mr. Hatcher thought she had not the self-respect to insist on a loving, respectful marriage.

"Take me home," she murmured. She should never have come to London. Never agreed to this farce.

Mr. Hatcher did not deviate from their course, and Lily repeated herself.

"We are nearly to the park," came the reply.

"I do not care about going into the park, Mr. Hatcher. I wish to return home. Immediately."

As he glanced at her, Mr. Hatcher's scowl spoke plenty though he remained mute.

Gathering her strength about her, Lily met his gaze. "If you do not turn this carriage towards my uncle's house, I will alight and walk there myself."

When he did not answer or do as bidden, Lily shifted as though to make good on her threat, though it was as empty as their false engagement. Mr. Hatcher shifted to keep her in her seat and then guided the horses to the first available street that would return her home.

Lily could not look at the fellow, and he did not deign to speak, which suited her. With any luck, Mr. Hatcher would see how ludicrous this engagement was, and she would be rid of him posthaste. But instinct told her the fellow was too stubborn to admit defeat so easily.

Hope as she might, Lily was forced to remain in this unhappy engagement until her parents returned.

Why had she been so hasty? Barring the others from writing her parents had seemed a good idea at the time, but that left her shackled until their trip came to its natural conclusion. Should Mama and Papa discover what had happened, they would return with all haste and save her from this torture, but the thought of her foolishness curtailing their travels did not sit well in Lily's heart.

Knowing that she needed rescuing only added to her embarrassment, anger, and general agitation. With so many consequences resting heaving on her shoulders, Lily would not add to the burden by robbing her parents of their long-awaited tour of the Continent. She could wait, and knowing that a reprieve was forthcoming was enough.

Jack was the first to admit that he knew little of ladies, but Lily was as inscrutable as any he'd known. Pushing the horses faster than he would have in other circumstances, Jack wove through traffic, determined to be done with this disastrous outing.

A morsel of guilt pricked at his conscience, like a rat nibbling on a discarded biscuit. It wasn't often that Jack lost control of his temper, but the way Lily was reacting to the engagement had struck a vulnerable part of his soul he hadn't known existed.

Lily spoke as though marrying him was repugnant. And though she took pains to hide her expression, Jack saw the way her lips trembled as she studied the passing buildings. Less than twenty-four hours into their engagement and his fiancée was all but hysteric over the thought of spending one more minute in his presence.

What had he said or done to disturb her so? Lily had been eager for his attention in that blasted library, yet in the light of day, she fought tooth and nail to be rid of him. The lady was ridiculous.

Luckily, her uncle's house appeared in a trice, but before Jack moved to assist her, Lily was out of the cabriolet and up the stairs, scurrying through the front door without a backward glance. With a sigh and a shake of his head, Jack turned his carriage homeward.

Chapter 8

Foot tapping to the music, Lily watched the dancers from the safety of her seat as the instruments' refrain buoyed her spirits. Ballroom music was not as enthralling as the opera or a concert, but any music was a pleasure. Though plenty of individuals found great enjoyment in spinning about the dance floor, Lily thought her position preferable. She was not forced to interact with her aunt's set and trip over the inevitable *faux pas* when she did not know so-and-so or react appropriately when faced with a piece of gossip that meant nothing to her.

Perhaps being engaged was not such a tragedy.

Life had changed with alarming speed. All of a sennight had passed since "the incident," and where Lily had been guarded religiously before, she was now at liberty to enjoy the ball as she pleased, and Aunt Louisa-Margaretta no longer snared young men for her unattached niece. Not that her aunt gave her complete freedom. No, Lily was still subjected to social calls and events she did not wish to attend, but Aunt Louisa-Margaretta no longer hovered at Lily's elbow.

It was quite liberating. Especially as Mr. Hatcher had not seen fit to visit again, and thus, Lily was not made to suffer through his company.

So, Lily sat on the edge of the ballroom availing herself of the only enjoyable aspect of a ball while her aunt danced the night away and her uncle lost himself in a card game. Mr. Hatcher's unceremonious announcement of their engagement had seemed awful, but at present, Lily could not deny that this horrid mess had its merits.

This evening was near perfection—if not for Mr. Hatcher looming in her thoughts.

Engaged yet unwanted. There was no other manner in which to view her situation, for the gentleman hadn't chosen her of his free will. If his behavior precipitating the engagement was an indication, Mr. Hatcher did not desire this marriage any more than she. Though Lily could not decipher the sudden shift in his behavior, it was clear that he viewed it as an obligation.

What a terrible word. There was nothing more unflattering than being a duty to fulfill. Lily had suffered through years of being an obligation, and she'd never dreamt that such a word would apply to her marriage. Where others celebrated the occasion, Lily felt a hollow ache in her chest.

Turning her gaze from the dancers, Lily looked at her gloved hands clasped in her lap. The pale blush of her dress was a stunning shade and the embroidery along the edges of her skirts was some of the finest she had seen, yet for all the finery, she felt like a sow's ear fashioned into a silk purse.

Lily fought against the sadness that crept into her soul, seeping into her like a malodorous vapor. Memories of her family's compliments came to mind, attempting to buoy her spirits, but they could not balance out the weight of her experience. Lily was no beauty.

This would not do. It was of no use to bemoan that which could not be changed. Lily would not allow despair to linger in her heart.

Holding her head erect, she watched sightlessly as the dancers turned about the room. The Walkers had purchased mountains of flowers that lined the dance floor and rose up to the ceilings. A blaze of candles hung from the chandeliers and sconces, burning like the midday sun, and the forthcoming dinner was likely to be utterly sumptuous. All things considered, it was quite a lovely party, and Lily ought to enjoy it.

"Miss Merriweather?"

As it was not her name, Lily did not respond until the gentleman repeated himself, coming to stand a few steps away. Lily looked at the fellow, and he gave a start.

"Oh, I do apologize," he said with a grin. "I mistook you for someone else."

Lily stared at the mysterious gentleman, though he hardly looked old enough for that title. She could not tell his precise age, but he was at least five years younger than herself.

"Think nothing of it, Mr...." Lily had begun the sentence without thinking it through and stumbled.

"Mr. Colin DeVere," he said with a quick bow and a growing smile that lit his handsome face. But that was not the correct descriptor. He was thin and lithe with delicate features and a mop of blonde curls, which made Lily think of him as more beautiful than handsome. "And though I have already been abominably rude, might I add to my sins by asking your name? I would seek a proper introduction, but it seems ridiculously *de rigueur* to seek one out when we are already speaking."

His gaze was not the penetrating glower Mr. Hatcher preferred, but it was earnest and fully fixed on her as though he truly cared about her answer, rather than a polite glance that accompanied a few moments of inane conversation before the gentleman scurried away.

"Miss Lily Kingsley."

That smile of his grew, and Lily's cheeks heated in response.

"Might I join you, Miss Kingsley? You were looking rather forlorn."

Though Lily did feel a tickle of pleasure over his concern, her lips pinched together as she muttered to herself, "Why does everyone seem to think they know how I am feeling?" Of course, she had been rather forlorn before he approached, but that was not the point.

"Pardon?" asked Mr. DeVere with raised eyebrows.

But Lily cleared her expression and motioned for him to sit beside her. The seat was unoccupied, and Lily doubted Mr. DeVere would linger long.

"And what has you so downcast tonight?" he asked.

Lily's eyebrows rose, and she glanced at him. It was the only thing she could do, for she could not think of a proper response.

Mr. DeVere gave a chagrined grimace. "You think me too forward, and I apologize. I simply was overtaken by curiosity as to why such a lovely young lady would look so distraught."

Lily blinked at Mr. DeVere, and her face burned to the tips of her ears. She could not think of a single time when anyone had called her lovely. Her. Miss Lily Kingsley. Of course, her parents and dearest friends used such words, but theirs were not unbiased opinions.

Colin did not think himself a vain man, but it was hard not to puff himself up when faced with unabashed admiration. From his first words spoken, Miss Kingsley blushed and tripped over her words, avoiding his gaze when possible and becoming all the more flustered when she didn't. There was something quite invigorating about knowing that he affected her so.

"Are you not dancing tonight, Miss Kingsley?"

Nibbling on her lips, she turned her face to the dancers to hide her expression from him. "I prefer to listen to the music."

"You can listen and dance at the same time."

Miss Kingsley shook her head. "I have no talent for dancing."

"I cannot believe that," he said, leaning closer. Not enough to be scandalous, but a subtle movement that drew her attention to his proximity. Miss Kingsley's eyes widened at it and the slight compliment, making Colin's chest ache for her. She may not be the physical ideal of womanhood, but Miss Kingsley seemed a sweet lady who deserved a bit of flattery.

"And where do you call home, Mr. DeVere?"

That diversion nearly had him laughing, as it was far from subtle. Though he wished to hurry things along, Colin allowed Miss Kingsley's change of subject.

"That is a complicated question," he said with a broad smile. "I hail from Wiltshire, though I did not spend much time there. At present, I count London as home."

The conversation paused for a moment, and Colin was content to wait as he knew Miss Kingsley was gathering her courage to ask the question. Vague statements may be a silly trick, but it was better to allow a conversation to be just that and not a lecture. So, he waited for her to prompt him, and she did.

"Then where did you spend your youth?"

"The sea," he said. A shiver ran along his spine as it always did when speaking of those years, but Colin held onto his affable smile. "I joined the navy when I was a lad, so that is more home than my family seat."

Colin had left the navy the moment he reached his majority and had not stepped foot on a ship in the three years since, yet ladies were always giddy for details. A simple mention was all it took, and their curiosities were piqued. Miss Kingsley's questions were more interesting than most, but they required little thought.

Which left him to stew.

Miss Aubrey was waiting for him; Colin had known it was foolhardy to attend both the Walkers' and the Thompsons' soirees in the same evening, but it was necessary. There was no time to waste—not that spending an evening with Miss Aubrey could ever be a waste, but neither was it conducive to his plans against Hatch.

The conversation bounced between them as Miss Kingsley took a vigorous approach to conversing. The lady had plenty to say on any topic broached, and one subject led to another, which led to another, and before long, their verbal path had meandered all over creation. Miss Kingsley hardly needed any help from him to ramble on about anything that popped into her head, and while she seemed a nice sort, Colin struggled to keep his attention on her.

He tried to push the ticking of his pocket watch from his mind, but he could feel it there in his waistcoat, warning him that his time with Miss Aubrey was flying away. It was like a second heartbeat, thumping against his stomach.

He had laid enough groundwork that it was unlikely to matter if he left now, but Colin could not leave Miss Kingsley. Not yet. Hatch wanted her, but she did not want him, and it would take little effort to turn Miss Kingsley's head. Colin needed to lay enough of a foundation to keep her from becoming attached to Hatch, but not enough to raise her expectations. She was an innocent, after all. Miss Kingsley would be a useful tool to punish Hatch, but she did not deserve to be hurt by Colin's machinations.

Though the scandal had raised some interest in the lady, Colin knew it would be forgotten soon enough; some gossip was bandied about for years, but Miss Kingsley was too overlooked to hold public interest for long. With a few well-chosen words in the right ears, Colin could help the rumors fade from memory, and then the lady wouldn't need to marry Hatch to repair her reputation.

Just a little flattery. A few compliments. Some time together. Hatch was such a difficult fellow that it wouldn't take much effort to sway Miss Kingsley from his side.

Finally, he retrieved his pocket watch and fought to keep the dismay from his face. Granted, Miss Kingsley may think it was due to his leaving her company, so Colin allowed some of it to show.

"I am afraid I must leave you, Miss Kingsley. The evening is waning, and I have another engagement."

There was a hint of disappointment in her gaze, and Colin knew he was well on his way to success.

"I understand, Mr. DeVere. Thank you for the lively conversation," she replied with a smile.

Standing, he gave her a low bow and tucked his pocket

watch away. Summoning all his charm, Colin fixed her with a warm gaze. "Might we drive out tomorrow to continue our discussion?"

Miss Kingsley sat there as though frozen, a confused flutter of her eyelashes her only movement. It was several quiet moments before she finally spoke. "I'm afraid I have a prior engagement that will commandeer the entire afternoon."

"And you cannot throw them over?" he asked, dropping his voice to little more than a whisper.

Pulling herself free of his gaze, Miss Kingsley shook her head, her hands clenching in her lap. "I have a standing appointment at a foundling home that I cannot miss." She paused, her cheeks reddening like an apple. "Though you are welcome to join me if you wish."

Mulling that option over, Colin was not happy to allow such an opportunity to slip by, but he did not wish to devote the entire afternoon to this. A few hours in a coach was one thing, but to waste most of the day was more than he desired. Besides, there was a chance Miss Aubrey would call on the Barlowes tomorrow, and that might allow him a few minutes in her company.

"I'm afraid I must decline," said Colin with a frown. When she met his eyes once more, he held her there, giving her a shadow of a smile that was filled with longing and disappointment. Sensing he had pushed things as far as he dared, he gave her another bow. "But I shall convince you to join me another time."

Biting on her lips once more, Miss Kingsley clenched her hands until he was certain she must have lost all feeling in them. She ducked her head with another blush and said, "Perhaps."

"Until next time, Miss Kingsley."

Chapter 9

A tea tray sat untouched on Jack's desk, and he slouched in his armchair, his clasped hands resting on his stomach as he stared at the far wall. It was pointless to pretend his mind was filled with anything but Miss Lily Kingsley, for his thoughts had not strayed from her since the moment she'd erupted into his life.

"Your tea is cold," said Silas, leaning against the door jamb, hands in pockets.

Jack grunted.

"I have heard the most remarkable rumor." Though Jack did not look at the fellow directly, he pictured that challenging expression Silas always had in such circumstances. He rarely demanded Jack to tell-all, but he was vastly irritating when he put his mind to it. So, the quickest way to avoid such megrims was to get to the heart of the matter as quickly as possible.

"I am engaged to Miss Lily Kingsley," said Jack.

Coming into the office, Silas dropped into the chair opposite Jack's desk. "Hearing it from you is no more believable than when I heard it from so many others."

Slanting his gaze to Silas, Jack raised his eyebrows. "And why is that so unbelievable?"

"You mean other than I heard you declare unequivocally

that you would not be offering for Miss Kingsley not one sennight ago? And to her uncle, no less?" Silas answered with a challenging raise of his own brows. "Or the fact that you have yet to mention it, though a fair amount of time has passed?"

With a sigh, Jack returned his gaze to the office wall, his eyes tracing the scrolling pattern of the wallpaper.

"The Jonathan Hatcher I know would never acquiesce."

"It was the right thing to do," said Jack in an off-handed tone. He had never noticed how gaudy the walls looked; they were a rich shade of burgundy, but the gold accent was a bit much.

"Certainly." It was a simple word, but there was a wealth of meaning in Silas's tone, both tentative and filled with curiosity. Jack heard the thoughts churning in his partner's mind.

"Both of us had a hand in the scandal that damaged her reputation, and it was only proper I do right by her," said Jack.

Silas grunted in agreement, though Jack did not look to see what expression accompanied that nebulous sound.

"I'm not opposed to marrying the lady."

This time, there was a distinct humor to Silas's grunt, and Jack turned his head to see his old friend watching him with laughter in his eyes.

"Such ardent sentiment," said Silas with a dry tone. "Though being 'not opposed' isn't the best foundation for a marriage, it is better than being opposed."

At that, memories of Lily's fury played through Jack's mind as his gaze drifted to the wall once more. If any word described the lady's opinion concerning their impending marriage, "opposed" would be it. His thumbs tapped together as he mused about his betrothed. Human nature was not hard to understand. People were a predictable lot, but Miss Lily Kingsley was a puzzle, and Jack was no closer to understanding her.

"She is an odd lady," mumbled Jack. He'd not thought that a particularly inflammatory statement, but it was met with a pregnant silence that drew his attention to Silas, who sat on the edge of his chair, watching Jack with wide eyes.

"What is the matter?" asked Jack with furrowed brows and a feeling of dread weighing him down.

"'An odd lady?'" Silas parroted.

"That is what I said."

"But what you meant is 'intriguing.'"

Straightening in his chair, Jack rolled his eyes. "I don't know what fantasies are brewing in your mind, but you'd best leave them be."

"I wouldn't say they're fantasies, Jack. Whether or not you are willing to admit it aloud, you are not one to offer marriage—regardless of duty. You could as easily bribe some gentleman in dire straits to offer for her or find some other way to fulfill your obligation."

There was truth to Silas's words, so Jack did not bother disputing them.

"And you are not free with your praise—"

"I said Miss Kingsley is odd. That is hardly praise," grumbled Jack.

Silas gave an appreciative nod but added, "From anyone else, that would be true. From you..." He let the words dangle off into oblivion, as though they could stand on their own without further evidence or support. Which was preposterous. Even if the image of Lily's eyes hung in Jack's memory, tantalizing him.

"She needs a keeper, that is all. From what I have seen of the lady, she is a tender, trusting soul who would wander into danger and thank it for its time. I have no desire to see that goodness crushed, and it will be if someone does not step in and watch over her."

Silas relaxed into his armchair, and that ever-present light in his eyes softened as Jack spoke, a gentle smile curling the edge of his lips.

"I hardly know the lady, Silas, so do not infer more to my feelings than I have expressed."

His partner gave a sage nod that embodied all the wisdom and experience of his far more mature years; the movement may have looked like an agreement, but there was a twinkle in his eyes that contradicted it. Although the fellow was nearly two decades older than Jack, Silas was an imp at heart.

"Then I shan't infer any more," said Silas. "But I will ask when you are to see her again."

Jack shrugged. "She doesn't wish to announce our engagement formally until her parents arrive home from the Continent, and then the wedding planning will take off in earnest—"

"I did not ask when you will marry her. I asked when you shall see her again."

Unbidden, Jack's lips pinched together as he remembered their disastrous outing. "I have no immediate plans."

Silas's brows pulled together, his expression wrinkling. "How do you plan to court her?"

Then Jack's expression matched Silas's. "Court her? We are already engaged."

Leaning forward with a sigh, Silas shook his head. "Courting does not end once you decide to marry. At least not in good marriages."

In the abstract, Jack was well familiar with what courting meant, but in real terms, it was as foreign as any word in Chinese. More so, for at least he knew a few simple phrases in that language. Scratching his jaw, Jack tried to think his way through that tangled mess. Did it mean he would be forced to spend hours on pointless outings like their failed venture to the park? Would she expect him to squire her to the usual insipid haunts? Evenings spent in ballrooms and parties when he had much more important things to do? Heaven help him, Jack could not stomach the thought of it.

Wasn't it enough that they were promised to each other? They had a lifetime to sort the rest of it out.

But when Jack emerged from his thoughts once more, he discovered Silas had abandoned him, leaving Jack to the silence of his office, a tray of cold tea, and a deluge of questions with no answers.

Chapter 10

F ingers running along the piano keys, Lily made her way through the interlude building to the song's finale. Taking in a deep breath, her voice came out in a bright, clear tone, rising above the accompaniment. The notes climbed, crescendoing to the highest reaches of her range. A brief shiver of nerves had her worrying she wouldn't hit that last lingering note, but it came out strong and controlled. There were times when the song felt like a runaway carriage, careening through the measures, haphazardly hitting the proper pitches and tone while only one misstep from disaster.

But in this instance, she made it to the journey's end.

Perhaps the forthcoming performance would not be an utter failure. Any musician would attest that one never performs before an audience as perfectly as one does in private, but Lily felt confident that all would be well; there was time enough before the concert, and she was already gaining confidence in the song.

Rising from her seat, Lily ran a final touch over the keys. The Broadwood was a beautiful instrument and entirely wasted on her uncle's family, as not one of them played with any proficiency. The frame was stained a deep reddish-brown, the strong grain of the wood adding a richness to the color. It was intended to be a showpiece, and it was a beautiful specimen.

A knock sounded at the drawing room door, and a footman entered a moment later, carrying a bouquet. Coming to stand before her, Gregory offered it to her, but Lily merely stared at it.

"For you, miss," he said, nodding at the flowers.

Of course, she knew what his motions had meant, but Lily could not believe the flowers were for her. Other than a time or two when her father or brother had sent her a posy, she'd never received a bouquet before. Lily took the blossoms and accompanying note, and the footman took his leave as she stared at the offering in her hands.

Pink and purple gillyflowers were gathered alongside small purple wildflowers, forming a frame around a single white rose and lily. Drawing them close until their buttery petals brushed her cheeks, Lily breathed in their scent.

Mr. Hatcher. The gentleman had finally acknowledged his horrid behavior and sent an apology. The irritation Lily had harbored for the past sennight faded at the sight of his lovely offering, but when she opened the accompanying note, she found Mr. DeVere's signature on the bottom.

Thank you for an enjoyable evening. I look forward to visiting with you again and hope you enjoy the flowers and their underlying sentiment.
Sincerely yours,
C. DeVere

Though he did not say it outright, Lily understood his meaning well enough. Hurrying from the drawing room, she snuck through the hall and into the library. Having never needed a flower dictionary, she did not have a copy, but as Aunt Louisa-Margaretta and Uncle Nicholas enjoyed sending each other little floral notes, Lily knew they owned at least one. Scouring the shelves, she hunted for the book. She clutched the flowers and note in one hand and yanked the volume free, though it was difficult to sift through the pages one-handed.

She could not be certain, but Lily was fairly confident that the wildflowers were Venus's looking-glass. Scanning the pages, she found the entry for that particular blossom and saw its meaning written directly below the name. Flattery. Lily smiled at that. Mr. DeVere certainly had flattered last night, so it was no surprise that he would do so with the flowers.

But she stopped when she landed on the entry for roses. Beauty. That surprise only increased when she read about gilly-flowers. Lasting beauty. Though the lily could be a nod to her namesake, according to Mr. Tyas's *The Sentiment of Flowers*, it also symbolized purity and modesty.

Mr. DeVere had sent her a bouquet that spoke of beauty, flattery, purity, and modesty.

Lily knew not what to do with that message. Perhaps she was inferring more than the gentleman had meant to imply. But it was common enough for ladies and gentlemen to send secret messages with a few flowers, and his note was quite pointed. However, Mr. DeVere may use a different dictionary that supplied less romantic meanings to his flowers.

Returning the book to its shelf, Lily clutched the note and bouquet and wandered to the window. The great thing opened to the sunshine, though there was little to be had that day. Staring out onto the gloomy street, Lily watched the carriages and people pass, wondering what Mr. DeVere meant.

A tiny prick of her conscience told her she was not free to accept Mr. DeVere's offering, just as it had told her she should not have entertained his flattery or longed to drive out with him. But was it truly wrong of her to enjoy Mr. DeVere's company when her engagement was a temporary and unwelcome arrangement?

A clock chimed a trilling tinkle of bells, and Lily realized the day had gotten away from her. Stepping into the hallway, she went in search of her things and gave the flowers to a maid to put in water. As much as she wished to sit about pondering this strange turn of events, she had more important things to do at present.

With a basket of goodies packed and a maid trailing behind her, Lily's footsteps led her along the path to the foundling home with little thought. Though eager for her day's work to begin, thoughts of Mr. DeVere and Mr. Hatcher haunted her steps. Her life had taken a strange turn. Flirtation, a kiss, and an engagement; Lily laughed to herself as she realized her dreams for the Season had come to fruition—merely in the wrong order and with different gentlemen.

Thoughts of Mr. DeVere's bouquet and tender words made Lily's footsteps quicken and her heart lighten. Never had she been so admired by a gentleman. Merely thinking of his honeyed words was enough to warm Lily's heart, pulling her lips into a smile; they were precisely what a lady wished to hear, which made them all the more difficult to believe—even if she dearly wished to.

Mr. DeVere was dashing and several years younger than she. Though such a gap did not bother her in the slightest, it was exceptionally bizarre that such a gentleman would take a fancy to her when none had done so before.

Of course, Lily had seen overlooked ladies receive an unexpected influx of admirers before, as though the gentlemen did not notice the lady until one of their kind paid court to her, making her desirable and forcing them to give chase. Not that Lily would call two admirers an influx, but for her, it was a veritable flood.

Instinct warned her Mr. DeVere was not earnest in his admiration, but no matter how she tried to puzzle it all out, Lily was no closer to understanding either his or Mr. Hatcher's motivations.

With a few hurried steps, Lily crossed the road and entered through one of the side gates into Hyde Park. It was too early for the fashionable crowd to clog the pathways, and she reveled in the calm. There were those traversing the roadways on horseback or in carriages, but it was a minor thing compared to the cacophony found in the rest of London.

Though dark clouds filled much of the sky, holes appeared between them, allowing shafts of sunlight to peek through. How she wished the rain clouds would clear. The weather had been so wet of late, and Lily was desperate to enjoy a warm and bright day. Too much of the world looked dreary, and she needed a dose of sunshine.

So caught up was she in her thoughts of the city, of suitors, and of the children she was going to visit that Lily did not see the path before her. It was straight and wide with no turns or twists to require her attention, so she allowed her feet free rein to move as they pleased with no prompting, not even noticing that one of the gentlemen who occupied her thoughts was standing in her path until she nearly collided with him.

"Mr. Hatcher," said Lily with a curtsy as the fellow gave a bow and tip of his hat.

The pair stood there, watching each other. His expression was as stony as ever, but Lily felt a blush enter her cheeks. Their last interlude had been so mortifying and infuriating, which only added to the general discomfort she felt in his presence. She only hoped Mr. Hatcher attributed her coloring to the crisp air.

"I see you are out wandering the city on your own again." The words were innocent enough, but there was no mistaking the disapproval in his tone.

Lily's eyes narrowed, her spine straightening. "As before, I am not alone."

Mr. Hatcher's eyes darted from Lily to the maid standing behind her. His brows rose, and the edge of his lips curled into a hint of a smirk. His expression wasn't belittling or snide, but it held a clear challenge. After their previous discussion on the subject, Lily doubted he viewed a single maid as an improvement over the previous footman. But it was not worth arguing over, as Mr. Hatcher's opinion mattered little.

Until he took the basket from her maid and dismissed the girl.

"What are you doing?" demanded Lily.

"As we are betrothed, there is no impropriety in me squiring you about alone. We do not need her services."

Lily reached for the basket, but Mr. Hatcher pulled it away and motioned for her to continue down the path.

When she did not move, Mr. Hatcher sighed. "What is the matter?"

A great many things were the matter. The sensible voice in her head warned her to be calm. This was an irritation—nothing more. There was no need to make a scene. Unfortunately, that voice was drowned out by her mounting frustration.

"Why must you be so irritating?" she asked.

"I wish to accompany you. Would you have your servant continue to do so when she is not needed and has work awaiting her return?"

"No..." It was true that Lily would have dismissed the maid, but that was not the point. "I will be gone most of the afternoon, and surely, you have other obligations that will not allow you to accompany me."

"Nothing that is as important."

The terse reply startled Lily. A gentleman like Mr. Hatcher must have a day full of business to be done, yet he viewed accompanying her as the more pressing matter. There was nothing admirable about his heavy-handed approach to the situation, but it was impossible to remain unmoved by the sentiment behind it.

"I can send word to my partner to shift my schedule," said Mr. Hatcher. "But my duty lies in escorting my betrothed."

And that cold assessment eradicated any warmth she'd felt; there was nothing so chilling as being deemed a "duty."

"I had an escort, though such a thing is hardly needed," she said. "If you had bothered to discuss it with me before dismissing my maid, you could have saved yourself the inconvenience of rearranging your schedule."

"If I see something needing to be done, I do it. What is the matter in that?"

Lily reached for the basket again, but Mr. Hatcher would

not let go of it.

"Please hand it to me," she said.

Mr. Hatcher glanced at the basket and then at her. "Is this why you are so upset? I wouldn't be much of a gentleman if I did not carry it for you."

"A gentleman would ask permission," she said, the words coming through clenched teeth.

That infuriating eyebrow of his cocked upwards again. "You would say yes, so what is the point?"

"The point is that you insist on making decisions for me and never solicit my opinions."

His head tilted to the side as he examined her. "So, you would have me waste time going through pointless motions when we both know you would accept my help?"

Cold disappointment filled Lily, dousing her simmering anger as she realized his meaning; Mr. Hatcher thought asking her opinion was a waste of time. And Lily realized she was wasting hers by fighting this immovable man. Only a little patience was needed until her parents returned, and then she would be free of him.

The lady was a confusing mess. At times, Lily was so sensible, but then her feathers would ruffle over the slightest issue, and Jack was at a loss to understand her. He was being perfectly courteous in escorting her and taking her cumbersome basket, yet she acted as though he'd impugned her honor in some fashion.

Lily moved forward, and Jack fell into step beside her. Yet as they walked along, the lady did not speak, and it was no pensive silence. Though Jack was heartily sick of the contention between them, he couldn't help but smile to himself. Yet again, she was accepting defeat, but she mounted a silent protest all the same. Jack admired that spirit. Even if it was irritating.

"Then you are unhappy with me?" he asked, unable to stop himself from baiting her.

Straightening, Lily halted and whirled around to stare at him. "The last time we were together, you insulted me. And you think I would simply forget?"

The accusation startled a scowl from Jack. "I did not, and I will not apologize because you chose to invent some offense."

Lily's cheeks flushed crimson, but it was not the demure, timid color she usually displayed. It was blazing. But before she could open her mouth, Jack raised a staying hand.

"Can we agree to let the past go?"

Though her posture softened, Lily's gaze held a smoldering fire waiting to unleash its fury.

Jack sighed to himself, but he managed to hide his impatience. Diplomacy was not his forte. Perhaps he should petition Silas to act as a mediator between them; that fellow was far more adept at handling delicate situations. But perhaps Jack could muster some finesse for Lily's sake.

"It's clear you are angry," said Jack, neglecting to add he was oblivious as to why she was, "but might we begin anew? Whatever has passed between us, we are engaged to be married, and at the very least, I would hope for us to manage some level of domestic peace."

Lily's expression shifted, and Jack saw the signs that she was coming to her senses. It was a pinching of her lips. A slight furrow of her brow. The faintest of scowls with a hint of begrudging acceptance in her gaze.

"I suppose there is wisdom in that course of action," she said, her shoulders slumping. "Though I may not have shown it properly, I do not care for contention and prefer there to be peace between us."

"Then we've struck a truce?"

With a nod, Lily continued on her way, and Jack fell into step again. However, for all their talk of peace, the lady seemed in no hurry to broach a conversation, either.

"Might I ask where we are headed?" asked Jack.

"A foundling home. When I am in Town, I assist with the children's music lessons." Lily paused before pointing to the basket he carried. "At times, I bring them treats and toys."

It was a simple statement, yet it roused both respect and frustration for his affianced wife. There were plenty who espoused charitable beliefs, but few went out of their way to act on them. While her services to the poor and downtrodden was heartwarming, Lily had chosen a ridiculous manner in which to do so.

"What is the matter, Mr. Hatcher?"

Jack shook his head and kept walking.

"You made a distinct noise," she said, glancing at him from the corner of her eye. "It was both significant and vague."

Diplomacy. Lily wished for honesty, something Jack prized, but speaking his unadulterated thoughts was likely to break their newfound peace. Thinking of Silas's manner in delivering such news, Jack hesitantly opened his mouth.

"Perhaps that is not the most efficient manner in which to aid those children."

Lily halted once more. "Meaning?"

Jack was forced to stop and look at her. "Though you may feel music is a worthwhile pursuit, I doubt it is valuable to those children whose futures will not afford them leisure time to enjoy such hobbies. They do need an education to improve their lot in life, but math, reading, and the like are far more valuable in that respect."

There was a subtle shift in Lily's posture and expression, as though every muscle in her body tightened, making her more rigid with each word Jack spoke. Perhaps he should have kept his own counsel, but he couldn't fathom marrying a woman with whom he could not be honest.

Lily gave a jerky nod and stepped around Jack, moving briskly along the path.

Chapter 11

Insufferable man! To think that she'd almost believed Mr. Hatcher's truce to be true. The gentleman clearly did not understand the concept. Or did not care. She wasn't clear as to which it was, but it did not matter. Either way, Mr. Hatcher was a domineering, self-important fool.

She need only suffer his company for a few more weeks. That was all. Why could she not grit her teeth and remain silent? Speaking only made the situation worse, and Lily did not understand what had taken hold of her tongue.

Why did Mr. Hatcher's opinion matter to her?

Lily knew well that she placed too much of her happiness on the judgments of those around her, but Mr. Hatcher elicited a degree of honesty unlike any other. Perhaps it was his forthright nature or the relative anonymity of their relationship, but Lily found it impossible to keep her own counsel.

Yet perhaps that was not a terrible thing.

Stopping, Lily whirled on Mr. Hatcher and gathered her courage, straightening her metaphorical and physical spine to face him.

"You may not think my efforts worthwhile, Mr. Hatcher, but that does not mean it is so. You may not feel that music is a useful skill, but it is to these children."

Lily half expected him to interrupt, but he merely stood before her, clutching the basket. As always, his face was impassi-
ble, but there was some sentiment gleaming in his eyes she
could not identify—nor did she care to. Now was not his moment. It was hers.

"Many of those young boys choose a career in the army, and
they have bands used for morale and ceremony. A majority of
their musicians are foundling home boys who learned how to
play classes like this. Not only are those well-paid positions, but
it keeps the boys away from the battlefield."

Mr. Hatcher merely stood there listening, so Lily went on.

"Even if they do not join the army, there is a demand for
musicians, yet those from social classes that can afford lessons
would never demean themselves by becoming hired workers.
And the girls can never hope to become teachers and governesses without some musical knowledge. You say they need an
education that will improve their lot in life, and that is precisely
what I am doing."

Whipping around, Lily stormed down the path. But another thought had her stopping to add one more defense.

"And even if that were not true..." Lily's words wobbled, her
throat tightening against the rising sentiments pressing against
her chest. Gritting her teeth, she wished she could keep her
voice from cracking and the tears from pricking her eyes, but
Lily had never learned how to rein in her emotions. It was like
a flood that washed through her, sweeping away her good sense
and decorum. It filled the whole of her with unstoppable
strength until it spilled out of her eyes unbidden.

Lily cleared her throat and tried again, though her voice
quivered. "Even if these lessons do nothing for their employment, it is not a waste of time and effort. These poor children
have so little love and happiness in their life, but for a few hours
every week, I can visit them and show the affection they crave.
I can teach them something that will be a joy to them, even as
life stretches before them into dreary nothingness."

How Lily wanted to remain strong, but speaking of those

little dears added to the torrent. Her heart cried out for them and all the poor children who were mistreated or unwanted by the very people who brought them into this world. Merely the thought of anyone suffering as they did filled her with such unbearable pain. She burned with a desire to protect and heal them, to erase the damage that had been done to them. Her breathing hitched, her vision blurred, but she forged ahead.

"There are plenty who are willing to hand over money to pay for buildings and caregivers, but they need more than a roof over their heads and clothes on their backs. I can think of no better use of my time than to give them that."

Turning, Lily strode along the path as tears wet her cheeks. She wiped at them, but she would not stop to retrieve her handkerchief from her reticule. A hand grabbed her arm, but Lily pulled away, only stopping when Mr. Hatcher spoke.

"Lily."

"I still have not given you permission to address me so informally," she replied, though the tartness behind her words was destroyed by the broken manner in which she spoke them.

"Yes, but it made you stop," he said, pressing his handkerchief into her hand.

Keeping her back to the gentleman, Lily stared at the linen as though she had never seen one before. She snapped out of her daze and dabbed at her cheeks with it.

"Thank you, sir."

There was silence for a moment as she sniffled and mopped at her tears. When he finally spoke, it was a phrase Lily had never thought to hear from him.

"I apologize."

Two little words, but they were startling. Glancing over her shoulder, Lily watched him with a furrowed brow, her breath hitching with the remnants of her tears.

Mr. Hatcher's teeth were not gnashing over the pain he'd caused nor was he prostrate before her, but his gaze was sincere. Somehow, that was more powerful than any passionate display of remorse. Though she couldn't help but wish for a little more groveling, Lily suspected Mr. Hatcher was not a man to speak such words lightly.

Mr. Hatcher's expression tightened, and he grumbled, "You needn't look so shocked. I am fully capable of apologizing when I have caused offense."

"You did not apologize the other times."

Mr. Hatcher held her gaze, and though others may not have recognized the shift of emotion there, Lily saw the subtle clench of his jaw, and even a hint of hurt in his eyes. Or at least, she believed it was hurt. It wasn't an emotion she'd thought to see from Mr. Hatcher, but it was there.

Nodding at her to move along, Mr. Hatcher said not another word, but merely waited for her to continue on their way. But Lily did not move.

"Have I hurt you, Mr. Hatcher?"

He nodded for her to begin walking, but when she refused, he sighed. "Don't be ridiculous."

"It is not ridiculous if it is the truth."

"I am not a fragile thing so easily broken," he replied before prodding her to move, but Lily held firm. After a moment of staring at him, Mr. Hatcher finally tacked on, "But I am not the villain you paint me to be."

The accusation lit a flicker of defensive anger in Lily's chest, but reason gave way before her mouth got the better of her. She did not care for his implications, but neither did she wish to prove Mr. Hatcher right by immediately attacking him.

And when given a moment to reflect, Lily's instincts whispered that this was no little thing for him—no matter how casually he spoke the words. She had caused him pain, and that did not sit right with her. But before Lily could address the issue, the gentleman began walking, leaving her to follow after him, and she suspected he preferred to leave the subject alone.

Their footsteps came together, matching each other pace for pace. Lily clutched Mr. Hatcher's handkerchief, and she tucked it into her reticule. They passed under the line of trees in silence, and Lily struggled to know what to do.

"It appears the peace between us could not last five minutes. That does not bode well for any future felicity between us." Lily had meant it as a jest, but her voice remained unsteady.

Her statement was met with silence, and Lily thought Mr. Hatcher did not intend to engage with her. Right when she despaired of him fully, he spoke.

"Then we will just try again. I do not intend to surrender so easily."

The words were simple, but his tone was not. Lily wished she understood the gentleman better, for she could not decipher his thoughts from those two sentences. His tone was earnest and determined, with some underlying emotion Lily could not identify.

Mr. Hatcher stopped them again, and Lily turned to face him. His eyes were a shade of rich blue, and they held her gaze with an intensity that had a weight all its own, pushing against her. "I do apologize for what I said. Too often, I see others pacify their conscience by assisting the poor and needy in the most useless ways."

Lily opened her mouth to speak, but Mr. Hatcher raised a staying hand.

"It was wrong of me to judge you by that standard," he said. He took a step closer, his eyes never leaving hers, and a low warmth simmered in Lily's heart. "You are too kind-hearted to do something so thoughtless, and I should not have assumed otherwise."

Yet again, his words were brief but spoken with a determined focus that brought such meaning to them. Earnest and honest. Mr. Hatcher may be a man of few words, but he used them well.

"May we begin again?" Mr. Hatcher hesitated, his gaze finally breaking from hers with a faint grimace as he added, "Again?"

Who was this man? There were strong aspects of his personality that gave Lily pause, yet there were glimpses of something beneath the hard exterior that had her wondering what she might find if she dug deeper. This did not alter her plans to rid herself of her unsolicited fiancé, but furthering their acquaintance mightn't be a terrible thing.

"Yes, Mr. Hatcher," she said. "And I apologize for getting a tad...emotional. Though your opinion did sting, there was no cause for becoming so discomposed."

"No," he said, his brow drawing together as his eyes captured hers once more in their stormy gaze. "Never apologize for caring so deeply. It is not a shameful thing."

Something about Mr. Hatcher seemed so dour, as though he rarely smiled or found joy in the world around him. His demeanor was hard and austere, like a boulder in a stream as the world flowed around it. Immovable. Still, there was a warmth to his eyes that belied that cold, aloof manner. As though during their short acquaintance, he had come to admire her. Though that was not quite the right word. Lily scoured her thoughts for how to quantify the emotions filling Mr. Hatcher's gaze, but she could not, nor could she understand why it filled her heart with a warmth that made the cool, damp spring day feel quite pleasant.

Lily did not know what to say in response, so she simply nodded. Mr. Hatcher turned to continue their journey, but he paused, offering his free arm to her. Lily stared at it. It was not as though she was ignorant of its meaning, but no gentleman ever offered one to her.

It was a small gesture, and rather unimportant to those viewing it from the outside. However, to Lily, it was something more. It was intimate. Some might think her ridiculous for putting so much meaning to such a simple thing, but one did not simply stroll along on a random gentleman's arm; it signified a deeper relationship than that of acquaintances or friends.

Of course, it made sense that Mr. Hatcher would do so. They were "engaged," after all. But there was something in his expression that made her believe it was no small thing for him, either.

Looping her arm through his, Lily wondered what to do with that hand. It was a silly thing to worry about, but letting it rest against his arm felt too forward. Other than holding a hand during the odd dance, Lily had hardly touched a man before. It was only an arm, but it left her flustered and discomposed.

She was such a ninny! It was only an escort. Lily had done far more intimate things with the fellow, but rather than comfort her, that thought made her blush all the more. There was nothing to get so bothered about, but the stance brought them close together and his legs brushed her skirts as they continued along the path.

Their first few steps were awkward. They bumped into each other, and Lily thought it preferable to have her arm free. But then their paces matched step-by-step, and the pair found a rhythm that blended together.

Chapter 12

The park was mostly unoccupied. Those of the lower classes had long ago begun their work, and those of the elite hadn't stirred from their houses. It was not empty but as close to it as one could find in the middle of London.

The birds and insects were dormant, for though the rain had not made an appearance today, it was thick in the air, promising a downpour later. Only the sounds of the pair's footsteps broke the silence. It was quite peaceful, even if the sodden world was far too gray to be deemed beautiful.

Mr. Hatcher was quiet beside her, though it was not an empty silence. There seemed to be thoughts aplenty in his head; he simply did not share them. Lily wondered what occupied his attention so thoroughly, and the more she thought, the more she realized just how little she knew the fellow at her side.

"Do you have any hobbies?" she asked, for that seemed as good a subject as any to broach. It was better than strolling along in silence.

He turned his head to look at her with a puzzled frown. "Hobbies?"

Lily fought back a laugh; his tone sounded so surprised that she couldn't help herself. "You look as though that is a positively mad question to ask, but I assure you it is quite a natural one. I cannot be the only one who has asked you."

Mr. Hatcher's eyes slid back to their path, and he gave a vague huff. "In all honesty, you may be."

Her brows shot upright. "I cannot believe that. Surely, you have some acquaintance or friend who has posed that question before."

"Believe what you will, but there are not many whom I can count as friends, and generally, my acquaintances only care about what advice I can give them concerning investments and finances."

But before Lily could respond to that surprising declaration, Mr. Hatcher continued, "But to answer your question, growing my business has not allowed me much time for hobbies in the past few years, but I do enjoy sewing."

Lily nearly tripped over her own feet at that declaration. "I do not know many gentlemen who would admit that."

Mr. Hatcher shrugged as though it was of no importance to him. "It was a necessary skill in the navy, and one I enjoy."

"You were in the navy?"

"Until I was four and twenty." He paused, and Lily glanced at him. Then he added, "I served with my business partner, Mr. Silas Byrnes, and we left together to open a shipping business. In the nine years since, we've expanded into other ventures as well."

"You've done very well for yourself, especially considering the present state of the economy," said Lily.

Mr. Hatcher glanced at her, his brows raised, though he did not voice the question written in his expression.

"I've read accounts in the newspapers, and I've heard my father and Uncle Ambrose speaking about such matters," she said, then added, "And I have the evidence of my own eyes, as the demand for charity has risen at an alarming rate. With the Corn Laws repealed, I had hoped things might improve, but I fear the Great Famine has taken too great a toll on the country with no end in sight."

Mr. Hatcher blinked at her as though she had been speaking Latin, which did terrible things to the fledgling goodwill she felt for the fellow.

"Believe it or not, Mr. Hatcher, but there are plenty of ladies who have an interest in the world around them and keep abreast of current events," she grumbled.

Walking at his side as she was, Lily could not fully see his face, but there was that same flash of emotion she'd seen during their last quarrel, and a sliver of guilt pricked her heart.

Mr. Hatcher stared down the road. "Even most gentlemen I know are not so well informed, and most begrudge the repeal of those laws that kept their coffers full at the expense of the less fortunate."

That sickening feeling spread, pressing on Lily's chest, as she realized she'd misjudged the situation. "I apologize for being abrupt, Mr. Hatcher. It appears I was too hasty in judging your meaning and took offense."

"I would hope for better common ground with my future wife than a tendency to judge too hastily, but I suppose it is something."

The statement was spoken with a dry wit, but it was said with wit all the same, and it elicited a laugh from Lily. "That is a dreadful beginning. But we both must learn to give the benefit of the doubt before assuming the worst."

There was a hint of a smile playing at the edge of his mouth. Though she only saw his profile, Lily swore it was there. But he gave a solemn nod that belied any humor she thought she read on his face.

"Do you miss the sea?" she asked.

"Not in the slightest."

Lily glanced at him. "I grew up listening to stories of my Uncle Graham's life in the navy, and it sounded like quite the adventure. Surely to see all those exotic lands was thrilling."

Mr. Hatcher halted in his steps, pulling Lily to a stop beside him. Turning enough to face her, he looked as sour as she'd ever seen him. "Men like your uncle romanticize naval life, but it is a brutal thing."

"Every profession has its drawbacks, but—"

"It is a life of blood and death." Holding her gaze, Mr. Hatcher leaned closer. "Even if you never see battle, life aboard a ship is filled with scurvy and floggings. I've seen sadists given command and their men beaten for the slightest infraction. Before I left home, my parents filled my head with romantic notions of the grand adventures I'd have and the many lands I'd see, but the reality of naval life was little better than hell on earth, with my life placed in the hands of a man who thought of his crew as slaves."

Lily couldn't breathe. Or more accurately, she couldn't let herself breathe. The pains in her heart grew with each of his words and doubled at the haunted look hiding in his gaze. Though he did not enumerate his wounds, Lily suspected they were many. Likely more than he realized.

"How old were you when you joined?" she asked.

"Almost ten."

Lily knew there were younger boys at sea than that, but the thought of any child being thrust into such a brutal world filled her with despair.

"I do not need your pity," he grumbled, turning to walk, and it was Lily's turn to stop him.

"It is not pity I feel," said Lily, forcing him to meet her eye with the same ferocity with which he'd held hers. "Pity is a shallow thing. It's a pat on the head with a few trite words of comfort. And what I feel is anything but that. My heart breaks for the little boy who had to face such difficulties, and I wish I could've shielded him from such suffering. I feel that pain as if it were my own, regardless of your objections. I cannot help it."

There was no good to be found in bemoaning the past, and Jack did not understand why she made such a to-do about it. But though he felt an inkling of embarrassment, it was touching to see her dander raised on his behalf. Not that she cared for him precisely; she sympathized with any child who was so mistreated.

Jack had never known anyone who loved so deeply and quickly as his Lily.

The lady seemed to need an acknowledgment, so he gave her another nod, and they fell into step once more—a perfect synchronicity as though they had been fashioned for one another. Though that was far too soppy a thought for Jack to entertain without laughing at himself.

Lily remained silent, and Jack sensed her thoughts were focused on his ridiculous confession. He wished she would forget his words. Plenty of people believed the fairy tales about the grand adventure that was the sea and waxed poetic about the freedom found aboard a ship, but hearing Lily speak such nonsense had demanded a response. Why had he said so much? Jack believed in being truthful, but there was nothing to be gained from bringing his history to light.

What good did it do to tell her of the scars marking his back? Or that the fingers on his right hand refused to straighten properly after a particularly violent row with one of his shipmates? Of the seamen who died not from an enemy's attack but the deprivations meted on them by their captain? Of the nightmares that plagued him on restless nights?

Lily should not be tainted by such things.

"I learned to sew for my benefit," he said. It was a silly topic to return to, but it was better than allowing the previous one to linger between them. Lily's expression cleared with each word, and he found more coming to his lips. "There weren't seamstresses aboard the ship, so I did my own mending. I have no interest in embroidery and am only passable at making clothes, but I enjoy stitching things together. Eventually, I took on other sailors' mending as well and earned extra income as the ship's tailor."

"That's a clever use of your skill," said Lily. "But I have to admit I detest sewing in all its forms. To do it well takes far too much precision, and I fear I have not the temperament to master it."

The lady drifted off into silence once more, and Jack scoured his thoughts for something that might draw her back into conversation.

"And you are musical?" he blurted, grasping on the first subject that came to mind.

"Yes," she replied, and though Jack did not turn to see her expression, he heard the smile in her tone. "I sing and play the pianoforte, though I am better at the former than the latter. I adore music."

There was a brightness to Lily when she spoke that colored her words, infusing them with a joy that could not be ignored. As though that love she felt consumed so much of her that even her voice was laden with it.

"I have often wished there was a way to bottle music so that I might carry it around with me always," she said.

"As a singer, you bring your instrument with you," Jack pointed out, and that elicited a laugh from Lily.

"Could you imagine how people would react if I were to burst out into song as though my life were an opera?"

Jack could imagine it, and that silly image brought a smile to his face as well.

"Even if I were to limit myself to moments when I was alone, it would not be the same. Not quite," she said with a shake of her head. "While I enjoy playing and singing, it is not like listening to a professional. For the most part, I do not care for London, but the city offers so many concerts and balls that I am blessed to listen to music played by those who are far more talented than myself almost every night."

She sighed. "And it takes such time to learn a piece well enough before I can lose myself in the music. At a concert, I can immerse myself in its beauty without needing to worry about anything else but my own enjoyment."

With a few slight prompts, Lily expounded on her passion with a vivacity that made Jack wish he had the power to give her that impossible dream of hers. He had never found much joy in songs, but listening to her speak about it with such intensity made him wonder if he'd misjudged it. Now that he thought about it, Jack wasn't certain he had ever attended an entire concert or performance. Certainly, it would be impossible not to enjoy an evening of music if his companion showed such earnest enjoyment as Lily.

"But I have allowed my mouth to run away with itself," said Lily, her tone colored by chagrin. "I apologize for commandeering the conversation, but I cannot seem to help it at times." Before Jack could assure her that her conversation had been anything but an imposition, she continued, "Do you live in London?"

It was a simple question, but Jack's answer was not a simple one. "I go wherever our business needs me. My partner lives here, and I stay with him and his family when I am needed in Town. But generally, I am not in one place long enough to claim it."

"It must be difficult living like a nomad."

In truth, Jack had not given it much thought. "I've never found a place worth settling."

"Do you have no family home?" Lily's voice was soft, and there was a disconcerting amount of something close to pity in it.

"My parents and sister passed away in a cholera epidemic just after I reached my majority, and there was no house once their creditors were done with them."

Lily pulled him to a stop, though Jack tried to keep walking. While there were many reasons he favored Lily's larger frame, the fact that she could slow him was mildly irritating.

"It must have been painful to lose them," she said.

Though she claimed her feelings were more compassionate than pitying, it felt like pity all the same, for he did not feel any pain with which to sympathize.

"I hardly saw them once I left home. It was no great loss to me."

"You last saw your family when you were ten years old?"

Jack shrugged. "I returned for a shore leave or two, but for the most part, I had no interest in doing so."

"Whyever not?"

That wasn't a question he was often asked. Or if it was posed, it was done with a suspicious or imperious air that demanded an answer. If Lily has spoken the words with even a hint of those emotions, Jack would have called it out as the impertinent question it was. However, there was nothing but wide-eyed curiosity and concern in her gaze, as though she could think of no worse thing to endure than being absent from his childhood home.

"My parents rarely wrote to me and never sent funds for me to make the journey, so I did not see the point in making the effort myself," he replied. Lily's eyes widened at the first half of his statement, but before she could speak, he added, "My parents were not wicked people. They were simply frivolous and empty-headed. It would not surprise me if they'd meant to stir themselves and simply never got around to it."

Before Lily could prod him further on the topic, Jack nodded for them to walk. "Now, if we do not continue on our way, you are going to be excessively late."

Lily was somewhat subdued as they continued on this interminable walk through the park, but Jack knew not how to revive her spirits and return that brightness to her eyes. He's never felt such a compulsion before, and as he was anything but an adept conversationalist, Jack was at a loss of how to proceed.

Luckily, Lily could not remain silent for long, and the conversation began on one thread before branching off into another. Soon, it became a series of strings woven together as Lily shifted from subject to subject before returning to a previous point and shifting to a whole new vein. Her mind conjured queries and made connections between various topics with a logic known only to Lily.

And though Jack could not claim familiarity with all the subjects and some were of no interest to him, the majority were engaging and ranged from the mundane to profound. At times, Lily prodded him for opinions but never forced the issue, allowing him to offer up his thoughts as he wished.

They spoke of the economy, art, music, travel, and even politics—a topic that generally irritated him when broached by anyone else. Every time Jack thought they'd exhausted their options, Lily posed another question and took them in a new direction. It was an odd string of thoughts, but Jack could not recall a more enjoyable conversation.

"But my mouth has run away with me once again," said Lily, her cheeks coloring. "I do apologize—"

"Why do you keep doing that? You have nothing to apologize for."

Lily Kingsley was a lady who stood out. Even if one discounted the effusive light that radiated from her, she was too large a woman to be ignored. Yet she shrank in on herself. It was a subtle shift with her shoulders curving forward as her expression dimmed, her eyes darting away from him.

"I don't always realize how long I've been talking," she said with a dismissive wave of her hand, though her red cheeks testified that the gesture was a lie. This mattered a great deal to her.

But when she did not continue, Jack said, "And what does that signify? Your conversation is lively."

Lily's eyes shot to his and then away again. "I've been told I'm too talkative."

Jack scowled. "What halfwit suggested such a thing?"

Lily shook her head, but he would not allow her to leave the question unanswered. He asked again, and she finally admitted the truth.

"When I was younger, a friend came to me and relayed a message from a young man of our acquaintance. He thought me charming at times but quite tedious at others because I never rein in my tongue and go into too much detail. He suggested my friend speak to me, as others would find me more engaging if I were more circumspect."

The whole speech was delivered with a casual air, but there was a brittle quality to Lily's voice, and Jack was not deceived by her performance.

She gave a false laugh. "It would be difficult enough to ignore the gentleman's opinion, for it was such a significant issue that it needed addressing, but the message was passed through a second party, who clearly felt the same or she would not have said a word. By the mouth of two witnesses, as the Bible says..."

Her voice trailed off, though Lily feigned a smile.

"Ludicrous." He hadn't meant to bark the word, but there was no stopping the force with which he spoke it.

Lily turned to look at him, her eyebrows raising.

"I assure you that your conversation is not tedious in any fashion," said Jack. "And you needn't ever apologize for it."

Her eyes turned to the path ahead of them, her spine straightening as they walked forward. Though he saw only her profile, Jack noticed a faint furrowing of her brow. When she turned to face him again, they were pulled tightly together.

"You do not mind me chattering on as I do?"

Jack huffed. "Nonsense. You do not chatter, and anyone who has told you otherwise is a lackwit."

Lily gave a vague noise that sounded intrigued, and she glanced at him with a question in her eyes, as though asking permission to return to the conversation he had been enjoying before she'd ended it so abruptly.

"You were speaking about a serial," he prompted. "Though I do not often read them, it sounds fascinating. I may have to try it."

Lily gave him a brilliant smile, that spark returning to her eyes. "I cannot wait until the final installments are published! I am desperate to know what will happen. I am so furious at Amelia! Her snake of a husband does not deserve her undying loyalty to his memory. She is a fool and doesn't deserve Dobbins' devotion..."

Chapter 13

J ack rarely had an afternoon free, and today was no exception. There were stacks of papers on his desk awaiting his return; a never-ending mass of inquiries and concerns that needed addressing. Though his appointments today were easily rescheduled, a sliver of concern worked its way into his thoughts—to follow Lily around would disrupt his plans.

But even as he recognized it was not the wisest course of action, Jack could not bring himself to take his leave. The longer they walked, the easier their conversation became, and the more difficult it was to pull himself away. Impossible, even. As fruitless as Luddites fighting against the inevitable march of progress. And it was not as though he could abandon Lily to her own devices; she needed an escort.

When they finally arrived at the foundling home, Jack wished for more time alone, but seeing Lily beam as they welcomed her was worth the sacrifice. The building was by no means inviting, as though the bricks themselves understood the sadness housed within, but when Lily stepped across the threshold, an air of vitality swept through it.

Tiny footsteps scuttled across the ceiling above them, and a servant at the door greeted her with expressions of genuine pleasure. Jack had no intention of leaving Lily's side, but he was given no choice in the matter, for they were ushered through the entry, up a narrow staircase, and into a spartan room.

The floor was bare, the wood was scarred and dull from years of use, and an array of childish drawings pinned to the walls provided the only adornment in the room. The few chairs and tables had been pushed to the edges, leaving the space clear for the gaggle of children who ran to greet them. The little ones clamored at the sight of Lily, wrapping themselves around her skirts as she bent to greet them with a little word here, a smile there, and as many embraces as she could manage before they were called to task.

"Children, please!" called a woman, though her voice lacked the harsh tone one expected when dealing with such a horde. "Remember your manners."

"Yes, Mrs. Bonneville," came the chorus of replies, and though the children obeyed, they were still abuzz with frenetic energy.

"Seats," Lily said with a smile, and most of the children scurried to the far end of the room and sat on the floor in a mis-shapen line.

"I will get there first," said Lily, taunting the few stragglers, and when she moved to take her place at the front, they scrambled to take their seats before her. Though reasonably still and quiet, the children wiggled in place as Lily took a moment to greet the teacher. Then, coming to stand before her pupils, Lily turned to a chalkboard propped to one side and pointed at the various notes.

Standing there with the basket in his hands, Jack didn't know what to do with himself or his burden, but Lily was occupied with other concerns as she quizzed them on scales. Jack took a seat on an obliging bench beside the wall that afforded him a view of his betrothed and sat the basket at his feet.

On the other end of the wooden plank was a lad who looked six or seven years of age and watched him with wary eyes. Jack moved to the farthest end, giving the boy more space—though the child scooted away until he was fairly hanging off the edge of the bench. Jack averted his eyes and focused on Lily as she and Mrs. Bonneville led the children through their lesson, though he felt the lad's attention on him, staring as though Jack were a monster ready to pounce.

Reaching into Lily's basket, Jack pulled back the linen protecting the bundle and searched the contents. There were toys and other trinkets that did not fit the bill, but then he spied a hefty paper bundle in one corner and discovered a bag of sweets. Keeping his actions hidden from the tiny eyes watching him, Jack snatched a caramel from the pile and tucked the basket away once more.

With a subtle slide of his hand, Jack placed the sweet on the bench between them. It sat there for several long moments before a tiny hand slid along the wood to snatch it. The child twisted in his seat so that he could reach it with his left hand, and his odd movement drew Jack's attention to his empty right sleeve.

Settling back into their seats, Jack and the boy watched the lesson as Mrs. Bonneville led the children in song and Lily pointed to the lyrics on the board. Jack reached into his pocket and pulled out his watch. Truly, he should return to the office, but he couldn't fathom returning to his letters and books while his mind was so firmly fixed on Lily.

The bench shifted, and Jack heard the sound of sliding across the wood. He did not look directly to his left, but he sensed the boy drawing slowly closer. Then the child stretched to get a clearer view of the timepiece in Jack's hand. Turning it, he gave the boy a better look without letting the lad know he'd been noticed.

But the sounds of footsteps entering the classroom startled the child, and he shrank away as Jack looked to see a middle-aged woman standing in the doorway with the air of one who was in command of her surroundings. No doubt this was the matron of this facility.

Tucking his watch into his pocket, Jack turned his attention to Lily as the boy beside him returned to his place on the far side of the bench. It was marvelous to see her in her element. Jack wouldn't have labeled Miss Lily Kingsley as confident, but she had a definite aura about her as she assisted Mrs. Bonneville and worked with the children. She infused the lesson with her enthusiasm but did so with a strong will—which was necessary when facing several dozen rambunctious children. Folding his arms, Jack watched her every movement.

That time they'd spent together in the market sprang to mind, and Jack remembered the possessive manner in which Lily had clutched that silly shawl of hers. She'd wanted the thing so desperately that she would've paid any price for it, and at the time, he'd thought it foolish. At present, Jack was coming to understand that desperation and desire. In the confines of his heart and mind, he could admit there was no price too high if it meant securing her as his wife.

This shift inside him made no rational sense. In a short period, Jack Hatcher had gone from a self-made man to being at the mercy of another. His heart thumped in his chest as though it were trying to beat some sense into him, but it was that foolish organ that had trapped him so thoroughly. If it were simply a matter of attraction, the sentiment could be dealt with, but every moment Jack spent in her company had become precious to him, though she seemed utterly unaware of the passion she inspired in him.

For his part, Jack wasn't certain if that were a good or bad thing.

"Might I ask you your name, sir?"

The matron's voice startled Jack from his thoughts, though he was quite grateful for the distraction. Getting to his feet, Jack bowed to her.

"Mr. Jonathan Hatcher. Miss Kingsley and I are engaged to be married, and I am playing escort for the afternoon."

The woman's brows rose at that revelation. "There has been no announcement."

Jack nodded, and though he'd been willing to accommodate Lily's wishes, he found himself quite displeased with that oversight at present. Though it did nothing to alter the truth of their situation, he wished for a far more binding agreement between them.

"We are awaiting her parents' return from the Continent, though it is no secret," said Jack.

The woman's only response was an indistinct huff that held a note of challenge. It was a sound Jack had made many a time when approached with a proposition that was neither wholly acceptable nor detestable. It demanded proof before support would be given, and with the calculating manner in which the matron examined him, Jack knew she thought it unlikely to happen.

"I am Mrs. Halliday," she finally replied, though she neither continued with their conversation nor moved away. Mrs. Halliday simply examined him as though she were trying to decide whether a cut of beef had gone off.

Where Lily's uncle had failed to instill any fear or respect, this woman's hard judgment was succeeding. Her dark eyes were unblinking and unwavering, and Jack's own warmed at the sight of her protective fury. Though he had set many people in their place when they overstepped their bounds, Jack's respect grew for Mrs. Halliday, who earnestly wished to safeguard his Lily and did not cower when faced with an opponent such as Jack Hatcher.

Mrs. Halliday's eyes narrowed, though the cold bite in her gaze softened a touch. "We will see."

She spoke no further words, simply turned to stand beside Jack and watched as the lesson ended and playtime began. Fetching her basket, Lily unleashed a whirlwind of giddiness as she plied the children with treats and toys. She was pulled from game to game as the children all vied for her and Mrs. Bonneville's attention. Lifting one of the smaller girls, Lily placed the child on her lap and sat on the floor as the pair played with a small doll.

"She is quite popular," said Jack.

"Miss Kingsley's family have always been beloved here,"

said Mrs. Halliday, tucking her hands behind her. "Her family has been our most faithful benefactor and supporter for as long as I can remember."

"You've been here many years?"

Mrs. Halliday stood silent for a long moment before replying. "I was raised in this home and became a maid, then teacher, and eventually matron. I remember Miss Kingsley's grandmother and mother visiting much the same as Miss Kingsley does now. Sweets and all."

Jack watched as Lily whispered something to the young girl on her lap, and the child beamed and hugged the doll tightly.

"They are the best of people," added Mrs. Halliday with that challenging air, and Jack gave the woman a nod in acknowledgment of the unspoken threat filling her tone. Jack had every intention of being a good husband to Lily.

The pair returned to their silent observations of the joyful chaos. Jack couldn't remember the last time he'd felt an urge to play, but part of his soul longed to join the melee. It was a ridiculous impulse, as he hadn't the foggiest notion how to do so. Nor did he find it comforting to have such a childish impulse take hold of him.

"Who is that lad?" asked Jack, nodding at the one-armed child with eyes far older than his years. He had moved from his place on the bench to a solitary corner of the room, watching the fun yet not participating in it.

"Gregor Jones," replied Mrs. Halliday. Though she did not add to that statement, her tone spoke of affection burdened by worry.

"Is he ill?"

Mrs. Halliday's brows rose. "No, sir, he is a robust child."

Seeing that his first guess was wrong, Jack clarified himself. "You sounded concerned about him, and with his injury, I had thought—"

But Mrs. Halliday shook her head with a sad smile as she watched Gregor in his quiet corner. "It does not pain him any longer. He lost his arm when it was crushed by a carriage, and it has healed nicely. It is not his health that has me concerned."

The matron was quiet for a long while, her expression growing more lined and tense as she watched the boy who sat apart from the others. Though the rest of the children varied in the games they played and the volume with which they did so, they each took part in the fun. Gregor simply watched, his eyes never turning away from the children while his shuttered expression hid his thoughts.

"Six months ago, I found Gregor living on the street not far from here. His family had abandoned him to his own devices after the accident. They could not afford to feed someone who could not work," said Mrs. Halliday. Her expression grew stonier, though her gaze softened as it rested on the poor lad. "We do our best to train the children and find them positions when it is time for them to leave our home, and many of them thrive. But what can we do when the children have injuries so great they cannot hope to perform the tasks required of a laborer or soldier? And even if their abilities are not hindered by their physical imperfection, too many employers will not hire an impaired worker when they can have a whole one."

Mrs. Halliday sighed. "I fret over all the children in my care, Mr. Hatcher, but those like Gregor cause me the most distress. It is difficult to ensure that each is provided with gainful employment, but with such an impediment, it is near impossible. We try to keep them on as teachers or servants, but we cannot help them all, and too many end up as beggars on the street."

Though Mrs. Halliday made a good show of keeping her emotions tamped, there was a hint of shine to her eyes. "We have saved Gregor for now, but I fear it is only delaying the inevitable."

Jack's throat tightened as he listened to Mrs. Halliday, his heart straining against his constricting chest. No wonder Gregor had such an air of hopelessness to him. He was old enough to understand what his family had done and what the future held for him. The way he'd snatched that sweet spoke of a soul that had learned the hard reality that life can snatch away even the smallest of joys. No child should bear such sorrow.

Pulling a calling card and pencil from his pocket, Jack scribbled a name and direction on the back of it and handed it to Mrs. Halliday.

"Mr. Shiller can assist you," said Jack.

Mrs. Halliday took the card in her hands, examining the inscription and note. Glancing at Jack with a clear question written on her face, she waited for him to explain. Though he preferred Mr. Shiller to handle the details, Jack knew more words were necessary.

"He heads a charity that finds work for those with physical limitations," said Jack. "He will assist you with Gregor and any other children when they are ready to join the workforce."

Eyes widening a fraction, Mrs. Halliday straightened as she stared at the card and then at Jack. But then her brows drew together in a hard pull. "But is he an honest and respectable man? There are plenty who claim to be charitable but are far from it—"

Jack raised a staying hand. "He was a fellow naval man who lost a leg during his time at sea, and when he was unable to manage aboard a ship, he was cast adrift with no means of supporting himself and his family."

His jaw tensed at the memory of finding the Shiller family wasting away in the workhouse. "He is the best of men, and I wouldn't have given him stewardship over that enterprise if he weren't."

Gripping the card in one hand, Mrs. Halliday offered the other to Jack, giving his a hearty shake.

Chapter 14

"Put the doll in the basket, Hetty," said Lily, pointing to the toy that had been tucked in the far corner of the room. "Julius, gather the soldiers."

It took much prompting from both Lily and Mrs. Bonneville before all the items were stowed in the basket, and a part of Lily's heart broke at the sad eyes that watched her as she lifted the bundle.

"We're not leaving the toys?" asked Mr. Hatcher. His question startled her—not the words themselves but their suddenness. He'd been on the other side of the room, deep in conversation with Mrs. Halliday seconds before. How had he snuck up on her?

Mr. Hatcher took the basket from her. The gentleman did not even recognize that once again he'd acted without asking permission. Lily knew it was petty to be bothered over such a little thing, but it was yet another sign of Mr. Hatcher's heavy-handedness.

However, Lily was equally annoyed at how grateful she was for that heavy-handed assistance. Even with the sweets distributed, the basket was ungainly and difficult to manage. And it was flattering that he did so without prompting. Perhaps it was her less than delicate frame that made others believe she did not need assistance, but even the most proper gentlemen forgot their manners when in her company and did not think to offer.

"I wish we could," she said. Little Daisy toddled over to her, wrapping her arms around Lily's skirts. Bending to lift the darling, she gave the child a hug farewell. "However, they do not have the space to store such things. They can house more children if they keep the unessentials to a minimum."

"Miss Kingsley brings us the toys and lets us borrow them," said William, rubbing his nose on his cuff.

"Absolutely not," said Lily, shaking her head in mock solemnity. "They are *your* toys. I am merely holding them for you."

William gave her a gapped tooth grin, which helped lighten her heart. Spending time with the children was such a boon to her spirits, but the initial parting was equally disheartening. They deserved so much more happiness than the foundling home could give them. Children should have toys and treats. They should be loved. Each time, she found herself wishing she could take them all home with her or that she might be able to spend more time with them, but it was not possible. Lily did what she could and gave what she had, but she did not have an unlimited supply of time or funds.

Mr. Hatcher helped her with her jacket, and Lily pulled on her gloves and bonnet as those thoughts pulled her into new worries. The list of things needing her attention grew as the charity concert drew closer. Lily had organized such events before, but that did not stop a shiver from settling into her stomach.

There was so much to be done. Her mind played through the people she needed to speak with and the various tasks she'd volunteered to oversee, and it was a good long moment before she realized Mr. Hatcher was waiting for her as she stood there like a statue.

Lily stepped forward but halted as she recalled the caramel in her pocket. Mrs. Bonneville had the children in hand and seated on their benches, their attention on their lesson. Gregor sat as far from the others as the tiny benches would allow; no matter how Lily attempted to engage him, he still would not join in the lessons or play. But she would not allow him to forgo everything.

With quiet steps, Lily snuck to his side and crouched to place the sweet on the bench beside him. His eyes darted to hers, his expression not changing from the blank one he always affected—though there was a hint of warmth and gratitude in his eyes. He spoke not a word, simply held her gaze as though that might convey all that was going on in his head, and Lily squeezed his remaining hand before slipping away.

Mr. Hatcher stood in the doorway, watching the pair of them, and when Lily caught sight of the expression on his face, her steps faltered. It was not so much that it showed any warmth or sorrow or emotion of any sort, but it was as though a grown version of Gregor stood before her. Even that same hint of something stirring inside him as he watched her. It broke her heart as verily as those young, sad eyes had seconds ago.

Stepping past Mr. Hatcher, Lily made her way down the stairs and onto the pavement as the gentleman trailed behind her. With a lift of his arm, he offered it to her, and Lily took it. The pair retraced their steps home in silence. It had hardly been more than a few hours since she had despised the gentleman at her side, and now, Lily wasn't certain what she felt or even what she wished to feel towards him.

"I see why you enjoy visiting the children," said Mr. Hatcher.

"Then it was not a waste of time?"

His brow furrowed. "I never called it a waste—"

"I was teasing you, Mr. Hatcher."

Though he did not push the previous subject, her words did not ease the unhappy pull of his expression. Lily thought through her words, trying to identify what it was that disturbed him so, though perhaps disturbed was too great a word for it. She wished she understood the gentleman's moods, but they were difficult to decipher. When no answer came to her, Lily decided that a more direct approach could not hurt things. At worst, they would argue once more, but as she had already weathered several of those, another did not matter much.

"Are you angry with me?"

Mr. Hatcher's brows rose, and he glanced at her. "No."

Lily sighed at that, for it was clearly not true. Or not the whole of it.

"You insist on calling me 'Mr.'"

That revelation was startling enough that Lily halted, but the street was busy, and there was no place for them to stand. Luckily, the park was in sight, and she waited until they were out of the way to pull him to the side so she could face him. Though his expression did not tell her much, it was easier than speaking to his profile.

"And that angers you?" she asked.

"As I said before, I am not angry," he said with a huff.

Looking at the hard lines of his face, Lily thought that was precisely what he was, but instinct whispered to her, insisting he was being truthful. Mr. Hatcher may be frustrating and difficult, but the more she spoke with him, the more she felt to her bones that he was an honest man. If anything, he was too free with those honest thoughts at times.

So, she studied his expression and thought over what had been said. The more she pondered, the more Lily wondered if he might be upset—hurt, even. She had seen a glimpse of it earlier, and there it was again.

"But it does bother you."

Though she had posed the question, Lily did not fully expect an answer, but he met her gaze and said, "Yes."

Lily's head tilted to the side as she watched him. She felt as though she were standing in a museum, examining a fine work of art. Not that his features were particularly handsome—though Lily saw a definite appeal to his strong features—but she found herself studying every aspect of his face, hunting for the little signs of the emotions he kept so securely locked away.

"Why does it bother you that I prefer a bit of formality when

I hardly know you—engaged or not?" she asked.

A twitch at the corner of his lips. The slightest tightening at his eyes. There were clear indications of something happening inside his skull, and Lily felt an urge to shake it loose. He stood there in silence for so long she assumed he would not answer.

"You treat me like a fool," he said.

Straightening, she asked, "How so?"

"Do you think I cannot see you have no intention of honoring our engagement?"

"Why would you say that?" Of course, it was the truth, but that was not of the utmost concern at present. Lily was more startled at his question's sudden appearance.

"If this engagement were real to you, you would not snap at me every time I use your given name nor insist on keeping me at a distance in this most basic manner," he said. "You hold to such formality because you view this as a temporary irritant and not a true betrothal."

Lily's eyes widened and her breathing paused as she watched him, but it wasn't the surprise of having her plans revealed that held her captive. Mr. Hatcher was no fool, and she had not hidden her feelings concerning this unwanted turn of events. Simply recalling the forthright manner with which she had rebuffed him during their last outing was enough to bring a flush to her cheeks.

But Lily had never imagined it would bother him.

"Why does it matter?" she asked. "Neither of us wished for this engagement."

She had posed a similar question to him not long ago, and he had not been forthcoming then, so she did not know why she thought to get an answer now. But this was not a question posed in anger or thrown out like a challenge. Lily truly wished to know his reasons, for she was at a loss to understand him. And at that moment, she longed to.

There was a shift in his expression, faint and slight enough that it was a mystery to her. But in his eyes, she saw a growing warmth. Mr. Hatcher's gaze held such power, and it was turned fully on her. Lily's heart stuttered in her chest, though she couldn't tell if it was an echo of the passion they'd shared in that one glorious moment or if her heart was truly drawn to him.

There were too many doubts and questions clogging her thoughts to see the truth. Was Mr. Hatcher acting only out of duty? Her mind said yes, but staring into his eyes, she felt a resounding "no" in her heart. But that could merely be her ridiculous sentimentality inferring more than he intended. Was this real?

Did she wish it to be? That was a complex question in its own right, but trapped as she was in that heated gaze, Lily wanted to lean in and close the distance once more. Those few moments of tender delight in the library had not been enough—especially not with his heated gaze fixed on her.

"Lily..."

This time his use of her name didn't raise her hackles. Lily had never heard it spoken in such a perfect manner before.

The pair stood there, ignorant of the passing crowds and carriages, and Lily stepped towards him.

And Mr. Hatcher stepped away.

That doused the fire in her chest as readily as a bucket of water. Lily watched him as he cleared his throat and turned his gaze away from her. If Lily were a silly creature, she may have even said that his cheeks held a touch of pink to them, but she knew better than to think Mr. Hatcher felt anything akin to embarrassment.

"My reasons are my own," he said in much the same manner as he had before. "They are immaterial, as we are engaged and breaking it off would be detrimental to your reputation. We must make the best of it, and we cannot do that if you insist on treating me like a slight acquaintance."

Make the best of it... That was what he was doing. That is all, so why should she be so pudding-headed and think that anything more lay beneath it?

Lily's stomach hardened and sunk as she realized she'd made a fool of herself once again. At least she'd stopped short of throwing herself into his arms and kissing him. But that was a small consolation. She seemed determined to make herself utterly ridiculous by accosting a man who had demonstrated nothing but a mild interest in her.

But even that was not entirely true. It was a mild interest in protecting her reputation. Nothing more.

Only a few more weeks before her parents returned home, and this whole situation would be resolved. A few weeks more of playacting. That was all, and Lily could not afford to forget it.

"...make the best of it?" Had those words truly come from his lips? That was the most ridiculous thing he had ever said in the entirety of his existence. It was as though the words had formed of their own volition. And though Jack prided himself on his honesty, they were entirely false.

Shaking his head at himself, Jack was at a loss to understand where his good sense had gone. He could not remember the last time he'd lost possession of his words or actions, yet he seemed to be struggling with both today.

He should have kissed her. Oh, how he had wanted to. Jack wished he could claim that prudence had kept him from making a spectacle of themselves in a public place, but when he'd stood there, staring into her eyes, he hadn't been aware of anything else in the world apart from Lily. Her gaze had begged him to close the distance, and Jack didn't know what had possessed him to step away and speak those idiotic words.

The more he came to know Lily, the more he realized that their meeting had been nothing short of providential. Of course, their situation was less than ideal. Namely, that his betrothed was determined to throw him over.

As Lily had said, the gossip would die away. The details behind their engagement would fade, and though breaking with him would not reflect well on her, it was a storm she could weather. With time, the arguments that had pushed her to accept his suit would lose their power.

And Jack could not force her to the altar, though that idea had some merit. An irrational, ridiculous voice in his head shouted for him to secure Lily by any means necessary. But sanity held sway, beating that lunacy back into the dark corners of his mind. Jack simply had to find some way to convince her that marrying him was for the best. Somehow.

"Your given name is Jonathan?" she asked.

Jack's eyes snapped to Lily. "Yes."

She took his arm once more and pulled him along, though he struggled to put one foot in front of the other. Walking wasn't a difficult thing, but with Lily so near, he couldn't remember how to perform that rudimentary action.

She sighed, and though it was not the type of sound one wanted to hear from his betrothed, Jack couldn't say he was bothered by it, either. Resignation was not happiness, but he had time to change it.

"I cannot call you Hatch or Hatcher," Lily said with a frown. "That is all well and good for men to call you either of those, but I think it strange for me to do the same."

She paused, and Jack kept only a slight amount of attention to their path, turning the majority of it onto Lily as he awaited her next words.

"And you do not look like a Jonathan," she mumbled, more to herself than to him, but she straightened and glanced at him with an apologetic smile. "I mean no offense."

"None taken." He'd never cared for it, so he couldn't fault her for disliking the name as well.

Lily's gaze turned to the world ahead of them, but her attention was far from it as she delved deep into her thoughts. Watching it was quite entertaining, for the lady was a thinker and spent much time lost in her head. Of course, she enjoyed speaking those thoughts aloud as well, and Jack found himself intrigued by what would come out next.

"Jack," she said.

His brows shot upwards.

"That seems fitting."

His heart clenched in his chest, and his breath quickened. That was a name he'd not heard in many years. No one called him Jack anymore.

"You don't care for it?" asked Lily with a frown.

"No."

Lily gave a curt nod and looked away, her hold on his arm loosening. Jack's mind sped through the words she'd spoken and his answer, realizing far too late what he'd said.

"Yes," he amended.

He stopped again, struggling to get his thoughts to form a coherent statement. How did he explain such a large emotion in words? "Jack" reminded him of home and family. It brought with it a myriad of memories and happiness. Of catching frogs in Mr. Bedford's pond and running along the heathered moors. Of eating toast and cheese by the fire with his family as the snow fell in fat flakes that covered the countryside. Of a world untainted by death and cruelty.

It was a name from a previous life that had died with his family.

"Call me Jack." That was all he managed to say. Fairly growling at himself, he pieced together possible things to say, scouring his thoughts for words that could explain to Lily how much it meant to him that she'd suggested it and how he longed to hear it on her lips.

"I like Jack." And that was the best he could do. Speaking was not a difficult thing, but for all his ability to negotiate business, Jack couldn't manage a simple courtship. Of course, it was difficult to focus when his heart felt like molten iron in his chest.

"Then Jack it is," she said with a decisive nod.

Chapter 15

From his place behind a tree, Colin watched the group of ladies strolling through the park and felt like a common footpad, lurking in wait. But this was his only recourse—to watch and wait, choosing his moment with precision.

Miss Aubrey was in fine form today, though Colin could not think of a single time when she was anything but in fine form. It was that fine form that had him so entranced. And the curve of her soft lips as she smiled. The lightness in her eyes when she laughed. The utter perfection of Miss Aubrey was visible even from this distance.

Seeing her in the flesh was a bittersweet agony, and Colin finally understood the scores of soppy poetry that expounded on the wretched misery found in a love never to be. Of course, that did not keep him from hoping that this romance was not a tragedy in disguise.

Miss Aubrey's head turned, catching just the barest hint of him, but her breath caught. Sending out a silent plea, he hoped she would find some excuse—any excuse—to join him. Though too far away to hear their conversation, he watched as Miss Aubrey gave a few friendly smiles and jovial words before turning away from the group.

"Just a moment, Mama!" she said, calling over her shoulder. "I must speak with Miss Jameson."

Colin could hardly hold himself steady as she hurried along the path, her footsteps coming faster as she drew near. Holding out his hand, he just about shouted with joy when hers slid into his, and he pulled her behind the tree.

"What are you doing here?" she asked with a smile, throwing her arms around his neck and burrowing into his hold with a contented sigh.

If only they could stand there and enjoy such a lovely moment, but with the park filling, they were bound to be noticed.

"We must be careful, darling," he said, pressing a kiss to her temple.

She lifted her head to gaze into his eyes, and her chin trembled. "I cannot keep doing this, Colin. It breaks my heart."

"I know," he said, brushing a tender touch across her cheek. How he wished he were not wearing gloves and could feel her soft skin.

Tears gathered in her eyes, and panic shot through Colin. He couldn't understand how those tiny things held such sway over him, but the very sight of them made his heart constrict.

"Please, do not cry, dearest," he said, wiping at the tears as they fell. "I will find a way for us to be together. I will."

"Can you not speak to Papa?" she asked.

"And ask him to give his beloved daughter to a gentleman who has nothing but his useless name to recommend him?" said Colin with a huff. "If he had any sense, he would have me drawn and quartered."

At the sound of footsteps drawing closer, Miss Aubrey straightened, though she allowed her hands to rest on his chest, lingering there as both their hearts fought against propriety and caution. Finally, she pulled free of his touch, her face cast downwards, and only the strongest sense of duty and honor kept Colin from sweeping her into his embrace until she smiled and laughed once more.

"I will find a way," he said. Reaching into his pocket, he

pulled out two flowers whose stems were bound together; a vine of honeysuckles entwined a small sprig of blue Canterbury bell flowers. Though he did not have the right to declare the depths of his affections aloud, those blossoms spoke for him. Constancy and the bonds of love gathered together. They were the perfect message for his dear Miss Aubrey.

Taking them in hand, she drew them to her nose, the silken petals brushing her skin, and she breathed in their scent. Her brown eyes captured his, her gaze telling him what her lips could not. At present, the flowers were the only words they were allowed, and it had to be enough.

For now.

"Miss Aubrey?" called one of the ladies.

"Coming!" she replied, her eyes holding firm to Colin.

They stood thusly for several quiet moments before Miss Aubrey finally compelled herself to leave, her gloved hand brushing against his in farewell. Colin watched her slow steps, his heart sinking with each one.

As he stood there, cowering behind the tree like the coward he was, Colin caught sight of another pair of lovers walking along the park's path, and his heart constricted again—but for a far more unpleasant reason.

Hatch held Miss Kingsley's basket and had her by the arm as the pair strolled along with the freedom their enviable state allowed. His heart burned in his chest like a flaming coal as he watched the couple. Fate had such a cruel sense of humor to flout Hatch's forced engagement in front of a man who wanted nothing more than to be married to the young lady pretending her heart wasn't breaking as the gaggle of ladies around her laughed and chatted.

Colin would not allow fate to be so cruel to him and Miss Aubrey nor so kind to the likes of Jonathan Hatcher. Perhaps today would be a good time to show his hand.

The couple meandered through the park, and Colin followed a few paces behind, choosing his time carefully. Miss Kingsley gave Hatch a broad smile, beaming at her companion as though he were especially amusing. Truth be told, there were moments when Colin had enjoyed Hatch's dry wit, but he thought it quite odd for Miss Kingsley to be so diverted. Even odder was the lightening of Hatch's expression as he glanced at the lady on his arm. It was not a smile per se, but as much of one as Hatch was wont to give.

This was not a good development.

"Miss Kingsley," said Colin, hurrying to catch them with a quick bow.

"Mr. DeVere," she said, pulling Hatch to a stop. Though she did not smile quite so broadly at his approach, there was still a spark of joy in her eyes as he came to a stop before the pair.

"Midshipman DeVere?" Hatch's eyebrows rose, and he freed his arm from Miss Kingsley so he could grip Colin's hand in a firm handshake. "I thought you were bound for America."

Colin had not thought Hatch one for play-acting, but he was doing a superb job of it. Of course, the bounder would not acknowledge that this reunion was anything but pleasant.

"Emigrating was not the best course of action, so I remained in Town," said Colin. There was no enticement great enough to separate him from Miss Aubrey.

"You are acquainted?" asked Miss Kingsley, glancing between the pair.

"We served together on my last ship," said Hatch.

Colin's jaw ached and he forced himself to unclench while keeping a pleasant smile on his face. He didn't know why he should be surprised that Hatch would gloss over so much of their history together, but now was not the time to broach that subject.

Hatch threaded Miss Kingsley's arm through his once more, and Colin forced himself not to snort in derision. It was so like Hatch to stake his claim in such a public manner, but he was a fool if he thought it would keep Miss Kingsley by his side.

Colin's smile broadened, his eyes warming as he looked at Lily. "When I saw you walking through the park, I could not waste the opportunity to spend a few minutes in your company.

I am crushed that you were otherwise occupied this afternoon. A drive is so much more engaging with a lovely lady at my side."

Miss Kingsley's cheeks heated, her eyes dropped away from Colin's, and though he noted the pleased smile on her lips, it was Hatch's dark scowl that held Colin's attention.

"You are ridiculous, Mr. DeVere," said Miss Kingsley with a shake of her head, though there was a distinctly warm tone to her voice.

"Absolutely not, Miss Kingsley. Is she not a breathtaking creature, Mr. Hatcher?" asked Colin, his eyes narrowing a fraction.

Hatch's brows pulled together, and his eyes darted between Colin and Miss Kingsley. But more importantly, he remained mute as Miss Kingsley's blush turned from pleased to uncomfortable.

"Yes," he finally said, and Colin nearly laughed out loud. Truly, the fellow was doing as much to ruin the situation as Colin. Miss Kingsley deserved far better than such a tepid sentiment.

Jack was an intelligent fellow. Though he had a reputation for being gruff, brusque, and unwavering, he was equally known for his quick wits and ability to fashion solutions to even the gravest of issues. Yet all those brains were for naught as he watched another man flirt and flatter his Lily.

Surely, there was some word he could speak to end this ridiculous display, but DeVere lavished compliments on Lily, making her beam like a midsummer's day, which was a far cry from so many of the huffy frowns she'd bestowed on Jack during their acquaintance. Though he'd mended the rift between them, it was a far cry from the warmth she exuded with each of DeVere's words.

Then there were the quick flashes of triumph that DeVere shot Jack whenever Miss Kingsley's gaze was turned away. He'd seen such looks enough times to recognize it for the gloat it was.

Of course, in those situations, it was generally followed by a tragic fall from grace as the fool who believed himself to have the upper hand was quickly put back in his place. But Jack didn't know what DeVere was trying to accomplish nor how to keep him from turning Miss Kingsley's head.

"And how are your preparations for the concert?" asked DeVere. "I am certain you will be the star of the night."

"Such flattery, Mr. DeVere." Lily gave a huff and a hint of a frown, but there was too much pleasure in her eyes for those tokens of irritation to be believed. "Things are well underway. I only hope all will go well."

"You needn't worry. I am certain it will be a raging success."

"What concert?" asked Jack, his gaze flicking between the pair.

"Our Miss Kingsley—"

Jack's teeth creaked as he glowered at DeVere's impertinence, but the lad was unfazed. He'd always thought DeVere sensible, but the lad's behavior was proving him a fool; Jack had never wished to knock the boy's teeth askew before, but he did in that moment, and if DeVere did not tread lightly, Jack was liable to do just that.

"—has organized a charity concert," said Mr. DeVere.

"I am working with a group of ladies from the Gilliford Music Society. I am hardly doing it alone," said Lily, with a faint blush coloring her cheeks. "*We* are organizing a charity concert for the Women's Aid Fund, which assists widows and their children."

"And she is performing in it," added DeVere.

Jack glanced between the pair as he tried to understand why it hurt to receive that news from a secondhand source and not the lady beside him. She had an abundance of conversation yet had not mentioned a word about it until DeVere's promptings.

"Along with several others," said Lily.

Jack's wretched mind moved as though soaked in molasses. Though he struggled for some semblance of intelligence, he stood there, mute, while DeVere gave his farewells. Lily chattered on as they made their way, seemingly unaware or unmoved by Jack's stunned silence.

His cavalier words to Silas that morning returned to haunt him. Courting had not been a high priority at the time, but it was clear Jack had misjudged the situation. He had a prior claim, but Lily was free to break with him. They were bound together in the slightest way possible, and Jack was not foolish enough to believe that it would be enough if she chose to be rid of him. Lily was too headstrong to do anything less.

Jack had known plenty of gentlemen who'd lost vast amounts of money and property by thinking they held the winning hand before the game was played out, and he would not allow himself to fall prey to such pride. And if that afternoon had shown him nothing else, it was that Lily was a prize, and if he did not venture forth with caution, he would lose her.

Lily did not scowl when DeVere was about. She laughed and smiled.

Her uncle's home was quickly appearing, and Jack scoured his useless mind for a plan. Silas had said he needed to court Lily, but Jack couldn't think of how to do that. The front steps arrived, and Lily moved to the door and grabbed the handle.

Jack grasped onto the first thought that emerged. "I can escort you about Town."

Lily stiffened and stared at him, and Jack tried not to flinch.

"Your aunt did not come with you today." The words he planned to say did not make it past his lips in the manner he'd intended.

"She is quite generous with her donations, but like many, she guards her time and does not wish to accompany me."

How close he'd come to doing the same. Of simply giving a passing greeting and going on his way. Of missing out on this perfect afternoon with his Lily. He would not allow another opportunity to slip by him.

"I enjoyed accompanying you," he said. "Should you require another escort, please send word, and I will come."

A hint of a smile played on Lily's lips, but her eyes said she did not believe him. "I am grateful for the offer, but I am certain you are far too busy to be squiring me about."

Jack wished he had the words to tell her how wrong she was on that score. For once, could he not have DeVere's silver tongue that was adept at conveying his convoluted tangle of feelings?

"For you, I am never too busy," he said.

Lily gave a hesitant nod, and Jack longed to see more acceptance and less trepidation in that little movement. She turned back to the door, and Jack fumbled for anything he might say to keep her there a moment longer.

"We should go for a drive tomorrow," he blurted. The muscles in his neck tensed at the clumsy manner in which he spoke, but Jack counted it as a victory that he had managed to say anything.

Lily paused and turned to face him. "A drive?"

Unable to formulate coherent words, he nodded.

She sighed, her lips pursing a moment before she spoke. Would she hesitate for DeVere? Jack fairly growled at his ridiculous self. What was the matter with him? He'd faced competition before and had handled it rationally; yet now, he was little more than a bumbling fool.

"The city is too crowded for it to be worthwhile, and our last attempt was not terribly pleasant," she replied.

Jack's mouth opened, though he was uncertain if he meant to convince or beg. This was ridiculous! There was no need to be so flustered. He had faced many challenges before and managed it with calm and aplomb, but with Lily's brown eyes staring at him and DeVere's specter haunting him, Jack was undone.

Before he could say a word, she added, "A different sort of outing then? It is abominable that you've seen so little of Town."

"I've been occupied with other things."

Lily's eyebrows rose in challenge. "That is a poor excuse."

Jack nodded and thought back to their conversation about London. "Westminster tomorrow, then?"

She straightened, her brows coming together. "Westminster?"

"You said it was your favorite sight."

"I did not think you were listening."

Brows knit together, Jack stared at her. Her conversation was delightful, and he had no idea why she kept assuming it was unbearable.

Lily reached for the basket and took it from him. "Westminster it is."

Unable to do anything else, Jack watched as she hurried through the front door and shut it behind her. Standing there like a confounded statue, he found himself wishing he had some excuse to follow her inside. Instead, he was left alone on the doorstep.

Dropping the basket to the side, Lily ignored the startled look from the footman and hurried through to the parlor. Cautiously, she crept to the window, peeking around the curtain to see if Jack was there.

He turned and walked away, leaving Lily uncertain what her heart was telling her. Truth be told, she was no closer to understanding the gentleman than she had been that morning, but there was something about him that drew her in. Not that she had any interest in marrying a fellow who only looked to "make the best" of their impending nuptials, but there were moments when she sensed something greater lurking beneath that hard surface of his.

If only she had some insight into the thoughts running through his head.

"For you, I am never too busy..."

Why did he go and say such wonderful things with such conviction? It was so much easier for her to dismiss Jack as a curmudgeon, but then there were those little moments that gave her the strangest flutter of hope and anticipation.

Stepping from the window, Lily shook her head at herself

and took off her bonnet, gloves, and coat and handed them to the footman who waited at the doorway.

It was ridiculous for her to dream of some grand romantic heart beating in that man's chest. She was a duty to him, nothing more. For her part, Lily was simply pleased to find that the afternoon had not proved a disaster. She and Jack conversed quite pleasantly and spent several amicable hours in each other's company.

Lily walked through the hallway, taking the stairs to her bedchamber. She was no closer to accepting this ludicrous engagement, but at least it was becoming less of a burden to partake of this farce. Jack was a pleasant enough fellow, and Lily would not mind knowing him better.

Chapter 16

C lasping her hands, Lily counted the days until her parents arrived home. A month and a half was not long, and having a set date of termination for this torment made it bearable. But still, having to endure six weeks trapped in parlors stuffed to the brim with callers was not for the faint of heart. The sofas and armchairs were occupied, and others stood, grouped together as her aunt traveled between them. It was not a raucous crowd, but that ever-present buzz of conversation made Lily feel as though she were trapped in a beehive.

A busy social calendar had sounded intriguing in the abstract, but as the Season wore on, Lily's nerves were wearing thin. She was never free from noise and movement, and even when she managed a decent night's rest (which was not often), any respite she'd found vanished the moment she waded back into the tumult.

Mama was not one for crowds. Though she had friends aplenty, Mrs. Mina Kingsley did not stuff her social calendar full, and Lily was more like that dear lady than Aunt Louisa-Margaretta. Lily hadn't thought it possible to fit so many people into a parlor; she doubted the lady ever turned away a caller or desired a moment of solitude.

Luckily for Lily, the horde ignored her and left her to the

privacy of her own thoughts. What would Jack think of such a crowd? She grinned at that foolish question. A fortnight ago, Lily couldn't have imagined longing for his silent presence, but he was the calm in the social storm. In moments such as these, a mute companion was a blessing.

"I hope that smile is for me."

Lily gave a start and turned to see Mr. DeVere standing beside her with that lazy grin of his. With that small act, he elicited a burning blush from her, and though she was long past the age of the tittering debutante, Lily had the strangest urge to giggle whenever he was about.

Leaning closer, Mr. DeVere glanced around before whispering to her. "Why are you standing in the corner?"

"It is much safer than venturing into the fray," she replied. "I did not hear you announced."

"I gathered as much, though I doubt anyone could hear a thing in this noise." Mr. DeVere surveyed the packed room. "I have visited many a crowded parlor before, but this is impressive."

Lily's smile brightened. "Yes, my aunt adores company."

"And you prefer to hide?"

"You make it sound so terrible, Mr. DeVere," she replied with a shake of her head. "With a stature such as mine, any opportunity to be overlooked is welcome."

The gentleman's brows drew together. "I wish you wouldn't speak of yourself in such a manner. You do yourself no credit by being so—"

"Honest?"

Mr. DeVere narrowed his eyes and said, "Unkind."

Lily turned her gaze to the room at large. Arguing the point would do no good, but neither would she concede.

"I see you won't listen to me," said Mr. DeVere with a huff of mock indignation.

Eyes sparkling, Lily glanced at the gentleman. "Those with beauty believe they understand the plight of the unattractive, but I assure you it's not easy to be on constant display for all the wrong reasons. To always look obtrusive and out of place. To be judged for something that is beyond my control."

Moving to stand before her, Mr. DeVere gave her a look that was all too serious for the jovial fellow. "I don't know who has filled your head with such ridiculous sentiments, but you should know that I find you remarkable, Miss Kingsley. And you have quite possibly the finest eyes I've ever seen."

Lily ducked her face, as though that might keep anyone from seeing the blazing red of her skin. The pair stood there for several quiet moments, and Lily did not know what Mr. DeVere was thinking, but she could not bring herself to glance up and read his expression.

For her part, she struggled between preening and scowling at the absolute flimflam Mr. DeVere was spouting—and at herself for being affected by it. Even if the fellow was earnest in his attentions (though Lily remained uncertain on that front), his compliments were too effusive and too ridiculous for her to believe them, even if her treacherous heart reveled in each one. No matter how she tried, Lily couldn't keep her pulse from speeding or her face from heating whenever he was near.

Finally, Mr. DeVere cleared his throat and returned to his place beside her. "I called to tell you that I quite enjoyed the Winstons' card party last night. You are a formidable partner."

With a laugh, Lily glanced at the fellow from the corner of her eye. "I'm afraid that Mr. Crosby and Miss Livingston expected an easy victory, and they may never forgive us for slaughtering them."

"You are a bloodthirsty opponent," said Mr. DeVere, his smile growing. "Remind me never to play against you."

From there the conversation shifted and flowed to their usual topics. Though Lily couldn't remember seeing Mr. DeVere before the Walkers' ball, she kept stumbling upon him at parties, morning visits, or strolls through the park; not a day passed without some moment spent in his company.

Not that she was unhappy about that development. Mr. DeVere was a lively conversationalist but never dominated. He gave her his full attention and looked as eager for her opinions as she was for his. And though he was fond of outrageous compliments, Lily couldn't say she minded it, for Mr. DeVere made her feel wanted and appreciated. Cherished, even.

Lily knew better than to trust his words—no matter how earnest he claimed them to be—but that did not mean she could not enjoy them. A handsome man called her lovely. Engaging. A catch. There was power in hearing such words, and they fed into the fantasy she'd dreamt of living when Lily Kingsley would stand beside her handsome, gregarious, and so very attentive beau, who loved her unabashedly.

How she longed for it to be real. That lonely part of her soul cried out for it, desperate to capture that fairy tale and drag it into reality.

Instead, she was bound to Jack.

At times, he said the most heartwarming things. Lily caught glimpses of something in his gaze that made her heart race. But he inevitably did something to break the spell. Lily supposed it was for the best; sweeping Jack into her flights of fancy would only lead to heartbreak.

Their outings together were enjoyable, and the more she came to know Jack, the more she liked him, but that was a far cry from being loved as a lady ought to be. She could no more imagine Jack becoming the swain of her dreams than she could imagine Mr. DeVere's motives being wholly honest.

"I fear I've stayed too long," said Mr. DeVere.

"It's hardly been five minutes," said Lily.

He gave a pained smile. "I know, and it's abominable of me to abandon you to this ravenous crowd, but I have a previous engagement I must attend to. I shouldn't have come at all, but I couldn't bear to miss the opportunity to see you again."

Lily's cheeks flushed red, and she gave an impatient huff. "You are too charming for my good, Mr. DeVere."

"Never," he said with a rascally grin and a parting bow.

Watching him leave, Lily shook her head at herself. It was so silly. He was little more than a boy and far too pretty for her tastes, yet she anticipated each of his visits.

Aunt Louisa-Margaretta waved to her, calling Lily to her side. With a sigh, she prepared herself for whatever quagmire of gossip her aunt had fallen into. Lily knew that pinched expression on her aunt's face far too well to assume it was anything but anxiety over some bit of tittle-tattle.

"My dear Lily," she said, pulling her niece aside. "Where in the world did you meet Mr. DeVere? I didn't realize you were acquainted."

"We met at the Walkers' ball last week."

There was a disapproving harrumph behind her, and Lily cast a glance to see Mrs. Bingham standing just to the side.

"That boy is going to break your heart, Miss Kingsley," said Mrs. Bingham with a disapproving sniff.

Aunt Louisa-Margaretta gave the lady a stern shake of her head. "Nonsense. She is engaged to Mr. Jonathan Hatcher."

Mrs. Bingham raised her thin eyebrows. "And yet she's been spied in Mr. DeVere's company nearly as often as Mr. Hatcher."

As Mrs. Bingham turned her gaze to Lily, Lily saw a touch of something there that looked like sympathy, though it felt far more like that dreaded pity Jack despised. "You must guard yourself, Miss Kingsley. Mr. DeVere and Mr. Hatcher have a history together, and I have it on good authority that Mr. DeVere is keen to avenge himself of some wrongdoing on Mr. Hatcher's part. I fear he is toying with you to annoy his adversary. And Mr. Hatcher is such a competitive fellow that he will not forfeit the challenge Mr. DeVere is posing. If you aren't careful, you will find yourself in great trouble."

"That is not possible," said her aunt.

"It makes perfect sense, Mrs. Ashbrook. Why else would a lady like your niece attract such attention if not for some ulterior motive?"

Aunt Louisa-Margaretta straightened, her normally bright features pinching together as she scowled with a ferocity that would put Jack to shame—even if she looked more like an angry lapdog than a slathering beast.

"And why should she not?" barked her aunt.

Mrs. Bingham's eyes widened, and she began to speak, but Aunt Louisa-Margaretta would have none of it.

"You stand there, speaking as though it's impossible for two gentlemen to show an interest in my niece, but why shouldn't they? She is an incredible lady who would make any man a fine wife!" she exclaimed with a swipe of her hand as though she were batting away the foul words Mrs. Bingham had spoken. "If other gentlemen are too foolish to realize what a gem she is, that is a reflection on them and not her. And I will not stand silent and listen to you cast aspersions against her."

Weaving Lily's arm through hers, Aunt Louisa-Margaretta clung to it, and Lily was grateful she wasn't called upon to speak, for she couldn't manage a single word at present.

Mrs. Bingham blinked at the pair, and it was then that Lily noticed how quiet the room had become. She could not bear to look around and see all the people witnessing the exchange— nor did she need to, for she felt their eyes on her.

"I didn't mean to offend," said Mrs. Bingham, but Aunt Louisa-Margaretta's eyes narrowed.

"That is precisely what you meant to do, and I have no wish to be party to such maliciousness."

Mrs. Bingham gave an ungainly gape at that. "Truly, it was not intentional. I hadn't thought—"

Aunt Louisa-Margaretta's brows rose. "—that I would be bothered by your words? Or that I would agree with them? I think it would be best if you leave."

That blustery lady's expression held none of its earlier haughtiness. With a sketch of a curtsy, she turned and hurried from the parlor with everyone watching. Aunt Louisa-Margaretta sent the others a look that had them returning to their conversations, and she pulled Lily close, patting her arm.

"Mrs. Bingham is a bitter harpy, and you mustn't let her words cause you one moment of pain. They mean nothing."

Her aunt's eyes were so earnest and her tone so impassioned that Lily couldn't bring herself to argue. Pasting on a smile, she gave Aunt Louisa-Margaretta a reassuring nod. "Simply ignore them" was a common refrain in her life, but if it were easily done, Lily would not need the advice repeated so often.

"Might I be excused?" whispered Lily.

"Darling, please give no weight to what she said." Her aunt clasped Lily's hands before patting her niece's cheek. "You are a treasure."

"Thank you," was all she could manage as her heart constricted in her chest. "But I would like a few moments to collect myself."

"Of course," said Aunt Louisa-Margaretta with another supportive smile before Lily was allowed to make her escape.

Lily did not run to her room. Or even jog. She would not allow herself to sprint for the shadows like the coward she was, but she did move at a clipped pace as she took the stairs to her bedchamber and shut the door behind her.

Not caring how her skirts and petticoats crumpled, Lily dropped onto her bed and stared at the wall opposite.

This was not the first time Lily had faced such cruelty, yet it made her heart feel like a leaden lump in her chest. She'd long ago accepted that she was invisible to most, but it was another thing to immunize herself against such blatant criticism. Lily wished she understood the motivations behind it or why she inspired such animosity. What was it about her that prompted others to put her in her place? Lily couldn't think of another person who was a more consistent target of such spiteful sentiments.

But as Lily thought about Mrs. Bingham's vitriol and all the rest she'd received over the course of her life, Jack's words came to mind. He'd spoken them with no expectation that she would take them so personally, but Lily returned to them repeatedly.

I am not the villain you paint me to be.

He'd been correct. Lily could admit that much. She'd assumed the worst of him and taken offense at the slightest provocation. But how could she do otherwise when experience had taught her to expect malicious intent?

Sitting there, Lily stared vacantly at the wall opposite her bed, her eyes not seeing the light blue flowers adorning the wallpaper, and she wondered what Jack would think of her caving under a few pitiful words and hiding in her room like a child. Though he did not speak of it, Lily knew his time at sea had been painful, yet he'd borne it.

But how could she protect her heart from such attacks? Not that Lily cared about Mrs. Bingham's opinions, but the lady gave voice to the dark, awful thoughts that plagued Lily's mind, allowing them to solidify and grow, taking firmer hold of her life. How could she dismiss them as mere insecurities when others told her in no uncertain terms that they were valid?

Lily had known Mr. DeVere's words were too smooth and insincere; hearing Mrs. Bingham confirm it shouldn't have bothered Lily, but the lady had crushed the tiny hope that wanted Mr. DeVere's feelings to be true. Lily was a fool, doomed to desire things never meant to be; hope could help one weather the greatest storms, but false hope was nothing more than a stone around one's neck, dragging its victim beneath the raging waves.

No, Lily had not harbored a serious tendre for Mr. DeVere, but knowing she was merely a pawn to him cracked her already fragile ego.

And Jack.

It was still odd to think of Mr. Hatcher as Jack, but the name did fit him quite nicely. Though he was stiff and distant, Jonathan sounded too formal. Jack was a name without pretension—exactly like the man himself.

Lily gripped the bedclothes, her fingers pulling on the linens as her eyes unfocused and her mind played through her memories. Since their truce, they'd spent many afternoons exploring the city together. Jack had experienced so little of it, and introducing him to her favorite sights had become the highlight of her days.

Though Jack was neither eloquent nor effusive, his company was enjoyable. He was such an interesting fellow, and though few, his words held great value, for they were enlightening and well thought out. And no matter how much she chattered away, he genuinely seemed interested in what she had to say. Jack simply watched her as she rambled on, his attention never wavering. There was a weight to it, as though his every thought was focused on the conversation—whether or not he was adding to it.

Jack Hatcher intrigued her. At times, Lily swore there was more to his behavior than duty. Those eyes of his whispered that something stirred in his heart. But then Jack would say something ridiculous and obtuse, and the spell cast over Lily would break, leaving her with a man who was far more frog than prince.

Was Mrs. Bingham correct about him as well? Jack was not the sort to be swayed by public opinion; he claimed his reasons for marrying her were his own, and perhaps they aligned with Mrs. Bingham's assertions. It was the more logical explanation. Mr. DeVere was using Lily to make Jack jealous, and Jack was simply responding in kind. It was just the sort of juvenile competition gentlemen adored.

And yet that felt wrong. Lily's heart prodded her, whispering that Jack was not so conniving and callous. Brusque and controlling, certainly, but the gentleman she'd come to know did not align with the picture Mrs. Bingham painted.

Grabbing a bolster pillow, Lily clutched it to her chest as she lay on the bed. She wore too many layers of petticoats for her to curl up as she wished to, so Lily contented herself with cozying into the pillows propped against the headboard.

That day at the foundling home had been infuriating and wonderful, and there was no denying that it had altered their relationship, but Lily struggled to remember what had passed before their run-in with Mr. DeVere. The arguing she remembered clearly, but those wonderful moments sprinkled between were muddled together.

Jack had grown markedly warmer throughout the afternoon, but had that been before Mr. DeVere or after? Was it a byproduct of genuine interest or merely a response to Mr. DeVere's obvious flirting? Or had she imagined it all? Perhaps Jack had been pondering investments and ledgers.

Yet Lily could not accept that. So often, he watched her with an intensity that was more like an embrace than a mere glance. For her part, Lily didn't know if she welcomed such sentiments from him, but there were moments when it felt as though an invisible cord were winding itself around them, pulling them together and binding them. As though gazing into his eyes was peering into a soul that reached out to touch hers.

If only she were as forthright as Jack, then Lily would simply ask him what his intentions were, but she had not the courage to do so. She couldn't bear the thought of hearing him say he harbored no romantic notions about her; her pride could not stand another blow at present.

It was best to simply guard her heart and await her parents' return. If nothing else, they had far more insight and would help her see the truth of the situation. Her elder brother might offer some clarity, but with his wife so close to her confinement, Lily refused to pull Oliver away from their home in the country. Her aunt and uncle were no help in the matter; they meant well but were convinced that any marriage was better than none, which couldn't be further from the truth.

All Lily could do was wait and see. If Jack were playing her false, then this engagement would suffer a quick and merciless death, but at present, she was willing to hold onto the hope that Jack was not a villain.

Chapter 17

A snap from the fireplace had Jack bolting upright, his muddled mind fighting to sift through the reality around him and the fading remnants of the dream. He clutched his mending, his lungs heaving as he stared into the flickering flames. Rigidly, Jack perched on the edge of the armchair, the sweat on his back having nothing to do with the fire's heat or the warmth of the leather seat.

The setting sun cast a few dying rays on his bedchamber, giving him a little light with which to see, but Jack could not turn away from the visions playing in his mind. It had been years since he had suffered from such vivid nightmares, but of late, those childhood phantoms had reappeared to plague him.

Captain Furton was long dead. As a lad, Jack had spent many an hour daydreaming about the justice he would mete out on that miserable soul, but cholera had stolen that opportunity from him. A sad and pathetic end for a man who took pleasure in breaking those in his power; Jack still felt the sting of the cane against his back. Long after the dreams faded, Jack saw the haunted hopelessness in the eyes of the crew.

With a few more breaths, Jack relaxed into his chair, letting his legs sprawl out in front of him as he straightened the nightshirt he'd been mending. But his hands would not cooperate.

A knock sounded at his door, and with a quick salutation, Silas entered, but his footsteps paused as he caught sight of Jack.

"Are you unwell?"

Jack leveled a look at the fellow, but Silas was not quelled as so many others were. Generally, Jack preferred his partner not to cower and scurry away, but at times like this, Jack wished he would. Crossing his arms, Silas leaned against the wall next to the fireplace and watched Jack as though an answer would appear with a little patience, but Jack had no desire to delve into that quagmire. Instead, he offered another.

"It occurred to me that I need a house," said Jack.

Silas watched him with knowing eyes, but the fellow allowed the change in subject. "I cannot imagine your new bride wishes to live under our roof."

"I must speak with our solicitor about it."

Stepping forward, Silas sat on the abandoned ottoman in front of Jack. "That would be sensible, though I suggest speaking with Miss Kingsley as well."

Jack tugged at the linen in his hands and readied his needle. "Whatever for?"

"She will have an opinion on the matter."

With quick work, he laid several stitches along the frayed hem. "A house is a house."

Silas gave a bark of laughter. "You are a brilliant man in many ways, Hatch, but in others, I fear your wits are sadly lacking. A house is not just a house. It will be her home, and Miss Kingsley will have an opinion."

Jack paused and sighed, his shoulders slumping. "It is four walls and a roof. What does it matter?"

But Silas merely shook his head in that infuriating manner of his as though he were the greatest sage and Jack were the greatest simpleton.

"At times, you have a talent for obtuseness, Hatch. For example, why are you sitting here in the growing dark when you are expected at Miss Kingsley's side tonight?"

Shoulders slumping, Jack leaned his head against the chair. His head and body ached at the thought of stepping out his bedchamber door. As much as he enjoyed Miss Kingsley's company, he couldn't stomach the thought of another evening out in public.

"I have work to be done," said Jack.

That was true enough. With Lily taking so much of his time and focus of late, many of his tasks had been piling into great mountains that he was struggling to keep at bay. His time during the Season was not one of frivolity, and keeping pace with Lily and his work was draining. However, even as he made that excuse, his stomach gave a sour twist. She'd spoken of this evening enough times over the past few weeks that Jack knew it was important, and he wanted to be at her side throughout it.

If only he could have one evening to himself, Jack could face another week of the social whirl, but just the thought of going out tonight eradicated the last of his reserves.

"She did not invite me," said Jack. "We've spoken about it many times, yet she never expressly said she wished me to attend. Her aunt and uncle will be there. And a concert is such a tedious way to spend an evening."

He didn't need to look at Silas to see the disapproving scowl on his face; Jack felt it well enough without the visual evidence. His own heart echoed the same sentiment at the treacherous words he'd spoken.

Pulling out his pocket watch, Jack was relieved to see there was time enough for him to change and arrive before the entertainment began, but it would be close. Getting slowly to his feet—for that was the only speed his exhausted body would allow—Jack gave Silas a brusque farewell and ushered his friend out the door before ordering a footman to ready a carriage. Quickly, Jack changed his clothes and was out the Byrnes's front door while his pocket watch counted the minutes.

Jack supposed he should be grateful to miss the inane conversation that preceded events such as this, but he still had to suffer through the concert itself. In his travels, he'd heard many fine folk musicians, but their music was lively and engaging; anything showcased tonight was bound to be pretentious and dull.

As far as Jack was concerned, there were only two blessings that would come from tonight. The first was that he'd arrive just as it began and make a quick escape after. The second was that his attendance would please Lily.

With quick work, Jack made his way to the Ollertons' townhouse and into their ballroom. The space was simply arrayed, though the gilded walls and ceiling required no further ornamentation; the Ollertons may claim no connection to the old or noble families, but their wealth was unparalleled and on display in the rococo flourishes.

The chairs were mostly filled, but Jack found an unoccupied one in the back and slipped into it as the music began—though he nearly shot out of it when he caught sight of DeVere near the front. As Lily had discussed this evening with the fellow, Jack should've expected to see him, but a thread of dissatisfaction worked its way through Jack's heart, which only intensified as he sat through several performances that sounded so similar that only the applause told him when one ended and the next began.

Reaching into his pocket, Jack pulled out this timepiece. Not yet a quarter of an hour, and there was likely much more to endure until he would be free to disappear into his bedchamber again. Jack fought against the urge to fidget and tucked the pocket watch back in its proper place and folded his arms.

Several more minutes of torture were endured until Lily finally rose and came to the front. Jack straightened, positioning himself so he had a clear view of her. The tension in her neck had his own straining, and his brows pinched together at the brittle smile she gave the audience. Eyes narrowing, Jack willed her to straighten her spine; the bright and fiery Lily he'd come to know had been replaced by a quivering coward that shook like a mouse staring down a hungry cat.

Broadcasting such nerves was foolhardy, and Jack wished he could tell her she ought not to cower.

The first notes of the piano filled the air, and all other thoughts fled at the sound of her voice rising above it. Her song wove through the irritation and exhaustion, erasing all else but her clear melody. It was a siren's call, entrancing him as no other performance ever had.

Jack Hatcher was no fool. He knew few valued Lily Kingsley, but he'd long ago accepted that most humans were gifted with little intelligence, and never was it more apparent than tonight: the lady standing before them was more than a mere woman. She was the personification of beauty and grace, kindness and compassion. She was so much more than Jack thought possible for one person to be, and as she sang, he watched that lovely creature and reveled in the warmth flooding through him.

His Lily.

Mr. DeVere was staring at her again. Of course, that was to be expected when one performed, but he'd chosen a prominent seat, and his ridiculous smile was too distracting. The first string of notes warbled, and Lily struggled to give them life. As much as she enjoyed his flirtation, now was not the time for Mr. DeVere's amorous glances.

As she tripped over the lyrics, Lily's cheeks flushed, which made her tremble all the more. This was her easiest piece of the evening, and if she had not the strength for it, there was no hope for the others. But those worries only added to her fluster.

Pulling her gaze from Mr. DeVere, Lily let her eyes drift over the crowd, seeing them but refusing to connect with any individual. Looking into their faces intensified the deep-seated nerves threatening to strangle her voice. And she did a reasonable job of ignoring the audience until she noticed the familiar dark hair at the very back.

Then her eyes connected with Jack's.

His gaze had weight and feeling, as though his eyes caressed her skin. Reason warned her not to read into his expression, but that invisible bond she'd felt stirring between them tightened as their gazes locked. Her heart flooded with warmth, casting her mind back to that moment they'd shared in the library, when he held her tenderly and captured her in that kiss. Her heart thumped in her chest, but the trembling in her hands ceased.

The audience faded from her awareness, and Lily sang for him alone.

Lily had chosen the song before meeting Jack, but she felt the lyrics in a whole new manner, for they spoke of her and her heart. She sang of the battle between fire and ice, hope and fear, confusion and clarity, and all the blessed and wretched sentiments battling for a home inside her.

Applause thundered, and the world came into focus, leaving her flushed and trembling at the realization that her performance had provided a musical window into her heart. Lily gave a quick curtsy before moving from the makeshift stage to her seat. The other musicians beside her whispered their congratulations, and Lily smiled and nodded, murmuring the appropriate responses, but she felt too raw and overwhelmed to do much else. Turning her eyes away from the next performer, she stared at the floor, but there was little solace to be found at present.

She did not understand Jack Hatcher, but Lily was coming to understand herself. There was no ignoring what had just passed between them. Perhaps it was only she who had felt that connection, but Lily knew she'd been deeply affected by it.

The minutes passed as she tried to make sense of her heart, but before she came to any conclusions, it was time for her next performance. Thankfully, it was a trio, which put less focus on Lily. Though they stood on stage as equals, the audience focused on the soprano and baritone, who provided the bulk of the sound, and not the mezzo-soprano who added the necessary harmony and little more.

However, that did not keep Lily's nerves at bay. Before her marriage, Mrs. Ridlington had been the darling of London opera, and Mr. Mills was one of the finest singers to grace the stage. Lily was both honored and terrified that they'd invited her to join them; Miss Morton and Mrs. Lowe had voices superior to Lily's, and far more stage presence.

Lily's gaze sought out Jack's again, and he straightened in his seat as the three performers took their places in front. Mrs. Ridlington reached over to give Lily an encouraging squeeze of her hand before the accompanist began the introduction.

Mozart was a favorite of hers, and in Lily's humble opinion, *Soave sia il vento* was among his best songs. The lyrics were a simple prayer for the safe travels of their loved ones, but the harmonies were breathtaking, resonating through her and resting in her ear with such beauty that it brought tears to her eyes.

And all the while, Jack held her gaze as though nothing else existed but her. His strength flowed through that invisible bond connecting them, filling her with a power beyond her own capability. And Lily infused the music with her heart, sending that passion back to him with each perfect note.

The song ended with more applause, and the singers gave their bows before the others left Lily alone for her final aria. Jack had so distracted her that she'd forgotten it was so soon, but though a shiver of fear ran along her spine, it faded into nothing. When she'd chosen this challenging piece, it had seemed a foolhardy thing. But now, Lily didn't know why she'd been so afraid. The opening notes played on the pianoforte, and Lily welcomed them with a smile.

The piece was flirtatious and confident, the song of a lady determined to seize the opportunity to love and be happy. It started slowly and built to trills and runs that stretched Lily's capabilities, but her voice soared with ease, and she found herself surrendering to the part she played, adding the mark of comedy and laughter the song demanded that she'd never felt comfortable displaying before. Lily threw herself into the music, drawing out the flourishes and meeting the dramatic end with strength and clarity.

When the final note finished, the room burst into applause. Her aunt and uncle got to their feet, and the others thundered their approval, but it was Jack's smiling eyes that Lily treasured.

Chapter 18

Giving the appropriate curtsies, Lily surrendered her place on the stage and was met with more hushed congratulations as she took her seat.

"You were marvelous," whispered Mrs. Ridlington, taking Lily's hand in hers. "I don't know if I've ever heard that performed so well. 'Tis a shame your talent is not showcased in the theater."

Lily blushed, a denial coming to her lips, but before the treacherous words escaped her lips, she held them in check.

"Thank you," she replied instead, allowing the compliment to warm her through.

The next performer took her place, leaving Lily free to her thoughts. She preferred a quiet corner to gather herself after such a performance, but this would have to do. Singing in front of others was a thrill that both enlivened her soul and wore her to threads.

The strains of the music filled the room, and Lily took a moment to compose herself. She did not know if it was her performance or the silent moment that had passed between her and Jack, but Lily's heart felt strained to its breaking point. The days of frantic preparation for this concert preceding this moment had weakened her, leaving her unable to withstand the emotions overcoming her.

Unfortunately, the applause sounded before Lily felt ready to face it. The others dragged her along as the performers gathered in front together to take their final bows. While at any other time, Lily might welcome such acknowledgment, now it merely added to the confusion raging in her heart and mind. As hostess, Mrs. Ollerton stepped forward to give another plea for contributions and the like, but Lily could not focus on the words.

The moment the lady finished, Lily wove through the others, hurrying to find a quiet place. She needed another moment or two or twenty before she'd be ready to face the masses. But she was not quick enough.

"You were perfection, Lily! Your voice is always so lovely, but tonight you were magnificent," said Aunt Louisa-Margaretta, grabbing Lily in a hug before glancing at her husband. "Wasn't she?"

"It's a shame your parents weren't here to witness that," said Uncle Nicholas, beaming at her as he wove his wife's arm through his. "We couldn't be prouder of you. And not just for the music, but all that you've done here. This is a triumph, Lily."

Looking at the mingling masses, Lily smiled, though her cheeks flushed crimson. "It did come together quite nicely."

"No modesty," said her aunt, tapping Lily's arm with her fan. "After such a rousing success, you are permitted to be ecstatic."

Someone caught Uncle Nicholas's eye, and he nodded in their direction. "If you will please excuse us, I need to speak with the Hamptons."

"Of course," said Lily. There was still plenty to be done before her part would be over for the evening.

"Come and find us when you are ready to return home," said Aunt Louisa-Margaretta, reaching forward to give Lily another embrace. "Truly, you were incredible tonight. Simply divine! I am positively jealous of your talent."

Lily's voice failed at that moment, so she nodded as the pair wandered off to greet their various friends, then she turned to escape. But it was not to be.

"Miss Kingsley," said Mr. DeVere with a deep bow. "You were a delight."

Boldness and Jack Hatcher went hand in hand. Even as a child, he'd known his mind and acted without fear, and years at sea and navigating the waters of commerce had honed that strength of spirit. If one were to poll his acquaintances, Jack would wager that not a single one would think him capable of nerves.

Uncertainty and fear were dangerous things, for they led to rash decisions and risky gambles; the ruination of many an investor was due to such fickle feelings, and Jack never allowed them a place in his heart. Yet Jack was plagued by both as DeVere arrived at Lily's side before him. Even worse was Lily's blush and smile as the fellow greeted her.

DeVere simpered and preened. "You put the others to shame, for none could match your performance."

"Mr. DeVere, do you ever run out of honeyed words?" asked Lily. Though her smile was tinged by chagrin, she beamed at the fellow.

Jack's gaze dropped to DeVere's hand, which still held Lily's.

Leaning in closer, the fellow said, "Not when I speak the truth."

Coming to Lily's side, Jack reached for the hand that DeVere had commandeered and threaded it through his arm. Rather than looking disheartened or put-out, DeVere's eyes gleamed, the corner of his mouth curling in mockery; Jack's brows furrowed as he stared at it.

"What did you think of our Miss Kingsley's performance?" asked DeVere.

Jack's eye twitched at his flagrant use of "our," and he

glared at the impertinent fellow. But then, he realized there was a question to answer. Both Lily and DeVere watched him, awaiting his response, and though Jack did not care two jots about DeVere's raised eyebrows, he was puzzled to see Lily sporting an equally quizzical expression. Jack's forehead furrowed as he met her gaze.

Joy blossomed in his chest as he recalled those special moments; he'd never felt such radiant peace and happiness as he had when she'd stood so proudly before the crowd, her voice ringing through the air like a heavenly choir. Something had shifted between them. Jack didn't understand the link binding their hearts, but he'd felt it there like a third heartbeat connecting his to hers.

Surely she'd felt it, too. And if so, how could she wonder if he'd enjoyed her performance?

Lily watched him, her smile seeping away as the silence drew out. Her eyes pleaded for him to say something, but Jack's mind failed him. No words could describe what he'd felt.

"It was enjoyable." And it was the only part of the concert that was, in Jack's humble opinion.

But when Lily's expression fell and DeVere's eyes widened, one would have thought Jack had impugned her honor with those three little words. Then DeVere's expression shifted perilously close to pity, but that fellow's feelings were of no consequence—not when Lily's eyes dimmed.

Apparently, his words were not enough, but as he did not have any more to offer, Jack scoured his mind for some borrowed ones.

"You were the highlight of the evening," he added, stealing a compliment he'd heard Silas use on many an occasion with his wife. But rather than grinning and blushing as Lily had done for DeVere, she gave Jack a weak approximation of a smile, her eyes averted.

Hatch did not deserve sympathy, but Colin felt decidedly

sorry for the fellow. Of course, the problem was of his own making. If Hatch could not manage even the simplest of compliments, he deserved every awkward, uncomfortable moment as he fumbled about to repair the damage he'd done.

Unfortunately, as much as Hatch deserved it, Miss Kingsley did not.

Righteous anger burbled in Colin's chest, giving him a sense of triumph as it burned through him. Miss Kingsley was a fine lady and ought not to be bound to such a man, and Colin was determined to make her see that. And frankly, Hatch was doing most of the work for him. The fellow didn't have a modicum of sense when it came to ladies. Hatch may be a commander in commerce, but he was a child when it came to courtship.

Miss Kingsley looked no more pleased with Hatch's half-hearted compliments than Colin, and the lady had the good sense to show it. Too many would overlook a multitude of sins in the hopes of becoming Mrs. Jonathan Hatcher.

But as Colin glanced between the pair, he caught sight of reddish curls, and his gaze shot towards them to catch a pair of hazel eyes watching them. Across the ballroom, Miss Aubrey stood with a rigid spine, her hands clasped before her, and though she held onto her composure and maintained an impassive expression, those lovely eyes of hers shone with tears and pain.

"Please excuse me," Colin mumbled, stumbling away from his companions.

Turning away from him, Miss Aubrey spoke a few hurried words to the matron beside her, and the pair made their way to the exit. Others called greetings to him, but Colin uttered passing remarks without stopping. Weaving through the crowd, he kept his eyes on Miss Aubrey as she fled from him.

Confound it! Colin tried to move faster, but there were too many between him and her, and he could not shout for her to wait—for all the good it would do.

In a flutter of silk, she was out the door and into a waiting coach before Colin could catch her, leaving him on the pavement alone. His strength abandoned him as he stood with shaky legs, his heart thumping in his chest as though he had run a great distance and not the length of a ballroom.

It was just a misunderstanding. That was all. In their precarious situation, they'd both been forced to flirt and smile at others, and though it rankled, it was their unfortunate reality until they were allowed to court openly. But as Colin retrieved his overcoat and hat, the betrayal in her expression haunted him. No other lady could ever have a hold on his heart as she did—surely Miss Aubrey knew that.

There was no question of his returning to Miss Kingsley's side; he'd done enough on that front, and he needed to find Miss Aubrey. She would understand. She had to.

Chapter 19

Lily stared after Mr. DeVere, blinking at his sudden departure. Something was the matter, but several days of frantic work culminating in this evening's performance had left her wits addled. It was more than mere exhaustion, for this would not be cured with a simple nap. She was desperate for solitude and rest from the cares weighing her down.

And from the gentleman silently holding her arm in his.

"Miss Kingsley," said a lady from behind.

Those two words sent a jolt through Lily. She took a breath, placing a hand on her stomach, as though that could somehow loosen the knot cinched around it. Giving herself a brief second to steel her nerves, Lily turned to face the lady and gentleman at her back.

"Mrs. Dosett," she said, hardly tripping over Phyllis's married name.

Lily released Jack's arm and dipped to give the appropriate curtsy, but before she could take hold of him again, Phyllis snatched Lily's hands in hers, squeezing them with a sickly-sweet smile.

"How wonderful to see you, Miss Kingsley. It has been an age."

"Yes," replied Lily, as that seemed the only response.

"And how is your dear brother?" she asked with an arched brow.

Lily tensed. "Oliver is in the country at present, awaiting the arrival of his second child."

The lady's smile tightened, her dark eyes hard and cold as flint. Lily tugged at her hands, but Phyllis did not let them go until she was ready to do so.

"Your dress is so daring," said Phyllis. "I am always too worried about others' opinions to take such risks, but you wear whatever you please. It's so refreshing."

Glancing at her brocade gown, Lily did not miss Phyllis's insult, though she could not fathom why the dress invited ridicule. The neckline was unusually high, coming to her throat rather than darting low as most did, and the style was simple to be sure, but that was part of the charm; it allowed the gorgeous fabric to shine. The base was a vibrant navy blue silk with a pattern of black flowers woven through it that only deepened the color further. It was rich and luxurious looking, and certainly not wholly unusual, though many of the others preferred lighter shades.

Of course, Phyllis's smiling insults did not need to be based in reality, for they found their mark more often than not. Lily knew she should give no consequence to the lady's spiteful words, but they gave voice to her hidden fears, finding her most vulnerable parts and exploiting them.

Phyllis took her husband's arm once more. "And how wonderful to see you perform! The organizers are so generous to allow you to add your little contribution to tonight's festivities."

But there, Lily felt a swell of pride. Whatever else Phyllis may criticize, Lily had done much to bring this evening's event together, and it was a rousing success.

"I assisted in organizing the concert—" began Lily before Phyllis cut her off with a sharp breath and nod.

"Of course. That makes perfect sense then. One of the advantages of setting the program, I imagine." Phyllis gave a tinkling laugh that set Lily's nerves on edge. She leaned in, as though to whisper to Lily. "And you mustn't listen to what anyone else says. You performed beautifully tonight."

Lily's teeth clenched together, and she sorted through her thoughts, trying to find some response. The only options that came to mind were banal and insipid and would do more to play in Phyllis's favor than defend against her subtle jabs. But what could she say? What defense could she mount against words that spoke to her deepest fears?

Standing center stage, Lily had felt confident, but as the glow of the performance faded, she was left wondering if she was simply puffing up her vanity and blind to the reality that her songs had been middling. Others had complimented her, but there were plenty of times when people gave kind but untruthful words in such moments.

Even Jack had said the performance was only "enjoyable." Such tepid words did not speak of a heart touched by her contribution to the evening.

Ridiculous tears began to prick at her eyes, and Lily attempted to bat them away, but she had not the emotional strength at present to withstand the pull of despair; she was worn too thin to do anything more than simply feel the pain Phyllis inflicted with each syllable.

However, that did not mean Lily must stand there and subject herself to this torment.

"Please excuse me," she said, fighting to keep the emotion from warbling her voice. "I still have much to do tonight."

Jack reached for her elbow, but Lily pulled it out of reach and, with what little reserve she had remaining, she walked out of the ballroom.

That fool, Mrs. Dosett, did not have the good sense to cower, but her husband proved himself to be of greater intelligence, for he was shuffling uncomfortably under the glower Jack fixed on him. While Silas was gifted in gently nudging others along, Jack preferred a more direct approach, and it rarely failed him, so he'd never felt a need to develop subtlety. But that did not mean he was oblivious to nuance.

Mrs. Dosett's attacks were finely crafted—enough so that Jack hadn't recognized them at first. But they found their marks. Lily had grown more brittle with each one, and before Jack could do a thing about it, she'd given a half-hearted excuse and fled. His heart burned in his chest, begging him to strike down Lily's attacker, but now was not the time to deal with Mrs. Dosett. Lily was in pain, and though Jack knew not how to heal her, he couldn't allow her to lick her wounds alone.

With a final look at Mr. Dosett that promised they would speak again, Jack followed after Lily. Of course, at the pace she moved, she was across the ballroom and out the door faster than Jack could follow. Various fools tried to stop him for a chat, but he brushed past them, getting to the door moments after her.

The sound of her shoes in the hallway drew him along, and Jack found Lily in the adjacent music room, busying herself with tidying sheet music.

"We practiced in here before the concert," she said, straightening the stack of papers in her hands. "Mrs. Ollerton was so kind as to host the evening, and I would hate to leave their music room in such a state."

"Lily?"

But the lady rambled on. "This is such a beautiful space, but hardly large enough to host a proper concert. Luckily, their ballroom was close enough that moving the piano was not difficult."

Coming to stand just behind her, Jack brushed a hand against her arm, but she did not turn. Lily reached for more sheets, tucking them into her stack and straightening them with jerky movements.

"Lily," he whispered.

"There is still so much to do," she replied, keeping her back to him. But her voice gave the faintest break.

Gently, Jack took hold of her arms; he wished he was not

wearing gloves so he could feel her soft skin. His thumbs caressed her, and he stood there, waiting for her to face him. Clutching the music to her chest, Lily glanced at him over her shoulder; tears clung to her lashes, and her brown eyes were circled in red. She dropped the sheets onto a nearby chair and ducked her face away from him, pulling free of his grasp to wipe at her face.

"It's silly, I know," she mumbled. "I shouldn't care one jot what Phyllis Dosett thinks of me. It means nothing, and I should not countenance it. I'm certain you think me weak to be so disturbed by a few words, but I cannot help myself. Mrs. Dosett and I were friends once upon a time, and she knows precisely how to wound me."

"You are putting words in my mouth," said Jack.

Lily gave a huff. "Are you claiming that the mighty Jack Hatcher does not think it excessively weak to be moved to tears over a few simple words?"

Coming to stand before her, Jack forced her to look at him. "I know the power of words, Lily, and only a fool would discount their ability to bruise as easily as any blow. I do not think it silly or weak for you to be hurt when she clearly meant to do so."

Chin trembling, Lily gave a watery smile. "Everyone tells me to be stronger, and I do try. I wish there were some way to turn off my heart at times—to harden it until such things do not bother me—but I cannot seem to do it."

"Harden your heart?" Just the thought of that had Jack's seizing in his chest. Lily continued to mumble more ridiculous notions about needing to be stronger. Once his heart started to beat again, it came in a thundering tempo, outpacing Lily's flowing syllables.

Staring at the magnificent woman before him, Jack could not think of anything stronger than someone willing to feel so deeply, even while the world assailed her heart. Merely the thought of her turning off that most beautiful part of her had adrenaline coursing through him, begging him to do something to stop such a thing from happening. Lily's heart made her beloved and special, and Jack could not stand the thought of her tamping it and closing herself off from the world.

It was then that Jack had the most startling revelation: he could not stand the thought of her becoming like him. The world had beaten him down from a young age, and he'd done what he needed to survive, but that would not be Lily's future. He would not allow it.

"No," he blurted, and Lily paused, blinking at him. Jack opened his mouth, but words were not his friend. He could not settle on the right descriptors for his horror and desperation; he hardly understood his thoughts and feelings, and thus, explaining them was impossible.

Standing there with wary eyes, Lily watched him as though he'd taken leave of his senses, and perhaps he had. With quick steps, Jack drew close and pulled Lily into his arms, capturing her lips in a kiss.

Eyes wide, Lily had a brief moment to be startled at the sudden turn of events before Jack's kiss upended all rational thought. There was a fire in his touch, burning through him and igniting her heart. He enveloped her in his arms, crushing her to his chest, and Lily clung to him. After the heartbreak of moments ago, she reveled in the desperate need emanating from him. It was overwhelming and confusing, but Lily lost herself in it, refusing to allow herself to think about the motives behind this kiss.

Their cord wound tightly around her, pulling her heart closer to his with that same invisible strength she'd felt before. Just as the power of it threatened to overwhelm her, the kiss slowed. Jack's breaths came in heaving pants, matching her own, and he took her face in his hands, turning her gaze to his.

"Do not close off your heart." The words were hard and unyielding, and his tone brooked no refusal. Where such dictates would normally spur her to anger, the kiss had left her light-headed and unable to do anything else but nod.

The angry lines of his face softened, and Jack's thumb caressed her cheek as he stared at her lips.

"Lily…"

Her name drifted off into silence, and when he finally closed the distance, his touch was gentle. Lily hadn't thought such a hard man capable of such affection, but where the other kiss was a veritable conquering, this was a plea. Where the other consumed and burned, this had her heart filling with longing and tenderness.

New tears came to her eyes, but these were not the mournful ones of a few moments ago. They were joyful and grateful, born of the bliss coursing through her. Lily could not help herself, and they spilled out. Pulling away, Jack stared at the tears, his brows knitted together.

"Sometimes my heart is too full, and they simply come forth," she explained, her voice hitching.

"You cry when you are happy?"

Lily gave a little laugh at Jack's incredulous tone. "I cry far too often about a great many things. I cannot help myself."

Jack nodded, releasing his hold on her to snatch one of her hands. Holding her gaze with warm eyes, he pressed a kiss to her palm, and Lily's heart melted at the warmth of his smile.

Then he released her and was across the music room before Lily gathered her wits. Blinking at the door that shut behind him, she stood frozen in place, listening to the silence as though that would provide some answer for the strange turn of events.

"Jack?" she called, but he was already gone.

With a shaky breath, Jack gathered the remaining shreds of his self-control. Being alone with Lily gazing at him in such a manner was not a safe place to be, for every ungentlemanly bone in his body had begged him to continue kissing her. But with his heart so full of her, a few innocent kisses would never be enough. Tugging his jacket and straightening his cravat, he turned his thoughts from the lady in the room behind him and how much he wanted to join her there.

Jack had other business to attend to.

Returning to the party, he scanned the ballroom. The Dosetts were standing to one side, and again, the husband proved himself far wiser than his wife, for he was gesturing to the exit and tugging at her, though she pulled free of him and frowned at him. Dosett's eyes met Jack's, and the fellow paled.

The sight brought a small, satisfied smile to Jack's face, but it wasn't enough. With determined steps, he made his way to the couple, though it required far less effort than before. It was as though the crowd sensed the simmering anger building in Jack's heart and simply parted the way between him and his quarry.

"Mr. Hatcher, I do apologize for any offense my wife might have caused—" began Dosett, but his words faltered beneath Jack's glower.

"Mr. Dosett, what are you on about?" growled his wife. "We have nothing to apologize for."

"Do not speak," Jack said with a growl.

"How dare you!" Mrs. Dosett turned her nose up at Jack and looked at her husband as though she expected him to defend her honor. But the lanky fellow was intelligent enough to know how such a battle would play out.

"Dearest, please," he said, taking his wife by the arm.

"I am not familiar with the history between you and Miss Kingsley, but if you ever speak to her in such a manner again, I will end you," said Jack, holding Mrs. Dosett's burning gaze. "I will destroy your family's reputation and investments, hunt down every debt you owe and call it in. By the time I finish, the only option you will have is to emigrate to some country beyond my reach—and I warn you, you will have to go far to find it."

There were plenty of men who would be appalled at threatening a woman, but a predator was a predator, regardless of gender. For all their supposed "weakness" as the fairer sex, women were as proficient and deadly as any man. And Jack would not allow anyone—*anyone*—to hurt Lily again. That precious heart of hers could not protect itself, and it no longer needed to. Guarding it was Jack's honor, and he reveled in the satisfaction he gained from that role.

Taking his wife by the arm, Mr. Dosett escorted her out of the ballroom, her whispered protests trailing behind. Jack fought back a triumphant smile, his chest threatening to burst as it swelled beneath the pleasure of vanquishing an enemy. Though it was more than that. It was vanquishing an enemy on Lily's behalf. Jack would hazard a guess that the vitriol of this evening was not the first time Mrs. Dosett had unleashed her cruelty on her, and it gave him a unique sense of pride to know this would be the last time.

Jack turned on his heel to stare out at the ballroom. The music was over, and he'd spoken with Lily, and yet he wasn't ready to return home. His earlier exhaustion had fled, and Jack felt the strongest urge to stay.

His eyes fell to a basket positioned not far from where he stood. There were others placed around the room, but the number of bills and coins filling them was meager. Though entrance to the concert had required tickets, the price was not what it ought to have been, and those in attendance could stand to put more into the donation baskets.

Too many needed incentives to be generous, and though Jack was by no means silver-tongued like Silas, that did not mean he lacked the skills to persuade and encourage; he'd used them enough times to get funding for his charity projects over the years. Of course, his approach was more akin to a hammer than a nudge, but that did not mean it was ineffective.

Searching the crowd for suitable candidates, Jack turned his attention to procuring more funds for his Lily.

Chapter 20

Head leaning against the armchair, Lily stared at the library shelves. Her eyelids opened and closed in slow, steady movements, each one happening without thought, for her head was quite empty at the moment. In fact, it was a blessed relief, even if she felt like a porcelain doll, propped in place and gathering dust.

Lily imagined sneaking back to her bedchamber for some rest, but this moment of mental silence was a ruse. She'd collapsed into bed the night before, quite certain that exhaustion meant a deep slumber, but a myriad of questions, thoughts, and worries had plagued her mind; she'd not had the strength to rise from her bed nor the ability to divert her attention from Jack and that devastating kiss. Her bed still called to her, but seeking it out was fruitless as Jack lingered at the edge of her consciousness.

Like a specter, he filled the shadows, waiting for Lily to give him life. Even a passing thought gave Jack more shape and substance, drawing more of her attention and giving him a stronger hold on her mind.

What she needed was conversation, but Lily had not the fortitude to seek it out, for the only options available were Aunt Louisa-Margaretta and Uncle Nicholas. She adored them—she truly did—but their conversation would not provide the distraction Lily craved. Even now, she heard the distant rumble of chatter as they entertained guests downstairs, and Lily could not face them at present.

What did last night mean?

Lily groaned as the question took shape in her mind. She'd dissected and pieced the evening together in every possible manner, and there was no more to be learned from it. But still, she could not cast the query aside. To her, the evening had been a revelation. If nothing else, Lily fully understood and accepted that a portion of her heart was lost to that inscrutable man.

But was it destined to be a blessing or a disaster?

And where did Jack's heart lie?

Lily would wager a hefty sum that he'd been moved during her songs as well; she was not the only one affected by that mysterious connection growing between them. But his tepid compliments did not speak of a lovesick man.

Yet shortly after, they'd shared those kisses in the music room. Even thinking of them now brought a flush to her cheeks, her heart growing so light that it could blow away with the slightest breeze. But then, Jack had abandoned her. He'd never shown an interest in socializing, yet he'd spent the rest of the evening being the busiest of busybodies. Was he only reserved around her?

It was pointless to logic herself into an answer. Lily had not the capacity for rational thought at present, and deciphering Jack Hatcher's motivations was an impossible feat at the best of times. Lily needed a distraction, something to take her mind off her present cares, and that left only one option.

Getting to her feet, she left the library in search of the parlor. But it was empty. Turning, she was startled to find the butler standing in the parlor doorway with a bouquet in hand.

"Pardon me, Miss Kingsley," said Harris with a bow. "These arrived this morning."

Lily took the flowers and accompanying note, her heartbeat coming faster as she breathed in the glorious white lilies bound by a twisting step of ivy.

"Thank you, Harris," she said, clutching the bouquet to her chest as the butler took his leave.

Going to the sofa, Lily laid the flowers on her lap as she broke the seal and opened the missive, her eyes falling straight to the signature.

C. DeVere.

Her heart sank like a stone, dropping from her chest as she stared at the name. The bouquet was not a sign of Jack's growing admiration but a manipulation. Mr. DeVere wrote to congratulate her on her performance, but Lily tossed the note aside. False words from a false man, and she was no closer to understanding Jack.

Some might say his kisses were proof enough, but their first had been impassioned while meaning nothing, and only proved Lily ought not to build up fancies in her head.

And then there was Mr. DeVere to consider. If Jack harbored genuine interest, was it merely a byproduct of pride sparked by Mr. DeVere's interest? As much as Lily didn't want to believe it, she suspected that was closer to the truth than the romantic tales she fashioned for herself.

With a huff and a silent growl at herself, Lily took her flowers and stood. She'd already spent hours pondering these thoughts, and doing so again served no purpose. Instead, Lily handed the bouquet to the nearest maid to place in water and went in search of her aunt and uncle. Surprisingly, the sounds of conversation drew her to the dining room rather than any of the usual places Aunt Louisa-Margaretta hosted guests.

But when Lily stepped through the doorway, she discovered why.

"Aunt Mary and Uncle Ambrose!" Lily practically threw herself at her newly arrived aunt and uncle. "I didn't know you were coming to Town. What a lovely surprise."

Wrapped in their embrace, Lily felt a prickle of tears growing, and she fought to keep them at bay, but she was in such desperate need of a confidant. Aunt Louisa-Margaretta was a well-meaning but poor option, and Lily had no friends in London. Surely, Aunt Mary and Uncle Ambrose would have some insight.

When Aunt Mary got a better look at Lily's face, her own expression grew worried. "Are you unwell?"

"I cannot see why she would be," answered Aunt Louisa-Margaretta. "Between her recent engagement and her triumph last night, our Lily must be euphoric."

With Aunt Louisa-Margaretta and Uncle Nicholas at an odd angle to her, Lily knew they could not see her expression, though Aunt Mary and Uncle Ambrose did. Pleading with her eyes, she begged them to assist her.

Turning his head slightly away from the others, Uncle Ambrose winked at her, and Lily felt a weight lifted from her heart. It was silly to be so relieved over something so simple, but she was desperate for anyone to speak sense to her. Aunt Mary squeezed her hands and cast a look at her husband, which Lily could not interpret, though he did.

"Lily, you must be famished," said Aunt Louisa-Margaretta, coming over to guide Lily to a seat. "You did not join us for breakfast."

Good food eased many a heartache, but Lily was well and truly beyond its comfort. The thought of eating anything made her stomach turn, but the lady was so insistent that Lily allowed herself to be maneuvered to the table.

Aunt Mary gave her a reassuring smile, and Lily could only hope she and Uncle Ambrose would rescue her soon.

"I'm disappointed we missed your concert," said Uncle Ambrose.

"She was splendid," said Aunt Louisa-Margaretta with a glowing smile for Lily before sipping from her teacup.

Lily colored and squirmed at the compliment, though she tried not to. "And Mrs. Ollerton and Mrs. Lowe informed me that the proceeds far exceeded expectations. People were especially generous last night, and it was our most profitable concert to date."

Finishing her bite of ham, Aunt Mary added, "I am so proud of you, Lily, and sorry that we missed it. If we had known, we would've arrived in time to see you perform."

"But what brought you to London?" asked Lily.

"We needed to speak with Lucas," said Aunt Mary.

"Our son has not been home in months, and he hasn't responded to our letters," added Uncle Ambrose.

Lily's brows rose. "Is anything the matter?"

But Aunt Mary shook her head. "Nothing particular. We've been worried, and when Ambrose suggested he speak to Lucas in person, I insisted on joining him."

"I would've thought you knew better than to get in a carriage with Ambrose," replied Uncle Nicholas with a chuckle as he returned to his luncheon.

"And I would've thought that you'd grow bored of that jest, Nicholas," said Aunt Mary with an exasperated smile that held a dose of familial patience. Today, it held more of the latter than the former, though Lily had seen plenty of times when that was not the case. Excepting Lily's mama, Aunt Mary was one of the few who faced down Uncle Nicholas, and the fellow was bullheaded enough not to learn his lesson. Yet the pair rarely got into rows. Lily wasn't certain how Aunt Mary managed it, but she did.

"But I thought Cousin Lucas was at home," said Lily. "I had hoped to see him during my visit but was informed when I arrived a few weeks ago that he'd returned to Lincolnshire for an extended visit."

Aunt Mary's lips pinched together, her gaze dropping to her plate as Uncle Ambrose took her hand in his.

"I am terribly sorry," said Lily.

"It is not your fault," said Uncle Ambrose with a furrowed brow. "He's been distant since he left for university."

Aunt Louisa-Margaretta dropped her teacup down with a

clink, and the blonde curls framing her face swayed as she leaned forward. "Oh, that is terrible, Mary. But I am certain it is just a misunderstanding. Lucas is such a good boy."

Standing, Ambrose dropped his serviette on the table. "I hate to interrupt, but Mary and I would like to take a turn about the city. She's not been to London in ages, and I thought we should take the opportunity while the weather is fine." Turning to look at his niece, he added, "Would you accompany us?"

Lily's faculties truly were impaired, for she thought it quite strange that the pair would wish to go for a drive after traveling such a long distance, but Aunt Mary gave her a pointed look that pushed Lily's slow wits to comprehend the situation.

"Yes, thank you," Lily replied before going to fetch her bonnet.

Squinting against the rare sunlight they'd received that summer, Lily joined her aunt and uncle in the hackney barouche they'd hired for their stay in London. Giving her the front-facing seat, her uncle took the rear-facing one, perching on the folding seat in a manner that could not have been altogether comfortable, but he refused to allow Lily to take his place.

"Now, what is the matter?" asked Aunt Mary, and Lily attempted a clear and rational response, but a hitching sob broke out, unleashing a torrent of tears.

Aunt Mary's arms came around her, holding her niece close as Lily gave in to the flood of emotion that was fed by confusion, frustration, and a heaping portion of exhaustion. It was ridiculous, but though Lily tried to gain control, she was worn too thin. Eventually, the tears ebbed, and Lily unraveled the whole convoluted tale from the moment she and Jack had been discovered in the Pratts' library.

Chapter 21

Turning the letter over, Jack broke the seal and read through the insipid contents. Too many people chose volume over value when it came to words, and Jack growled at the fool who had written the unnecessary missive. The wasted blunt to send it in addition to the time spent writing and reading it made Jack's jaw clench together.

Crumpling the paper, he tossed it into the fireplace; it was of more value there than in his hand.

Jack retrieved the next and continued to sort through his correspondence. The pile had grown significantly, and it was difficult to keep abreast of the work that had been shunted to the side in favor of repeated outings with Lily, who was far more important than this dribble.

His chest twinged, and Jack counted through the days before Mr. and Mrs. Kingsley would return. A month was not an interminable length of time, but Jack would not rest easy until the wedding was over. Leaving things on such uncertain footing went against his nature. Negotiations that lingered on in such nebulous terms rarely ended in success.

Certainly, their engagement was progressing nicely. The kisses they'd shared last night were not a mistake or convenience. Lily had accepted his every touch and kiss, matching his passion with equal measure.

Him. Not DeVere.

But Jack didn't know what Lily did when he was not around. That thought brought an unpleasant shiver along his spine and settled in his stomach. She had entered into their engagement unwillingly and may not feel bound to it. Was she bestowing such tokens on DeVere as well?

Slamming the letters down, Jack cursed at himself for entertaining such a thought. Lily would not toy with others in that manner, and she had returned his affection with fervor. She cared for him, and it was ridiculous for him to—

His office door swung open, and Mr. Ambrose Ashbrook marched in. The affable gentleman Jack had met during their business dealings was nowhere in sight; before him stood a soldier staring down the enemy, ready to charge.

"What did you do to my niece?"

Not long ago, another Ashbrook had pushed his way into Jack's office, but where Nicholas deserved a few flippant remarks, Jack felt no desire to twit Ambrose.

"First, you compromise her, and then you use her good nature against her to manipulate her into an engagement she did not desire," he said, staring at Jack with a hard glint in his eyes.

Jack had no defense against the first accusation, but the second demanded rebuttal. "I only made her see that an engagement was the best choice for her. She needs to be protected."

"She needs to be cherished."

"Would you rather her face shame and ostracism?"

"An unwanted marriage is not an improvement," said Mr. Ashbrook, crossing his arms. Behind him, Jack caught sight of Silas in the doorway, watching with wide eyes.

"Your brother did not agree," said Jack.

Mr. Ashbrook narrowed his eyes. "My eldest brother is short-sighted and refused to act as her father would. I am here on Mr. Kingsley's behalf."

"What father wouldn't wish for a prosperous and honorable

son-in-law?"

But Mr. Ashbrook huffed. "If my daughter had found herself in Lily's situation, I would move heaven and earth to ensure she was not consigned to the misery and loneliness of a forced marriage. I would sell my property and move us to a new country—even beggar myself—before I would allow her to suffer like that. Lily's father would do the same, and he would be livid if he knew what our brother had done in his name."

Jack's teeth ground together. "You assume a life with me would make her miserable."

Mr. Ashbrook's brow rose in challenge. "If the number of tears she shed today are any indication, I would say she is well on her way to it."

A cold shock swept over Jack, freezing him as he gaped at Mr. Ashbrook. "She was crying?"

Leaning back on his heels, Mr. Ashbrook stuffed his hands in his pockets as he watched Jack with an appraising eye. Casting a glance over his shoulder to Silas, he said, "You were right."

"He's a bungler, but a lovestruck one," replied Silas, coming to stand beside Mr. Ashbrook with that irritating superiority he sported when he had the upper hand over Jack.

"I am not here for your amusement, gentlemen," said Jack through clenched teeth. Turning a hard look at her uncle, he demanded, "Is Lily truly unhappy?"

"I am not here to discuss Lily." Mr. Ashbrook sat on a chair opposite Jack, and Silas occupied the other. Leaning forward, Mr. Ashbrook held Jack's gaze with stern, unflinching eyes. "As her father is not available, and my brother has not seen fit to do so, I demand to know your intentions before I allow you anywhere near my niece. I know you are a good man, but 'good' is not good enough for our Lily."

Human nature was not a complex thing, though philosophers were determined to complicate it. Often, it took only a few minutes to determine how a gentleman conducted his business, and in Jack's experience, that was indicative of how he approached the rest of his life; an unscrupulous investor was never a saint in other aspects of his life. Lily was not business, but Mr. Ashbrook's fierce defense of her told Jack everything he needed to know about the gentleman and made him one of only a few people in the world whose good opinion Jack wished to earn.

"My intentions are..." Jack struggled for the right words. Turning his eyes to the pile of letters on his desk, he thought through the words. Writing to a colleague was no difficult thing, but that gave him time and privacy to pen it. And there was no matter of business that equaled the gravity of defending his honor to the guardian of the woman he loved.

"...honorable." There. That was truthful. "Lily is...unique."

But that did not come close to capturing what he wished to convey.

Jack paused, his fingers tapping along the desk, beating out a rapid staccato. He hemmed and hawed as his muscles tensed. Jack tried to ease the pull in his neck, but it did no good. Shifting in his seat, he grabbed one of the letters and stood it on end, but that did not keep his hands still, for he began bouncing it up and down, knocking the folded edge against the wood.

"I will marry her." Jack gave an internal cringe against those inane words, but the one that lingered in his thoughts was too large a one to declare. Yet still, those four little letters did not explain his heart.

Glancing at the gentlemen sitting before him, Jack found Mr. Ashbrook's brows high on his forehead while Silas openly gawked.

Mr. Ashbrook looked at Silas. "Am I wrong in thinking that the Jonathan Hatcher you know is unflappable?"

Silas watched Jack for several long moments before answering. His expression shifted, his gaze growing contemplative. "I can think of only a few times I've ever seen him thusly. Hatch has always prized control, but he feels things far more deeply than he shows."

Jack gritted his teeth, fairly pounding the desk with his fingertips. "I do not care to be examined, Mr. Byrnes."

Though using such formal address in company was not a foreign thing, the tone with which Jack spoke it could not be ignored. Rather than having the desired effect, it made Silas smile. Mr. Ashbrook's eyes moved between the pair, and Jack sensed the fellow did not miss a single detail.

"You love her," said Mr. Ashbrook as he crossed his arms. It was no question, though he awaited confirmation.

Words were such useless things that easily twisted the truth, and actions spoke louder, as they were wont to say. A man's behavior bespoke of his true intentions, and Jack's were clear. He saw no value in adding words to them.

As Mr. Ashbrook's question-that-was-not-a-question required only a single, simple word in response, Jack could manage that, though his throat tightened around the reply.

"Yes."

With a nod, Mr. Ashbrook added, "And this engagement is not about duty."

Again, no complex response was required, so Jack replied. But only just. "Yes."

Mr. Ashbrook gave another sharp nod and straightened. "Then how do you plan to secure her heart?"

Jack blinked at that. "You wish to aid me in winning her over? The fellow who made her cry?"

Just speaking the words made Jack's heart chill, his chest aching at her unhappiness. Lily had seemed content the night before, and he did not understand how it had changed so rapidly. But Jack would find a way to make her smile once more, and then ensure she never felt such pain again.

"In my experience, men give women many reasons to shed tears, however unintentionally," said Mr. Ashbrook with a hint of chagrin coloring his cheeks.

Silas's expression pinched, and he gave a guilty nod. "As much as I am loath to admit it, tears are an unfortunate part of courtship. When there is so much at risk, it is easy to be over-wrought by the simplest of things."

"And I am not aiding the man who made Lily cry," added

Mr. Ashbrook with a cock of his eyebrow. "I am aiding the man who loves her and will do his best to make her happy. What Lily has told me and what I've witnessed here leads me to believe you are him."

Jack mulled over those words, and though he did not wish to ask the question, it came unbidden to his lips. "What did Lily say about me?"

Silas gave a snorting laugh, though he tried to cover it. Jack scowled at him, and the fellow raised his hands in surrender.

"I apologize, Hatch, but between the tone and question, you sounded like a schoolboy asking for gossip about the girl he admires."

The scowl deepened as Jack made to stand. "I will not sit here and be mocked, Mr. Byrnes."

Silas winced and came to his feet. "I didn't mean to make light of the situation, Hatch. I apologize for giving offense but seeing you in such a manner..." Silas sighed, motioning for Jack to sit once more. "It was like seeing myself when I met my dear Judith. I was in my forties, previously married, and a father, yet I was just as lovestruck as a lad half my age. When love strikes for the first time, it makes fools of us all—no matter your age."

Mr. Ashbrook gave a low chuckle. "Having your heart fully engaged is marvelous and terrifying all at once, especially when you are uncertain of hers."

But restless energy had taken hold of Jack, and he couldn't stand the thought of sitting again. And being forced to discuss his courtship was more than his battered heart could handle at present. Jack needed to be alone. Or a stroll might clear his head.

"I appreciate your concern, gentlemen, but I have things in hand," said Jack as he moved to where his coat and hat hung beside the door. It wasn't a lie precisely, but it was true enough; he didn't know if he would feel fully confident until the marriage vows were spoken.

Mr. Ashbrook stood as well, his eyes displaying more doubt than Jack cared to see, but Jack had faced greater odds and emerged victorious. He simply had to hold onto that hope.

"I apologize if we offended you, Mr. Hatcher," said Mr. Ashbrook.

"Please, call me...Hatch." Jack nearly let slip the other name, but as much as "Jack" had become a part of him, it belonged to Lily, and he would not share it with anyone else. "And I am not offended. I simply have business to tend to."

Mr. Ashbrook nodded, though he did not look as though he believed it any more than Silas did. "But before you leave, I would like to give you the advice Lily's father gave me when I was courting my wife: never give her reason to doubt your affection."

Jack paused in putting on his overcoat and looked at Mr. Ashbrook with raised brows. "Lily knows where my heart lies. Hers is the one in question."

Tucking his hands behind him, Mr. Ashbrook watched Jack with an inscrutable expression. "I will not break Lily's confidence, but I will tell you something I learned from hard experience."

Mr. Ashbrook paused, his gaze turning to the wall as he sorted through his thoughts. "When someone has been taught to believe they are inferior, it can be..." Mr. Ashbrook paused again. "...difficult for them to believe someone does love them."

"Mr. and Mrs. Kingsley—"

But before Jack could finish that thought, Mr. Ashbrook gave a vigorous shake of his head. "They love her as much as any parents can, and our family dotes on her. But too often others tell her she is lacking, though I cannot fathom why. That leads her to doubt herself."

Silas grunted with a sad smile. "Those steeped in insecurities are adept at inferring insults where none were intended simply because they assume all people think ill of them."

Jack's brows rose as a string of memories played in his mind, showing those early arguments in a new light. But such miscommunications had lessened in the intervening weeks, even disappearing altogether. His behavior had shown how much he admired her, and Lily could be in no doubt of his intentions. And if there were any residual uncertainties, those would be overcome with the surprise he was planning; Lily could not overlook the effort he'd expended to bring it about nor the meaning steeped in it.

"Do not leave her in doubt of your heart," said Mr. Ashbrook.

Jack pulled on his jacket and held his hat in his hands. "I appreciate your candor, and I assure you I am doing my best to earn her trust. I will not break it."

With a nod, he fled his office, but Mr. Ashbrook's parting words followed Jack long after he'd gone.

"I said that as well, and I was wrong..."

Chapter 22

"You promise you have no idea what he's planned for tonight?" asked Lily as she leaned closer to the lady sitting beside her on the carriage seat. Though it was too dark inside to see for certain, Lily sensed Mrs. Byrnes's smile. Of course, it was a feeling the lady exuded at all times, though her face may not always show it.

"I assure you Hatch has not spoken a single word about tonight's entertainment," she replied. "I am terrible at keeping secrets. I cannot seem to keep from blurting out the truth."

There was a low chuckle from across the way as Mr. Byrnes added, "And Hatch knows better than to say a word to me, as I am equally terrible when it comes to keeping secrets from my dear Judith. We are a hopeless pair."

Lily covered her laugh with a dramatic sigh. "Then I suppose I must consign myself to waiting."

Mrs. Byrnes chuckled and added in a low voice, "I can say that our Hatch is quite pleased with himself. He has been in high spirits ever since he arranged this surprise."

Turning her gaze to the shadows where Jack sat, Lily thought that an apt description of his behavior of late. Strangers may be forgiven for missing the subtle hints, but his mood had lightened over the past sennight. Of course, Lily's own had improved after a good rest and many long chats with Aunt Mary and Uncle Ambrose.

Her cheeks heated (as they were wont to do) when she recalled how she'd sobbed like a fool when they'd first arrived. With age, Lily had learned some control over such outbursts, but her heart was too much of a whirlwind for her to manage it at all times.

"I do wish to apologize for Silas," Mrs. Byrnes whispered, her voice hardly loud enough for Lily to hear. "He has been most anxious to make your acquaintance, and I fear our conversation at dinner was more of an interrogation."

Lily chuckled and whispered back, "Your husband reminds me of my uncle, who is too charming for his good. It was a subtle interrogation and did not frighten me off. If anything, it is good to know that Jack has such loyal friends. Everyone should."

"We may need to be careful, Hatch," said Mr. Byrnes in a stage whisper. "I fear they may be plotting against us."

Jack said nothing in reply, but Mrs. Byrnes gave a huff like many a wife has given when her husband is acting the fool.

"As we don't know where we are headed, what else do we have to occupy our thoughts? The only sensible thing is to plot against the menfolk," said Lily.

"Patience," came Jack's rumbly reply, though she swore she heard a smile in his tone.

Between Silas and Lily, the conversation never lagged for long, though the mystery of the coming entertainment lingered in the back of her thoughts. When the coach came to a stop, Jack and Silas stepped out and helped the ladies. Weaving her arm through Jack's, Lily found herself standing on the pavement before a townhouse not far from her aunt and uncle's home—though in a finer part of Mayfair.

Lily looked at Jack with a questioning raise of her brow, but he remained mum as he led their party up the steps. At the door, Jack gave the answering footman his name.

"Mr. and Mrs. Kempthorne invited us for the evening's entertainment," said Jack.

Lily sighed. His statement had given no clues as to what the entertainment would be, nor did the footman say anything of value as he divested them of their jackets and hats. They entered the drawing room, and Lily spied a few lines of chairs facing a pianoforte.

"A concert?" she asked with a smile.

Jack gave her a nod, but there was something in his eyes that made her suspect there was more to the surprise. If it had been Mr. Byrnes or her Uncle Ambrose, Lily would say the fellow looked mischievous, but she could not imagine Jack Hatcher ever called such a thing.

Leading them to a row of chairs, Jack motioned for them to sit.

"I thought you didn't care for concerts," she said, thinking back to his tepid reaction of the last one.

"Not unless you are performing." Jack tone held none of the ardent air such a compliment deserved. He tossed the words out as though they were inconsequential. A mere fact. But they sent a surge of warmth flowing through Lily.

That simple statement meant more than all the practiced compliments Mr. DeVere spouted. If Jack had delivered such uninspired sentiments in the first days of their acquaintance, Lily may not have understood their significance, but she knew Jack Hatcher was not one for false compliments. And he'd deemed her the only musician worth hearing.

"But tonight isn't about my enjoyment," he added, nodding towards the piano.

Lily's gaze flew to the instrument and found a pair of gentlemen conversing beside it. The older had the bearing of gentry, and from his position in the room and the fine quality of his clothing, Lily hazarded a guess that it was their host, Mr. Kempthorne. She suspected the younger man was the musician, for he had the dark, wild air of a Gothic character.

"Is this to be a solo performance or an ensemble?" asked

Lily.

Jack gave her the only hint of the evening. "Solo."

Turning to meet his gaze, Lily's eyes brightened. "And the musician's name?"

But Jack shook his head, one corner of his lips twisting in a hint of a smile.

"You are determined to hold onto your secrets and drive me mad with guessing—" But Mr. Kempthorne interrupted Lily's fruitless protestations with a call for the guests to take their seats.

"We welcome you here tonight for this most special occasion," he said. Her anticipation had Lily holding her breath, but the fellow extemporized, thanking various people and babbling about the great honor it was to host the event until Lily longed to shout at him to get on with it; the mysterious musician looked no more pleased with the overly long introduction than she.

"We are overjoyed that Monsieur Chopin is visiting our shores—"

Lily gasped loudly enough that several people around her glanced her direction, but she could not help it. Her gaze shot from the pianist to Jack, her breath frozen in her chest.

"How...?" Lily didn't know which line of questioning to pursue first, though each started with that single word. The corner of Jack's mouth curled in a lopsided smile, his eyes gazing at her with such pleasure that Lily wished they were alone, for she had the strongest desire to throw herself into his embrace.

But Jack did not respond to the unspoken questions. He merely nodded to the front again, and Lily turned to see M. Chopin taking his place at the pianoforte. Leaning to the edge of her seat, Lily waited as he placed his hands on the keys.

The chords rang out, loud and clear, filling the room with a resounding staccato like a bugler calling his brothers in arms to war. Then the piece began in earnest, the notes building as M. Chopin's hands marched up and down the keyboard. Reaching over, Lily rested her hand on Jack's forearm, though she didn't know if it was to give him a sign of her deep gratitude or to draw on his strength, for the beauty of it threatened to overwhelm her.

The music sounded like a spring storm—a pounding torrent one moment before moving into a happy melody that tripped along like a thawing river and then, the first joyous notes of a songbird welcomed the awakening world. Lily had to keep herself from leaping to her feet when the song ended; while the others gave a hearty show of their admiration, Lily thought M. Chopin deserved a standing ovation. How she detested having to wear gloves, for having her hands muted in such a fashion made it far more difficult to give what she felt was an appropriate display of gratitude; as it was, she contented herself with being the last lingering clap when the others had finished. A few guests gave her sideways looks, but Lily ignored them.

The music began again, and Lily was swept away with another piece, another melody. There were times when the notes blended into a cacophony, like a powerful train barreling along the tracks with abandon. Then they would shift into a delicate sound, clear and pure, filling the room with sweetness and joy. Emotion resonated through the notes—anger and sorrow, passion and joy.

More than that, there was indefinable beauty to his playing. Describing it to those unaffected was like explaining the radiant glory of a sunset to those who'd never seen one. But as the concert wore on, Lily clung to Jack's arm and stopped fighting the emotions M. Chopin's masterpieces elicited. She didn't know if the music itself pulled the tears from her or if it was the knowledge that once the concert was over, it would be gone forever. Lily had attended concerts featuring his pieces before, but they paled in comparison to hearing them played by their creator.

When the final note rang out, Lily sprung to her feet, and it was shameful how few of those in the audience did. Far too many claimed an appreciation of music but had no true understanding or love of it. The evening may have been wasted on them, but Lily was determined to show the composer how beloved his music was.

M. Chopin stood and took his bows, though he was unsteady on his feet; there'd been reports that he was ill, and it disturbed Lily to see the toll the concert had taken. His already pale complexion had grown ashen, and he moved as though a light breeze would knock him over. When the applause was finished, Lily felt quite as spent as M. Chopin.

Chapter 23

With a discreet movement, Jack pressed a handkerchief into her free hand. Lily glanced at it and then to his face. His brows were drawn tight together, and Lily leaned closer to him.

"They are happy tears," she assured him. Using it to dab at her cheeks, Lily glanced at the Byrneses on Jack's other side.

Mrs. Byrnes smiled at her. "He plays with such passion that it is impossible not to be moved by it."

Lily wiped at her face, though it was difficult to stem the damage she'd done. "I adore his music and was thrilled when I heard news that he was visiting England, but he scheduled no public concerts, so I thought I would never have the opportunity to hear him play."

Turning her gaze to Jack, she added, "I don't know how you managed an invite, but I cannot begin to describe how much this means to me."

Jack shifted uncomfortably, looking away from her as she spoke, and though Lily wished to expound further, she sensed that Jack preferred she didn't.

"No false modesty, Hatch. You went to great lengths to arrange this outing," said Mr. Byrnes with a grin, but Jack leveled a hard look at the man. That only made the gentleman's smile broaden, though Jack's eyes narrowed.

"Leave him be, Mr. Byrnes," Lily ordered while giving the fellow her own narrowed gaze. Her glare may not be as intimidating as Jack's, but she would not allow Mr. Byrnes to tease Jack in such a manner—no matter how good-naturedly.

Mr. Byrnes's brows rose, but he gave a deferential nod. "Yes, Miss Kingsley."

At his side, his wife held back a laugh, but it was Jack's tiny upturn of his lips that held Lily's attention. Threading her arm through his once more, Lily clutched his handkerchief in her other hand, for she feared that with the way the evening was progressing, it would not be the last time she needed it.

"Though I am very pleased we were invited, I fear it was wasted on me," said Mr. Byrnes with an apologetic smile. "M. Chopin's work is too modern for my tastes."

Mrs. Byrnes patted her husband on the arm and gave a put-upon sigh. "You are so unrefined, Silas."

Lily laughed at the jest. "And you would not be alone in this crowd. I doubt many of them have heard of M. Chopin before tonight, but he is popular among the musical elite, so they must feign devotion or risk being out of fashion. I fear he has not been given his due in England."

"Do you wish to meet him?" asked Jack, nodding at the growing group of people surrounding the composer. Jack moved in that direction, but Lily stopped him.

Turning her gaze to M. Chopin, Lily watched the teeming mass of people. As much as she did wish to express her adoration for his talent, she could not bring herself to do so. The poor fellow looked weaker with each moment, and there was a hint of something in his eyes that made her think he wanted nothing more than to escape. Recalling her own performances, Lily understood that instinct. And anyone who deferred playing in larger venues in favor of more intimate but less lucrative settings was bound to be someone who did not care for crowds.

"I think he'd rather be left to his own devices than hear anything I have to say," said Lily.

"Then he's a fool," replied Jack.

Lily's gaze jerked to him, but he was looking off at someone on the other side of the room. He'd spoken with the same tone as his earlier compliment, and its sentiment struck with equal force—a mere statement of fact to Jack, but Lily reveled in every syllable. She squeezed his arm, and Jack glanced at her, a question written in his eyes. That he clearly did not know how he'd pleased her only added to the charm of the moment.

"Thank you," she said. But his brows rose higher.

"Mr. Byrnes and Mr. Hatcher, what a pleasure," said a gentleman, stopping beside them.

"Mr. Makey," greeted Mr. Byrnes with an affable smile. Jack turned to acknowledge the fellow, but did not speak; though he didn't dismiss Mr. Makey entirely, there was a tightening of his muscles that made Lily wonder if Jack disliked the gentleman.

"I wish to speak with you about one of your ventures," said Mr. Makey. He smiled readily enough, looking to all outward appearances as congenial as Mr. Byrnes, but a tickling at the back of Lily's neck gave her an instant distrust of the fellow.

"I'm certain you do, but you know our terms," said Jack, his eyes turning from Mr. Makey to glance around the music room.

"And it is admirable, but I have no interest in your waterworks scheme. The railroad, on the other hand—"

Jack opened his mouth, but Mr. Byrnes spoke before Jack could.

"We appreciate your enthusiasm, but we have substantial investments for the railroad and must be circumspect in how we proceed," said Mr. Byrnes.

Mr. Makey's eyes narrowed. "Preposterous."

Mrs. Byrnes released her husband's arm and grabbed Lily's while saying, "Let's take a turn about the room."

Lily hardly had time to process the words before Mrs. Byrnes marched them away. Once out of earshot of the gentlemen, she slowed their pace.

"I do apologize, but I thought it best if we withdrew," said

Mrs. Byrnes with a grim glance back at the gentlemen. "Mr. Makey is not a pleasant fellow in the best of circumstances, and I fear the conversation would take a turn for the worse if we remained. Silas and Hatch can manage him, but Hatch would not react well if Mr. Makey's careless tongue slighted either of us. Best not to tempt fate."

Lily straightened at the implication. "Would it not bother your husband?"

Mrs. Byrnes gave Lily a twinkling smile. "It would, but Hatch has far less patience and a stronger protective instinct than Silas. Where my husband would approach it with discretion and care, Hatch would barrel in and eviscerate."

With a laugh, Lily said, "Jack is not subtle."

"And Mr. Makey is certain to be disappointed, which will not improve tempers."

Nodding at that wisdom, Lily allowed Mrs. Byrnes to guide them along. There was no one in the company to whom Lily could claim an acquaintance, and she had no interest in approaching strangers, so it was quite the ideal situation. As Mrs. Byrnes did not steer them towards anyone, Lily guessed the lady felt the same.

"It is a bit odd that Mr. Makey is so set against investing in waterworks," said Lily. "Railroads may be all the rage, but water is a good investment."

Mrs. Byrnes's brows drew together as she glanced at Lily. "Hatcher and Silas have no plans to make it profitable. It is one of their charity projects."

Lily came to a stop and turned to look at the lady. "What do you mean?"

"Most of their ventures are profitable enough that they can take on the occasional unprofitable one. Things that are of benefit but not financially sound," said Mrs. Byrnes with an airy wave of her hand. "Hospitals, tenements, schools, and many others. They have enough investors clamoring for the profitable ones that they can leverage them into donating to the charitable ones, and this waterworks project will be their most ambitious yet."

It was a good thing Lily still held Jack's handkerchief, for she felt decidedly overwhelmed by that revelation.

Charity work was a part of life in the Kingsley household, and Lily had been raised with an eye towards aiding the less fortunate, but it was more than a duty. She truly enjoyed the giving, but she had neither the means nor talent to do more. No wonder Jack had thought her offerings to the foundling home so paltry, for next to the efforts Mrs. Byrnes had listed, they were.

Her mind swept back to the charity concert and saw it in a new light. The amount they'd earned was remarkable and far greater than anyone could have anticipated, and the only difference that Lily could see between that evening and those in the past was Jack's presence. The question was whether Jack had donated the funds himself or used his position to sway the others towards generosity.

Lily suspected it was a bit of both, and her limbs felt weak, trembling as though they struggled to hold her upright; yet her heart was so light that it did not matter. It had to be Jack's doing. Without a word or hint of his actions, he'd done what he could to make the evening a success.

"Much of London does not have sufficient access to water," said Mrs. Byrnes. "Though waterworks companies are sprouting up to solve that issue, too many of them are unscrupulous. Silas and Jack wish to supply water without beggaring the recipients, but it is an expensive endeavor, and they will need significant investments to fund it."

Mrs. Byrnes paused and her expression pinched as she looked at Lily. "Has Hatch not mentioned it?"

As much as this revelation had set a simmering joy burning in her heart, that question doused it just as quickly.

"No, he has not," said Lily. She turned away and took Mrs. Byrnes's arm as though to continue their turn about the room, but Mrs. Byrnes stopped her. Standing before Lily, the lady waited, her eyes drifting away as she sorted through her thoughts. It was several silent moments before Mrs. Byrnes spoke.

"I would never wish to break a confidence—" she began.

"And I would not ask you to," said Lily, but Mrs. Byrnes lifted a staying hand.

"But you need to understand that Hatch..." Her words drifted off, her brows pinching together. "I have known Hatch for over nine years, and he is as much a brother to me as he is to Silas." She paused. "Though I suppose brother is probably not the right word for it. In many ways, he is more like a son to us. Outside of Silas and our children, he is my only family, and we are his."

Mrs. Byrnes took a deep breath, holding it as she dropped her gaze to the ground. Another moment passed before she met Lily's gaze again. "He was so young when he was sent out into the world, and it was not kind to him. Hatch may seem cold and aloof at times, but it is not because he feels nothing. It's because he's learned to protect himself."

Blinking, Lily tried to keep her eyes from filling, but it was impossible to keep the emotions swelling in her heart from pouring out of her eyes.

"Oh, please don't do that," said Mrs. Byrnes, casting a glance at her husband and Jack.

Lily shook her head, taking in a cleansing breath. "I apologize. I cannot help but become emotional when I think of it. I cannot imagine a child bearing such brutality."

Mrs. Byrnes straightened, her brows rising. "He has spoken to you about it?"

"In passing. I don't think he meant to share as much as he did," replied Lily.

Taking Lily's hands in hers, Mrs. Byrnes smiled. "My dear, if I knew nothing else, I would dub you a miracle for that alone. I have known him for many years, and all I've learned about his time at sea is from my husband. Hatch is plagued with nightmares at times, and I hear him pacing the floor when he should be sleeping, but he never speaks of it to anyone."

Blinking at Mrs. Byrnes, Lily tried to understand the lady's meaning.

"Though it may be little, he does speak to you," said Mrs. Byrnes, squeezing Lily's hands tight. "You may not see the difference you have made to him, but I have seen him changing since he met you. Little things here and there, but I promise you are having a profound influence on him and making him a better man than he already is."

Mrs. Byrnes had known Jack for nine years and still did not know him as well as she ought. If it only required patience, Lily could manage it. Deep inside, she felt Jack was a man deserving of it, but a niggling fear had her wondering if patience would be enough.

There was no questioning that Lily knew little about the gentleman. Even after several weeks in each other's company, she knew little more about him now than when she'd burst into the Pratts' library. There were tidbits—little snippets of information she pieced together—but too much of his mind was shrouded in silence. And Lily wondered if she would ever fully know him.

"Please do not abandon him," said Mrs. Byrnes.

Glancing over at Jack and Mr. Byrnes, Lily watched the pair speaking with Mr. Makey and others who had gathered around them. Mr. Byrnes was all congenial smiles, while Jack had the resigned expression of a child forced to sit quietly during a sermon. His blue eyes met hers, and there was a hint of a plea in them, as though he wished for her to rescue him from such drudgery.

Lily hid a smile and took Mrs. Byrnes's arm again. "I shan't."

Chapter 24

Dimly aware of the swirl of dancers, Colin wove through the crowded ballroom. When it came to parties, the Youngs took the term "crush" far too literally, and Colin let loose a silent string of inappropriate words as he was bumped for the fifteenth time in the last minute; he felt like bellowing at the others to get out of his way.

"Tuck!" he called out, and after a few more tries, the gentleman turned and made his way towards Colin.

"What a crush." Tuck sounded pleased to find it so, but Colin was heartily sick of the teeming mass.

"I believe you have the next set with Miss Aubrey."

Tuck's eyes narrowed, a knowing smile tugging at his lips. "Yes. What of it?"

"Might I have it?" The question was hardly out before Colin wished it unspoken. Tuck was not generous and being indebted to him was unwise, but the evening was waning, and Colin could not wait for another opportunity.

Greed gleamed in Tuck's eyes. "I would love to assist you, DeVere, of course, but if Miss Aubrey did not see fit to save you a set, I don't see why I should oblige you."

Someone bumped Colin, knocking him forward, and it took considerable self-control not to shove the person away. The past sennight had been miserable, and his mood was souring with every moment spent speaking with this fool.

"I will give you a guinea for your troubles," said Colin. It was the worst bargaining position to take, but he had not the slightest interest in bartering any further.

Tuck's brows shot upwards, and he reached forward, shaking Colin's hand. "Done."

The coin changed hands, and Colin began the arduous journey to the edge of the dance floor.

His heart pounded in his chest, beating in time with the music as he watched Miss Aubrey twirling about in another man's arms. Her lips were turned upwards, but her smile was a mere shadow of its usual brilliance, lacking her warmth or spirit—and even that fled when her fine eyes met his. She and her partner passed by him, and with each turn and step, her gaze remained fixed on Colin.

Her eyes held the same desperation and pleading as Colin's, though he suspected her feelings stemmed from a desire to avoid him as she had since that wretched charity concert. If he were a better man he might honor her wishes, but Colin could not let things lie. For both their happiness, he would not cry retreat.

The music came to an end, and Colin did not wait for her partner to escort her from the dance floor.

"Miss Aubrey," said Colin with a bow.

"I am promised to Mr. Tuck for the next set, Mr. DeVere," she replied, nudging her partner to continue past Colin.

"And he graciously offered that honor to me," he said.

"My dances cannot be bartered about."

Stepping closer so only she heard his whispered plea, he said, "Please, Miss Aubrey. I need to explain."

Her partner glanced between the pair but waited for Miss Aubrey's nod before he released her and took his leave. The instruments gave a few warning notes for the dancers to take their places, and Colin was all the more relieved to see that luck was with him for once.

The slow strains of a waltz began, and Colin stepped closer, waiting for her to move into position. Miss Aubrey gave a sigh that did nothing for his peace of mind and placed her hand on his shoulder. Taking her hand in his, he ushered them into the winding steps.

"Please, allow me to explain," said Colin.

"What is there to explain, Mr. DeVere?" she replied, her eyes firmly locked on anything other than her partner. "If the rumors I've heard weren't enough, I witnessed the truth with my own eyes. I saw how you fawned over her."

Her chin trembled, and Colin tried to speak, but Miss Aubrey continued. "Not that I can blame you. Miss Kingsley is a wonderful, kind-hearted lady, and quite striking. She comes from a good family and..." But her words caught, and she blinked, turning her face away from Colin.

As grateful as he was for the opportunity to speak with Miss Aubrey, Colin cursed the public manner in which they met, for he longed to pull her into his embrace; a kiss would assure her of his affections far better than words.

"You are the only lady who holds my heart," he said.

Her eyes met his, and Colin fell into their hazel depths. He wanted to tell her everything he felt, but there was too much to tell, and words were too weak to describe the way his heart twisted in his chest at the sight of her gathering tears.

"I do not care for Miss Kingsley as anything other than a friend," said Colin, and that much was true, though it was not the whole of the story. But before he could gather his courage to tell it all, Miss Aubrey prodded him.

"From what I hear, you see her daily. At parties and balls. On drives and walks."

Colin sighed and fought to keep his feet moving in time with the music while his thoughts struggled to coalesce. "Only to make Hatch jealous."

Miss Aubrey halted for a moment, though a near collision with another pair snapped her into action. "You were using Miss Kingsley?"

With the most shameful part out in the open, there was little reason to hide anything else, so Colin told her all.

"How could you?" she gasped.

"I swear it's over and I've not seen Miss Kingsley since you spied us," he said. "I never meant to hurt you, and my heart aches to know that I have. I will never give you reason to doubt—"

"How could you do that to Miss Kingsley? You toyed with her heart," she said, her brows pulling together in a fierce scowl. "The gentleman I love would never have done such a selfish thing."

Colin's eyes widened. "You love me?"

But Miss Aubrey's eyes narrowed, her lips pinching together. "That is not a revelation, Mr. DeVere."

"Yes, but you have never spoken those particular words."

Her cheeks pinked, and her gaze fell away from him. "*My* heart is not in question."

"And neither is mine," replied Colin. How he wanted to lean in closer and press his lips to hers, but to do so would be inexcusable.

"Perhaps, but even if I believe you, your honor is not as sterling as it once was." The words stung as they rightly should, but before Colin could defend himself, Miss Aubrey continued while holding his gaze in a steady, unyielding manner. "You have allowed this petty argument between you and Mr. Hatcher to fester and grow. It has tainted you and your character, and I cannot accept that."

"I own that my behavior has not been sterling of late, but my anger towards that man is justified. He treated me cruelly—"

"He did the right thing, Mr. DeVere," she replied with a challenging glint to her eye.

"He promised—"

"A position but not a partnership. You decided what you wanted and would not accept anything you deemed beneath your dignity. And rather than searching for a position elsewhere, you've allowed your anger to fester and waited for an income to fall in your lap. I've held my tongue hoping you would see the folly in your actions, but I cannot stand it a moment longer. What you've done is despicable!" Her expression tightened, growing fiercer with each word. Colin opened his mouth to argue, but Miss Aubrey shook her head.

"How could you do such a thing, Mr. DeVere?" she whispered, her chin trembling. "You toyed with a good lady's affections and broke my heart in the process, and all in the name of getting revenge on an honorable gentleman whose only offense was to offer you something you were too entitled to accept."

Miss Aubrey went silent as they turned about the dance floor. She held herself stiffly in his arms as though she wished to be free of his touch, and Colin could not blame her. While his pride had shielded him from the truth of the matter, hearing such a stark assessment of his character from such a kind creature cast a light on the truth. The guilt he'd so easily hidden came rearing into focus, and Colin couldn't deny that he deserved it weighty presence.

"I have behaved like a bounder," said Colin, his brows scrunching together as he gazed into her eyes with all the heart he could muster. "You are unequivocally correct, and I wish I had some better response than 'I apologize.'"

The grim lines in her expression softened, her eyes growing misty. "I cannot think of a better one than that. People do not say it often enough." Blinking, she turned her attention to the dancers. "But that doesn't mean I forgive you."

There was a hint of her usual sauciness in her tone, and Colin smiled at that. "I would not expect you to without more groveling on my part."

Miss Aubrey's eyes darted to him and narrowed. "And what would that entail?"

Colin resisted the urge to pull her closer, but he gripped her hand gently in his, his thumb brushing against her palm. Miss Aubrey's cheeks glowed as she gazed at him.

"First," he said, his voice a husky whisper, "a vow to never behave like a cad again and to make reparations if I can. I have already sent Miss Kingsley a note to make a break of things."

The corners of her lips turned up. "That is a good beginning."

"And second, I have an appointment with your father to speak with him about my intentions." Just speaking the words sent a spike of panic flowing through him, but it subsided at the brilliant smile Miss Aubrey gave him. Her eyes sparkled with radiant joy, and she looked ready to throw her arms around his neck.

"I fully expect him to bar me from your house, but I shall try to make him see reason," said Colin. In all honesty, he didn't know how he would manage it, but the time was long past for him to try. They could not go on as they had.

"We shall convince him together," she added, her hand squeezing his.

"Together," he echoed. Colin rather liked the sound of that.

Chapter 25

H olding a leaf between her fingers, Lily twirled it as she walked along the park's pathway. In a rare display of glory, the sun was out with not a cloud in the sky. Though her aunt would be horrified to see her niece risking her fair complexion, Lily turned her face towards it, basking in the rays. Luckily, Aunt Louisa-Margaretta was holding court to one side of the walkway and too occupied to notice.

For once, the day was warm enough that one did not need jackets, and though it had taken some work, Lily found the right dress to match her shawl. It was a silly way to choose an outfit, but she couldn't help herself. She'd not had the opportunity to use it, and today was too perfect a day to do anything less.

The dress was the perfect shade of dove gray. Lily normally shied away from such dull colors, but it was the ideal complement to the bright shawl; the rosy tint to the muted neutral color paired perfectly with the bold reddish-pink. Lily may be a grown woman, but she felt like twirling about the park with her shawl fluttering behind her. Though that might have more to do with the memories of the day she'd purchased it.

Lily broke into a smile. She couldn't help herself. Even a fleeting thought of Jack had her beaming. Nearly two days since M. Chopin's concert, yet Lily was still grinning like a fool.

"Miss Kingsley!" called a gentleman, and Lily dropped the leaf and turned to see Mr. Dosett guiding his wife towards them—though guiding was too kind a word for it. Phyllis looked as eager as a prisoner marching to the gallows while Mr. Dosett prodded her along.

"How good to see you this lovely afternoon," he said with a bow. His wife gave a faint bob, but Mr. Dosett scowled at her. Straightening, Phyllis glared at him and then at her, though Lily had not the foggiest notion as to why the lady so clearly blamed her for this imposition. Then, with stiff movements, Phyllis gave a proper curtsy and brittle smile.

"Miss Kingsley." Her tone was cold enough to drive away the warmth of the summer sun.

Mr. Dosett leaned over and hissed something in her ear, and Phyllis took a deep, shaky breath, her muscles tensing. With a sigh, the lady's expression softened, though her eyes were as glacial as before.

"I do admire your shawl, Miss Kingsley," she said.

Lily nodded, though she couldn't think what to say in response to the first civil words she'd received from Phyllis in years.

"Though I have yet to see an announcement in the papers, I hear we're to congratulate you on your upcoming nuptials to Mr. Hatcher." Phyllis's jaw tensed as she smiled at Lily. "Quite fortuitous—"

"Darling," interrupted Mr. Dosett, with a pointed tone. Turning to Lily, he smiled. "Mr. Hatcher is quite the lucky fellow to have captured your heart. We wish you both well."

Taking his wife by the arm, Mr. Dosett led her away but paused as he passed Lily. He leaned forward and asked in a low voice, "You will tell Mr. Hatcher that we spoke with you today, won't you?"

"If you wish me to," said Lily, her brows drawing together.

"And that it was quite congenial,'" he added with a pointed look.

Lily blinked at the odd man. "Certainly."

Mr. Dosett bowed in farewell and nudged his wife, who gave her another curtsy. Lily watched the pair walk away, as Phyllis hissed and scowled at her husband, though he did not budge in whatever argument they'd been having.

"That was quite odd," she said to no one in particular, and as no one was paid her any heed, it was of no consequence.

A strange thought popped into her head, and though Lily could not quite countenance it, she could not dismiss it, either. At the best of times, Phyllis was a two-faced shrew. At all others, she was merely a malicious, cold-hearted shrew. The only difference was how pointed she was in attacking her prey.

Yet Lily could almost say this interaction had been innocuous. Strange, certainly. But there'd been no veiled insults. Lily was not fool enough to believe Phyllis's behavior was of her own volition. Anyone could see that she'd held her tongue under duress. And Lily could think of only one person who could inspire such a significant change and would put forth the effort to do so for her.

Jack had not seemed overly concerned with Phyllis's behavior during the charity concert, but this had to be his doing.

"I do hope that smile means you are in a particularly fine mood," said Mr. DeVere.

As she turned to greet him, Lily's smile broadened, though it had nothing to do with the gentleman before her. Simply having him comment on her fine mood reminded her of why she was in a fine mood, which made it all the finer. She was being a bit ridiculous, but her heart expanded every time she thought of Jack.

"I am, Mr. DeVere," Lily replied. "And yourself?"

"Better than I've been in a good while," he replied, tucking his hands behind him with a nod.

Stepping closer, Lily batted her eyes at him in a most audacious fashion, but she knew it was time to end this farce. There was no good to be had from it anymore—though Lily had no intention of giving Mr. DeVere an easy escape. She may not have much experience with gentlemen, but nothing terrified flirts more than true intent. Banter was fine and well, but hint at something serious beneath it, and they fled like a fox from the hounds.

"Is it because we are together?" she asked with a simpering smile and a step closer. Lily wished she dared to brush his arm or do something more flirtatious, but she couldn't be that forward.

"I wanted to speak with you," he said, stepping away.

Widening her eyes, Lily gasped. "Certainly, Mr. DeVere!"

Colin stared at her, his mind moving slowly through the implications of her tone. Miss Kingsley kept batting her lashes, drawing closer any time he remained in place for more than a heartbeat. He kept putting a respectful distance between them, but the lady moved forward with a determination he'd not seen from her before. It had them inching along the pathway, moving farther from the rest of her group. Though Colin appreciated the privacy for what he needed to say, Miss Kingsley's behavior had him sweating at his temples.

It was difficult enough to confess without this lunacy.

"You received my flowers after your performance?" asked Colin. He tugged at his jacket as she gave yet another simpering grin.

Surely she'd understood the bouquet's meaning. Ivy was a sign of friendship, and the accompanying note had been polite—nothing more. It was a simple token of admiration for her talent and could not be taken as anything more. Yet she kept gazing at him as though he were the sun in her sky, all while batting her eyes in a most bizarre manner.

"They were so lovely," she replied, her voice dropping into a whisper. "But you wished to speak with me?"

"Over the past few weeks, I have come to value our *friendship* dearly." Colin put a none-too-subtle emphasis on that innocuous word.

"Oh, Mr. DeVere," she said in a breathy tone.

Behind Miss Kingsley was a clear path. An easy exit. Simply turn tail and flee. There was no reason to beleaguer this point. Colin's pride told him to remain mute, and if not for a promise he'd made to Miss Aubrey and his guilty conscience holding him there, he would've taken the coward's way out. But acknowledging his behavior and taking the consequences was the only honorable thing to do, and Colin was done with playing the cad.

"I need to apologize, Miss Kingsley." Gritting his teeth, Colin closed his eyes to gather his courage and his words. "I have used you abominably and behaved in an unseemly manner, leading you to believe my feelings run deeper than they do in order to annoy Mr. Hatcher. It was unfair of me to toy with your affections, and I ask your forgiveness, though I do not deserve it."

When Colin opened his eyes to meet Miss Kingsley's gaze, he found no tears or pained expressions. Miss Kingsley gave him a narrowed look, her brows drawing together.

"You are ruining my fun, Mr. DeVere."

"Fun?"

"You are supposed to be running away in fear," she said with a frown. "And instead, you are behaving rather honorably."

Colin stared at her. "And you wish me to behave more dishonorably?"

"I wish you to give me the satisfaction of getting one over on you."

Mr. DeVere's brow was pulled tight, his expression all scrunched together in such utter confusion that Lily didn't know whether to laugh or pat the lad on his head and send him home to his mother.

"I am no fool, Mr. DeVere. I was aware of your intentions, and though I cannot claim I was unaffected by your deception, it did no lasting damage."

Glancing at his feet, Mr. DeVere's shoulders sagged. "I don't know if I should feel relieved or ashamed."

"A bit of both, I suppose," replied Lily. "But you have ruined my grand plan. I thought it time to end the charade, so I was going to make you think I expected us to get married. I'd expected you to escape posthaste and never return."

Mr. DeVere's head snapped up, his eyes wide, though that shock faded into chagrin. "I suppose you have every reason to think I would be that despicable. I'd planned on quietly disappearing after sending that bouquet, but after speaking with someone dear to me, I knew you deserved a proper apology."

"A lady?" asked Lily with a smile.

Eyes darting away from Lily, Mr. DeVere's cheeks pinked, though his lips held a hint of a smile. "She is exceptionally patient and far better than I deserve."

"I do hope you tell her that."

Mr. DeVere gave Lily a tender smile, his gaze softening as he looked at her. "I apologize for behaving so terribly. You deserve far better as well."

"No harm was done, Mr. DeVere. I only hope you will be careful how you treat others in the future."

"I swear it," came the quick reply, though the speed did not lessen the sincerity with which he spoke the vow. "Sometimes it is hard to see how far astray we've gone. Luckily, I have a good lady who sees more clearly than I and is willing to set me straight."

Lily smiled at that. "We should all be so lucky to have someone like that in our lives. But in truth, I would like to thank you for your compliments over the past weeks. It is not often that I hear such lovely things said."

Mr. DeVere's brow furrowed. "You deserve to hear them often." •

With a chuckle, Lily clasped her hands behind her. "That is the second time you've claimed I 'deserve' something, but I cannot help but think you are too free with that word. There are so many unmet needs in this world that I hardly think I deserve any more blessings than I already have. My life is so full, how can I *deserve* more?"

His lips pulled into an appreciative smile. "May I at least say that Hatch does not deserve you?"

"You may," she said, cocking her head to one side, "but I disagree. I don't know what has transpired between you two, but he is an excellent man."

"Then you are happy with him?" asked Mr. DeVere. It was a forward question, but the entire conversation had been rather forward, so Lily took no offense at it. Of course, she didn't need to answer his question aloud, for that bright smile of hers broadened, filling her face, and Mr. DeVere's grew in response.

Reaching forward, Mr. DeVere took her hand in his, bowing over it and placing a respectful kiss on her knuckles. "I thank you for your kindness and wish you nothing but happiness, Miss Kingsley."

Lily's cheeks flared as they always did when Mr. DeVere was particularly gallant, and she gave him a curtsy in reply. "And the same for you, Mr. DeVere."

With another bow, he turned and went on his way. It was not the exit Lily had intended him to take, but it was far better and added to her joy. She'd not thought it possible for her heart to feel even fuller, but it did. Lily fairly skipped to her aunt's side, quite certain she did not need anything more, for life had already given her more than any person deserved.

Chapter 26

Leaving the pathway, Jack crossed the open lawn, weaving between flocks of children and their harried nursemaids and governesses and the gaggles of gossiping ladies and gentlemen. Most days, he preferred straight and open pavement, but today, he felt the urge to revel in the open sunshine. The sun hung high in the sky, and though there was a lingering chill in the air, the temperature was rising.

The summer had been a wet and miserable mess. It had been an age since anyone had seen such downpours, and more than social calendars were suffering for it. While there was a lingering worry in his thoughts for all the farmers and laborers impacted by it, Jack's heart was brimming with contentment. The only other time he'd felt this peaceful was when he'd disembarked his last naval ship, and his unshackled feet stepped once more on solid ground.

Smiling to himself, Jack thought of Lily and the rousing success the piano concert had been. If not for her, it would've been a tedious evening, but instead, it was a treasured moment. Merely the memory of her enraptured expression during the music was enough to bring a spring to his step—if Jack were capable of such foolishness.

Yes, it had been a triumph. An offering given with his whole heart that had been accepted with unrestrained eagerness.

Jack wondered if Lily was still joyous over the concert. Duty and responsibility prodded him to return to work, but his feet pulled him towards her uncle's home; meetings had kept him from visiting her the day before, and Jack wasn't about to allow two days to lapse without her. Besides, locking himself in his office was hardly efficient when his thoughts were consumed with her.

His eyes drifted over the sea of people, though Jack did not meet anyone's gaze and risk being compelled to stop. It was as though all of London had decided to steal a moment outdoors, but even the suffocating crowd could not dampen his spirits.

And then he caught sight of her.

Even in the greatest throng, Lily stood out like a candle in the darkness. She was not proportioned to others' standards, but Jack could not think of a lady whose figure rivaled his Lily's. He itched to pull her into his embrace and feel her pressed close to him. A phantom scent that belonged only to her filled his nose. He couldn't pinpoint the components of the fragrance; Jack only knew that it smelled of his Lily.

But thoughts of those delights fled his mind as he saw DeVere standing before her.

Jack's feet moved faster to join them, for the lad needed yet another reminder that Lily was not free to receive such overt attentions, but his steps halted at the sight of her blinding smile turned to DeVere. Lily's eyes glittered in the sun as she gazed at the fellow with unmitigated pleasure.

An invisible weight dropped on his shoulders, pressing down on him before settling in his stomach. Standing like a statue, he watched DeVere bow over her hand, giving it a gallant kiss before parting, and Lily was aglow as she returned to her aunt's side.

After everything he'd done to secure her affections, Lily was in love with someone else.

The warmth disintegrated, the sunshine dimming as a chill seeped into his heart like mud in a shoe, filling it until the organ froze in his chest. In a flash, Jack saw the future stretching before him. Lily happily announcing her engagement to DeVere. Standing before a vicar to exchange their vows. Beginning a life together. And Jack stood like a starving beggar at the edge of a feast, unable to partake as others gorged themselves to bursting.

His time in the navy had given Jack a low standard for happiness, but Lily had shown him how much greater life could be. He couldn't return to the quiet nothingness of business, and Jack knew if he spent the rest of his life searching, he'd never find anyone to rival his Lily. The thought of losing her had his frozen heart fracturing, the tiny shards of ice penetrating every part of him.

Wild thoughts filled his mind, begging Jack to toss Lily in a carriage and force her to the nearest church. Do something—anything—to secure her. A dozen scenarios cropped up, and Jack fought against their enticing—but ludicrous—call.

"Jack!"

Mind occupied as it was, Jack hadn't Lily's approach. His thoughts struggled to coalesce; he needed time to formulate a plan that would show her she belonged with him. The pressure in his head grew, begging to be unleashed, but to do so might hurt Lily, and the thought made Jack's heart recoil.

Coming to stand before him, Lily grinned. "How lovely to see you."

Jack gave a vague nod, for that was all he trusted himself to do. That pressure spread through him; somehow it both expanded and constricted in equal measure, making him feel as though he was stuck between exploding and crumpling.

And suddenly, he was the lad he'd once been—powerless and at the mercy of someone capable of destroying his entire world.

Lily spoke a few more words, though Jack did not hear them. His breath came in quick bursts as he tried to gain control of himself. But how could he? This situation was not something he could control. Lily was free to do as she pleased. Engagements were broken every day. His claim to her was informal and flimsy, and she would leave him. Disappear forever.

Reaching forward, she touched his arm. "Is something the matter? You look quite unwell."

Her brows were knit together, her eyes brimming with concern, but Jack could not speak as he stared at her hand against his arm.

Shaking his head, Jack found the strength to move once more. He needed to gather his thoughts. He needed to think. He needed time. Jack knew he could win the day, but images of Lily in DeVere's embrace clouded his mind, and the more he thought on it, the more erratic his thoughts grew until it felt as though his mind were a foreign thing, autonomous and independent of his will.

Lily pleaded for him to speak, but words were not his strength. No doubt DeVere could string together a glorious explanation for cacophony consuming his heart and mind, but Jack couldn't think of a single coherent word to give Lily.

For the first time in his life, Jack retreated.

Lily could not interpret the expression on Jack's face. There was a pinch of impatience around his eyes and lips, but a hint of what looked to be panic in his gaze. Or confusion? And frustration? Whatever was going through his thoughts was certainly of great import and stirring up strong emotions, but Lily could not decipher them. And Jack would not speak.

With a few steps, he moved around her and walked away without speaking a word. Not even a greeting. Where was the Jack of two days ago who had gazed upon her with such longing? Sickness gripped her stomach, filling her with a sour, queasy feeling.

"Jack, please tell me what is the matter," she said, reaching for his arm, but Jack tugged away from her grip.

"Jack—" But her voice cracked, betraying the growing emotions Lily was trying to keep at bay.

He halted, casting a wary glance over his shoulder at her. Blinking, she tried to dispel the gathering tears while cursing herself for being so ridiculous and unable to control her emotions. This was merely a misunderstanding, surely. Something easily mended.

"We are engaged." Those three words were all that Jack supplied, and they gave her no better insight into his behavior. But as Lily tried to make some connection to his present ill temper and what had happened, a sudden answer came to her thoughts.

"Are you speaking of Mr. DeVere?" she asked, and when Jack scowled, Lily swiped at her eyes with a smile. Her heart sighed at that innocuous issue. "We are just acquaintances, Jack. He is a nice young man, and I enjoy his company, but that is all."

However, a morsel of guilt sunk into her stomach, and Lily knew her behavior towards Mr. DeVere had not always been so innocent as her tone implied. Examined from her present position, Lily knew she'd given Jack reason to believe the worst.

"I promise that no matter how it appeared, Mr. DeVere and I have no understanding nor do I wish for one."

But Jack merely watched her, silent and still. His expression was unreadable, and Lily's stomach twisted as she tried to decipher what was going through his mind. Clutching the shawl tight around her, she took a breath to calm the anxious flutters in her heart as her instincts told her to say more. But to admit why she'd welcomed Mr. DeVere's flirtations was to expose those shameful parts of her heart she preferred to keep hidden. Her feet longed to flee, and her mind dredged up every rational and irrational argument why she should do so, but Jack deserved to understand.

Glancing around at the passing people, Lily wished they had more privacy for such a discussion. At least they were standing between a row of trees, which provided some protection from onlookers.

"I've never sought out Mr. DeVere's affections, but I did welcome his flirtation," she began as her cheeks heated. "I know it was selfish of me, but I wanted to know what it was like to be admired."

Dropping her gaze to the ground, Lily focused on the folds of her gown. "I wanted to hear someone tell me I'm beautiful. To flirt with me. I've seen so many young ladies and young men participate in the courtship dance, and for once, I wished to join in."

Though she kept a tight rein on her tears, she couldn't control them completely, and they made her voice wobble. "It was silly, and I shouldn't have allowed it to go on as it has. But it was harmless, and it is not going to continue."

Lily couldn't bear to look at Jack after having admitted that pitiful desire, but he did not speak, and the silence became more unbearable, and she met his gaze. Jack stared at her, mouth agape and brows pulled tight together, but then his expression shifted into his favorite scowl. His jaw clenched and his features pinched, giving an angry cast to his face.

But worst of all, Lily saw disappointment burning in his eyes.

Some residual rational thoughts called for Jack to calm himself and think before acting, but Lily's desperate words had the pressure building inside him until he was certain his skull would crack.

After everything he'd done to win her heart, Lily desired DeVere's foolish flattery? Jack had done everything he could to show her his heart. What was left to be done? That sad organ in his chest shattered, leaving Jack with a gaping wound.

"I am not some pitiful creature, Jack Hatcher. I am not proud of my weakness, but you have no right to judge me for it," she blurted, and Jack's eyes darted back to meet hers. Though there was a flicker of sadness in her eyes at that confession, Lily straightened her spine and raised her head in defiance. "I simply wanted to feel beautiful for once in my life."

Jack had heard plenty of ridiculous things in his life, but that dwarfed all others. Lily was gorgeous, and his heart ached at the thought that she felt the need to seek out validation of that fact. How did she not understand the power she held over him? The awe he felt when she smiled? Jack had known many ladies in the course of his life, and not one of them rivaled his Lily.

If his greatest offerings had not convinced her of that, what more could he do?

"I knew Mr. DeVere's words meant nothing, but still, he made me feel desirable, and I will not apologize for wanting that." Her voice quivered, and though her body thrummed with agitated energy, a sheen of tears came to her eyes.

Taking Lily's hand in his, Jack pulled her forward, bringing his lips to hers, but Lily reared away.

"What are you doing?" she demanded.

Lily's hand never moved, but Jack felt the slap all the same. Taking a step back, Jack ground his teeth together as yet another of his offerings was rejected, and Lily scowled at him with such fury that his mind could not scrape together coherent thoughts. For a moment, he thought of attempting another kiss; Lily could not mistake that ardor for anything less than the truth. But even as his body itched to show her his heart, Jack stood there like the useless lump he was.

In truth, there was only one thing he could think to do. Turning on his heels, he strode away from Lily. She may hold him at arm's length, but Jack knew there must be some way for him to win her heart. To show her the depth of the hold she had on his. He had to.

Chapter 27

L ily clutched her saucer and teacup; the drink was cold by now, but still, she held onto it. Mindlessly, she lifted the spoon and gave it a cursory turn in her cup as though that might revive the tea.

Her eyes ached, and though Lily believed her tears were spent, any time her thoughts turned to Jack, they threatened anew. In fact, her whole body was plagued by pains; it begged for proper sleep while her heart pleaded for relief from the concerns pressing on her.

"All is not over, Lily," said Aunt Mary, glancing at her niece over the top of her newspaper.

"I wish I had your faith," replied Lily.

"In my experience, disagreements look far bleaker to those involved than they truly are. Give it time, and you will discover whether you are well-suited or not."

"It seems clear we are ill-suited."

Folding the newspaper, her aunt turned her full attention to her niece. "This is merely a miscommunication, which is not the death knell of a relationship or no one would ever marry."

Lily set aside her teacup with a clink of china against the side table. "You didn't see him, Aunt Mary. He was disgusted with me."

With a sigh, Lily clasped her hands in her lap. Turning her attention to the window, she watched the passing traffic. Replaying the scene for the thousandth time during the last day, Lily saw it clearly in her mind.

"I cannot fault Jack for thinking me enamored with Mr. DeVere. I was foolish and vain, and Jack has every right to be upset with my behavior. But his expression, Aunt Mary..." Turning her gaze to the lady before her, Lily's brows pinched together, her heart dropping at the memory. "He is so strong and confident, and it is only natural he would view my behavior as weak and revolting."

Aunt Mary gave her a sad smile. "I've found that deciphering another's motives is often a hopeless cause, for my understanding is colored by my fears and opinions. You cannot know what his thoughts were."

Lily gave her an acknowledging nod, but her heart found no comfort in that. "But how am I to understand his thoughts when he refuses to share them?"

"Not everyone is as free with their words as you," replied Aunt Mary with a smile, but Lily was in no mood to find the humor in the situation. "There are many who express themselves through their actions—"

"The speedy manner in which he escaped spoke volumes."

But Aunt Mary replied with a challenging raise of her brow. "And what does it say that he attended your charity concert, though he doesn't care for such things? Or that he worked to make it a success? Or that he arranged for you to attend a recital given by your favorite composer? Again, attending it with you, solely because you enjoy it? Or the many hours he's spent forgoing his own pursuits to spend time in your company?"

Lily's gaze fell to the floor, her chest tightening with each word. When listed in such a succinct manner, it did seem as though she was terribly shortsighted. "But what if he's only doing so out of duty or honor? How am I to know if he does not tell me? I don't think I am asking for the moon and stars by wishing my betrothed to give some clear indication of his feelings."

At that, Aunt Mary gave a vague noise, and Lily looked up to see her aunt gazing off at nothing. A moment later, her eyes focused on Lily, and she gave her a sad smile. "Is it going to be enough, Lily? If he tells you everything you dream of hearing, will you finally trust that he cares for you?"

"Certainly."

But her aunt gave another challenging raise of her eyebrows. "The issue is not that you distrust him. It's that you distrust his feelings for you. I struggled with the self-same issue when I met your dear uncle. He tried winning me over with his silver tongue and then showed his devotion in so many ways, but still, I doubted him—because I doubted I could inspire such feelings."

Lily knew there was no defending herself against such words, for they were true. Jack certainly had behaved strangely yesterday, but she'd been quick to forget all the signs of his devotion in favor of assuming the worst of him. When she thought about his actions as a whole, Lily wanted to believe he was in earnest.

Desperately.

Jack had stolen her heart, and she wanted to believe that she'd stolen his.

However, there was a lingering little doubt that lay hidden in her heart. That niggling, awful whisper, which said he was only tolerating her. But even as she listened to its poisoned words, her heart recalled their time together. Those looks he gave her. The kindnesses he bestowed. The time he sacrificed. Taken objectively, they were the signs of a tender beau. Yet she allowed her fears to cast a pall over those joys. Once again.

Certainly, Jack's behavior was bizarre, but she'd leaped to the worst assumption. With little prompting, she'd made him the villain. Once again.

Leaning forward, Lily covered her eyes. Not that she held all the blame in this situation, but neither could she lay all it on

Jack's shoulders, either. Like most disagreements, there were two parties involved, neither of which was entirely guilty or innocent.

"You are right," she murmured, meeting Aunt Mary's gaze. "I assumed the worst of Jack, which is unfair of me."

She twisted her hands in her lap, her shoulders falling. "But how can I come to understand him when he won't speak to me? I accept he is not one to chatter on, and he speaks freely about many subjects, but if the conversation turns too personal, he remains mute. I begged him to speak with me and explain his thoughts, and he simply walked away. How can I have a happy life with someone so distant?"

With a sigh, Lily's heart deflated. "When I first met him, I thought him domineering and insufferable, but I've grown to adore his company. There is something in him that inspires me to be stronger, as though being with him makes me more confident and capable somehow."

Aunt Mary's smile turned from sad to contemplative as her gaze grew distant. "From what I've heard, Jack is much improved as well, and that is the mark of a good match. Marriage is not just about finances, social standing, or even love. It's two people banding together to become something greater than they can be alone."

Each word fanned the longing in Lily's heart until it consumed her. She could not imagine a better sort of marriage and wished it could be hers.

"But that said," added Aunt Mary, "even the best pairings do not guarantee never-ending bliss. You both come into it with shortcomings and flaws. Are you willing to shoulder your Mr. Hatcher's weaknesses as well as his strengths?"

A shadow of desire clung to Lily's heart. Despite everything that had happened in the last few days, it still resided there, begging her to try again. But the pressing fear of what heartache the future may bring balanced it out, leaving Lily unsure of which to choose. Like many others, she'd dreamt of finding love, and the phantom grooms she'd constructed in her day-dreams were nothing like the stoic and unyielding Jack Hatcher.

Lily fiddled with the folds of her skirts. "I know many young ladies marry, hoping their groom will change for the better, and that only ends in disappointment."

"There is a difference between loving someone for their potential and loving them for who they are while seeing their potential. I fear too many young ladies don't understand that," replied Aunt Mary. "But you needn't decide your future with Mr. Hatcher at this very moment. Now, you need only decide whether you're willing to explore the possibility."

Aunt Mary unfolded the newspaper once more, perusing the contents. Lily was no closer to understanding her heart than she had been that morning or the day before, but there was no use in belaboring the issue any further.

"I did not realize you were such an avid reader of the newspaper," said Lily. It was a weak change in subject, but it was better than wallowing in confusion and uncertainty.

"It is important to improve one's mind," replied Aunt Mary with a distracted tone. "And as your uncle has not the time to keep abreast of current events, I read through it for him and give him a report of the important points."

"Is there no news of Lucas?" asked Lily with a furrowed brow. Her stomach felt heavy as she realized that while she'd bemoaned her heartaches, her poor aunt was struggling with her own.

"We believe he's traveling with friends, but Ambrose cannot find anything concrete," she replied. Though Aunt Mary's eyes did not leave the newspaper, strain pulled at the edges of her mouth and eyes. "I am certain everything will be made right in the end."

Aunt Mary's words were light, but her tone was too stilted for Lily to put any stock in her deflection. However, if Aunt Mary wished to feign nonchalance, Lily would not press the matter.

"I wonder when Aunt Louisa-Margaretta will return," said Lily.

It was a silly thing to say, for she was quite enjoying a bit of peace with Aunt Mary at present and had no desire to rush her other aunt's return, but that thought brought with it a wave of guilt. Aunt Louisa-Margaretta was a good and kind lady, but after weeks of spending so much time in the lady's care, Lily longed to return to her own home.

Aunt Mary straightened, her eyes widening as she stared at the newspaper.

"What is it?" asked Lily.

But her aunt merely murmured, "That fool of a man."

Glancing from the paper, Aunt Mary looked at Lily with a deeply furrowed brow. She sat there, silent, her expression growing more pinched.

"What is the matter?" Lily pressed.

Aunt Mary sighed and folded the paper into a smaller size before handing it to Lily. With a frown, she took it and cast her eyes to the row of text. It took a moment of searching to discover what her aunt was referring to, but then Lily saw her own name printed in black and white.

Buried among bits and pieces about social functions and entertainment, which was little more than thinly veiled gossip, was a section announcing engagements and marriages. And right in the middle was a short paragraph concerning Miss Lily Kingsley's future wedding to Mr. Jonathan Hatcher. Lily's hands clenched the edges of the paper, crumpling it as she stared at the words. While a small part of her heart leaped at the sight of their names paired together, her stomach churned as a chill skittered along her spine.

"He agreed to wait until my parents arrived home." Lily looked to her aunt, the woman's features blurring with the tears that sprung to Lily's eyes. "He agreed to an informal engagement until then."

But quick on sorrow's heels came a fire that melted away the cold gripping her heart. "He agreed to this and has gone back on his word!"

Tossing the paper aside, Lily got to her feet as her fury pushed her to pace the room.

"Why would he do this? Why?" Lily nearly shouted the question at Aunt Mary, though that dear lady had no more answers to this puzzle than she. "If you'd seen the way he behaved yesterday, you would've thought him more likely to break with me than formally announce our engagement."

Aunt Mary opened her mouth, but Lily spoke over her. "And to break his word? I cannot make heads nor tails of it, Aunt. It makes no sense."

"I dare say it does to Mr. Hatcher," Aunt Mary replied. "Dear, please sit before you work yourself into a proper dither."

Begrudgingly, Lily sat on the sofa beside her aunt.

Reaching over, Aunt Mary took Lily's hands in hers. "There may yet be an explanation. Before you go charging in, temper flaring, it would be best to take a moment and think this through."

Lily's shoulders drooped as the fight seeped out of her. "How can I trust him, Aunt? He seems determined to do as he pleases, regardless of my feelings on the matter. My father would never do such a thing to Mama."

"Dearest, I know it seems bleak at present, but no relationship is perfect from the start," said Aunt Mary, wrapping her arms around Lily's shoulders. "I am not saying you must continue courting Mr. Hatcher, but I would hate for you to surrender over something that could be merely a misunderstanding."

"How else can I interpret his behavior?" asked Lily, leaning away to give her aunt a stern look. "What he has done is unforgivable."

"You would be surprised how much is forgivable with a bit of context."

Lily sagged at those words, and though she agreed with the sentiment, she struggled to see how this situation could be made any better. "But I am no longer certain I want to fight through this. It cannot bode well for a marriage when a mere courtship is so disastrous."

Pulling Lily close, Aunt Mary took her in her arms, but Lily had no more tears to offer up.

Chapter 28

I f Jack were a drinking man, he'd be tempted to disappear into a bottle and not emerge for days. Then he might have an excuse for such ludicrous behavior. But as much as he wished to have something or someone to blame for his foolishness, Jack knew it rested on his shoulders. Of course, accepting the blame did not help him face the consequences.

Sitting in a quiet corner of his favorite coffeehouse, Jack stared at the flaking paint on the wall. He hadn't bothered going into the office, as Silas would have a few choice words for him, and though he longed to go and pass the afternoon with Lily, Jack knew what awaited him if he did; she had every right to eviscerate him. When had he become a man who hid from problems?

His cup sat beside him, growing cold, and Jack could not bring himself to drink it. Other patrons gathered together in groups, chattering away as though this were a perfectly fine day, and Jack wondered how they did not feel the storm clouds gathering. The only blessing to be found at the moment was that his seat was obscured from general view, giving him a semblance of privacy.

How had he come to this?

Jack had been approached by many men who longed to invest in wild schemes and attain the fortune and glory of which they dreamt, and Jack turned them out on their ear because such men were prone to desperation, which led to foolhardy decisions. Rationality was Jack's hallmark, but clearly, he'd taken leave of his senses; if any associate had bungled business as Jack had done with Lily, Jack would've washed his hands of the fellow and wished him good riddance.

Scrubbing his hands through his hair, Jack rested his head against the armchair. His fingers tapped against the arm, ticking off the seconds that passed as he hid there.

"You have the look of a dying man."

Jack stifled a growl. "You are possibly the last person I wish to see at present, DeVere."

Hands in his pockets, the young man stood to one side and dipped his head in acknowledgment. Though he rocked on his heels, DeVere did not leave. "I need to speak with you."

"I think you've done enough," grumbled Jack. "After what has happened, I doubt Miss Kingsley will forgive me. The field is free for you to conquer."

DeVere winced at that, and Jack regretted the metaphor, but he had far greater regrets at present.

"I owe you an apology," said DeVere. And instead of scurrying away at Jack's glower, the insolent pup took a seat. "Though I hadn't planned to speak with you, my conscience won't leave me be. I apologized to Miss Kingsley, but you deserve one as well, for it is you I was aiming to hurt."

Jack straightened in his seat, his eyes narrowing on DeVere. "What did you do to Miss Kingsley?"

DeVere raised his hands. "Nothing terrible." He paused. "At least not wholly terrible."

Jack's gaze bore into the young man's pale eyes as DeVere hurriedly added, "I treated her callously, but I assure you, I spoke with her and made amends."

The building pressure in Jack's chest eased at that, though he couldn't relax.

The young man's face heated, his eyes darting around the room, though they refused to land on Jack. DeVere cleared his throat. "My behavior towards her was a ploy. I knew flirting with her would make you jealous. By doing so, I toyed with both her affections and those of the woman I love."

"You don't love Miss Kingsley?" Jack's brows shot upwards, his breath catching in his lungs. The idea was ludicrous, but Jack needed to be certain he understood the fellow.

"I'm courting Miss Aubrey Valentine." Though a somber tone clung to the conversation, DeVere broke into a silly grin at those words, but it disappeared at the sight of Jack's scowl.

Miss Aubrey Valentine? What fool in his right mind would choose that chit over Lily? It was absurd. He supposed Miss Aubrey was pretty enough and seemed a good sort, but Lily was superior in every aspect. Clearly, Jack had been correct in thinking DeVere would never thrive in business, for he lacked sound judgment.

DeVere stared off into the distance with a smile tugging at his lips until Jack cleared his throat and drew him back to the present.

"I toyed with Miss Kingsley's heart, and it was wrong of me, but I have already spoken with her about it," said DeVere, shifting in his seat. "I came here to offer my apologies to you."

The fellow sighed, shifted in his seat once more, and stared at the floorboards as though they were terribly interesting.

"I've been angry with you—unjustly so—and I used your regard for Miss Kingsley to punish you," said DeVere. "It was wrong of me to interfere with your courtship and treat you both so poorly."

Jack's brows drew together. "You've been angry with me?"

DeVere sighed and reclined in his seat. "When you and Silas left the navy to start this grand adventure on your own, I was desperate to join you."

"But you couldn't resign yet," added Jack, hurrying the narrative past that which he knew. "You came for a visit later but then disappeared."

He grimaced and gave a quick nod. "It was childish of me, but I believed we would be partners like you and Silas, but you offered me a position as a glorified laborer."

"Of course I did," said Jack with a scowl. "You're a fine fellow, but you've no head for business, and I will not risk our employees' livelihoods for you."

DeVere gave a low chuckle and shook his head with a rueful smile. "Your honesty still borders on brutal, Hatch."

"But I offered to help you find something better suited—"

"And I did say that my behavior was childish and was unjust." DeVere scratched at his jaw, his expression falling. "You were generous to me, but I took offense and allowed my pride to keep me from following your sound advice. Luckily, Miss Aubrey is exceptionally patient and willing to be similarly brutal when I need a good shake."

A ghost of a smile played across Jack's lips when his thoughts turned to another lady with similar talents, but it faded as he reflected on the mess he'd made of things.

"Thank you for your kindness to a silly, blind fool, and I apologize for any hurt I may have caused," said DeVere.

Jack gave a nod and examined the young man sitting before him. "Have you found a position?"

DeVere's brows rose. "After all I've done, you would help me get one?"

"You've admitted your mistake and earnestly expressed remorse," said Jack with a shrug. "That already marks you as a man worth helping. And I cannot imagine you've changed all that much from the young man I knew. You were a poor sailor, but you've a good heart and a sharp mind."

With a sigh, DeVere dropped his head. He rubbed his forehead for several quiet moments before finally speaking. "You are a far better man than I ever knew, Hatch."

Straightening again, DeVere met Jack's gaze and added, "I thank you for your offer, but I've already taken steps to follow the advice you gave me all those years ago. I took a position as a clerk to Lord Dewhurst. It's a lowly start, but I have high hopes that it will lead to something more substantial."

"He is influential in the House of Lords and the Department of the Treasury," said Jack with a thoughtful nod. "Impress him and you'll have plenty of lucrative offers before long. I think you will do well in politics."

DeVere's cheeks colored. "Yes, as you told me before. I just wish I hadn't been such a prideful fool to ignore your sound advice for so long; I might've been well established and married to Miss Aubrey by this time."

Jack huffed and shook his head. No matter how he tried to reconcile it, he could not fathom why DeVere would choose a lady like Miss Aubrey over Lily. And Jack told him so. DeVere stared as though he were a raving madman, but Jack knew it was DeVere who'd taken leave of his senses.

"Even if I wished to pursue Miss Kingsley, she has no interest in being pursued by me," said DeVere.

Jack's fingers tapped a rapid pace along the arm of the chair. "Well, I offer my congratulations to you and Miss Aubrey."

"There is nothing to congratulate quite yet. Her father has only allowed me to pay court to her at present. Until I can prove myself a 'steady chap' with a decent income, I am not free to go any further. But we have hope and that is enough for now."

Leaning forward with a smile, DeVere smiled at Jack. "But you are deserving of congratulations."

Jack's heart fell from his chest, landing with a thud on the floor, and it sunk even lower when DeVere continued.

"I saw the announcement in the newspaper. The engagement is formalized, then? When is the wedding?"

The void in his chest collapsed in on itself, leaving Jack shrunken and shriveled inside. He had no reply to give, for anything other than the truth was unacceptable, and Jack couldn't bring himself to speak the words aloud and admit the full breadth of his mistake. He'd come to this quiet, out of the way coffee shop for the sole purpose of avoiding anyone who would ask him such questions.

"That is not the expression of a happy man," said DeVere, his brows pulling together. "Has something happened? The last I saw Miss Kingsley, she was enamored."

Jack stiffened, his eyes searching DeVere's for the truth in his words. The fellow seemed to believe them, though Jack could not accept them so easily.

"What did you do?" asked DeVere. At Jack's puzzled look, he added, "Miss Kingsley is a sweet lady, and if a rift has formed, I doubt it is of her making."

A quick defense came to Jack's lips, but he had enough sense to keep it tucked away. As much as it would be gratifying to lay the blame on Lily or DeVere, Jack deserved most of it. DeVere may have struck the match that led to this burning ruin, but Jack had laid the kindling and nursed it into a proper blaze.

"I will not press you for details, but I would like to help. It's the least I can do," said DeVere.

Leveling a look at the young man, Jack wanted to send him on his way, but he paused. From the beginning, Jack had known he lacked the skill to court properly, and he'd already been foolish enough to turn aside Silas's and Ambrose's offers of aid. And DeVere had shown himself adept at turning Lily's head.

"You have the look of a fellow who has ruined everything and doesn't know how to repair it," added DeVere. Jack gave him another questioning glance, and the young man shrugged. "It's the same look I sported a few days ago."

When Jack did not respond to that, DeVere added, "I think you'll find an apology will do most of the work."

"I am beyond that."

"I didn't think I would live to see the day when Jonathan Hatcher surrendered. I've seen you take on greater odds without flinching."

Slouching in his chair, Jack rapped his fingers against the leather arm as he thought through his behavior of the past few days. "But I knew the variables and how to handle the situations. Miss Kingsley is a mystery I cannot grasp and never behaves as expected."

Jack's head dropped against the chair, and he stared at the ceiling as his spirits darkened.

"Giving your heart to someone is a terrifying thing, isn't it?" DeVere phrased it as a question, but his tone said it as a fact. "You cannot control whether they will accept it or give theirs in return."

DeVere paused, examining Jack with a long, quiet look. "I don't know what has passed between you two, so I will not pretend to understand the situation in its entirety, but you should talk to Miss Kingsley. Be frank. Honest."

The words were spoken as though they were a little thing, but Jack's pulse quickened at the thought of it. Honesty did not trouble him in the slightest, but there was too much to explain, and the few times Jack had tried to speak his heart to Lily had ended in disaster.

"Apologize, Hatch," said DeVere as he rose to his feet. "Trust her. Miss Kingsley cares deeply for you."

He turned to leave, but Jack could not leave that final statement unchallenged.

"She does?" At least he'd managed to ask that desperate question in a calm, collected tone.

DeVere paused, turning on his heel to stare at Jack. "You don't see it?"

"She flirted and fawned over you."

With a snort, DeVere laughed. "There was only one time in our acquaintance in which she did so, and that was to exact revenge for what she knew I was doing to her. Otherwise, she was only kind and gregarious, but she is that way with everyone."

Jack watched him with a furrowed brow, pondering over the words though too afraid to hope they were true.

DeVere shook his head and gave a frustrated huff. "In the time I've known her, there is only one person for whom she brightens as though the world did not exist until he stepped into view. With you nearby, it's as though she expands and her already large heart doubles."

And with that, DeVere took his leave, abandoning Jack with only that dim light of hope to chase away the growing shadows threatening to overtake him.

Chapter 29

The sun had set by the time Jack made his way home, and the streets were black with only the gas lamps lighting the way. Workers turned their carts to home as the wealthy trundled about in their carriages, heading to their various evening engagements. The smell of rain hung heavy in the air, mixing with the stench of the city, promising that tomorrow's weather would be as bleak as the rest of the summer had been; their short period of sunshine had ended in a blink.

But Jack didn't notice any of it.

His feet moved along the pavement, following the pathway home without conscious thought, pulling him through the crowds. Luckily, he knew the way well enough, leaving him free to think about Lily.

Could an apology be all he needed? Jack had broken her trust. If the manner in which they'd gotten engaged had angered Lily, Jack knew his announcing it to the world—expressly against her wishes—could cause irreparable damage. DeVere did understand ladies better than he, but Jack couldn't imagine a simple apology would be enough to mend this.

Reaching the Byrnes's front door, Jack let himself in, divesting himself of his hat and gloves and giving them to an obliging footman who appeared moments later.

A hand grabbed him by the arm, and Jack turned to see Judith standing there.

"I was calling to you, but you didn't answer," she said.

"I didn't hear you," said Jack. And he hadn't. In fact, he hadn't noticed the footman disappear or her approach, either. "I shan't be joining you for dinner tonight."

But Judith waved that away. "You are needed in the parlor."

Jack tried to give excuses, turning towards the stairs that would lead him to his bedchamber, but Judith blocked his way, herding him towards the dreaded parlor. Though normally, he welcomed an evening at home with the Byrnes family, the thought of being surrounded by people soured Jack's stomach. He needed solitude.

But Judith would not be thrown over, and Jack had to either follow her directions or shove past her. So, he followed and stepped to the doorway; he took several steps inside before seeing Lily. Blinking, Jack stared at her, wondering if his wits had finally abandoned him altogether, leaving him haunted by her memory. That had to be the case, for Lily was not sobbing nor berating his honor. But even as he contemplated that possibility, the truth slapped him in the face.

Lily was here to take her leave of him.

Judith disappeared, shutting the parlor door behind them, and Jack felt torn between the need to flee and the desire to sweep Lily into his arms and burrow into her hold, as though it could hide him from this impending doom.

Motioning for him to sit, Lily took the seat across from him. A tray of tea and cakes sat on the side table (though only remnants remained), and a book and several magazines rested beside her.

"As you decided to go to ground, I had no choice but to wait here for you to return," said Lily. "We need to have a frank discussion."

Grasping her skirts to keep her hands from shaking, Lily took a silent, calming breath. In the abstract, speaking to Jack had seemed the only course, but the thought of laying her heart bare before him made it shudder in her chest. But there was no helping the situation. As much as she longed for a cowardly retreat, that would only bring her a lifetime of misery. At least this course of action held the possibility of a joyful resolution.

"You aren't angry with me?" His question came out in a halting manner, as though he struggled with each word.

"I am angry." Lily's eyes narrowed on him. The memory of the agony she'd felt came rearing into her forethoughts, and she fought against the tide of emotion that accompanied it. "Three days ago, I had the most wonderful evening in my life, but since then, you have been distant and combative, leaving me confused and hurt."

Jack shifted in his seat, but before he could say a thing, Lily continued. "However, as someone once pointed out to me, I tend to misinterpret your motives, so I am finished with subtlety. I need to know what is going through your head."

Reaching over, Lily retrieved the newspaper and tossed it on the table between them, displaying the accursed announcement. Jack's fingers tapped against the arm of the sofa, thumping a muted beat over and over, but he said nothing.

"Why did you go against what we had agreed?"

His fingers beat faster like a hummingbird's wings, but his mouth remained shut.

Many a fellow had tried to intimidate Jack, but none of their paltry efforts generated even a particle of the terror Lily inspired with a few simple words. He'd never thought himself a coward, but when faced with Lily's pleading eyes, there was no denying the abject fear that took hold of him.

It was only the two of them in that parlor, but it felt as though they were standing amid a busy thoroughfare, the confusing mess of noise and movement pulling Jack's thoughts every which way. His mind fought to gain control, but he could hardly recall his own name, let alone express that which was inexpressible.

"I see," she murmured, getting to her feet. Face turned away from him, Lily crossed the room in several quick steps before Jack could react. When his sluggish thoughts arrived at the present, he was across the parlor in a flash. Lily gave a squeak when his arms came around her, turning her to face him and trapping her against him.

"Please, don't leave me," he murmured.

Lily's eyes widened as she stared at him, but Jack didn't have the strength to meet her gaze. His insides roiled as he struggled to find the words that would not come. His strength ebbed until it felt as though he was clinging to Lily, and she was the only thing keeping them upright.

Taking a breath, Jack forced himself to look at her. "You terrify me."

Her brows rose and then sank down again, drawing together as she stared at him. Her expression fell as she turned her face away from him. "That is not what I'd hoped to hear."

Though Jack was loath to let go of the hold he had on her, he freed one hand so that he could tilt her chin to face him. As he could not bring order to the raging mess in his head, Jack spoke without thought.

"For most of my life, I've lived at the mercy of others, and I fought hard to be my own master. My life is in my control, and I find peace in that. Then you swept in, disrupting everything, and my life is no longer my own."

Lily's eyes began blinking furiously, and she tugged her chin from his hold, turning as though she wished to leave, and Jack cursed his ineptitude.

"You terrify me because I cannot control you—I do not wish to—but at any moment, you can choose to walk away, and I cannot do a thing about it. I am at your mercy, and I have fought long and hard to never be in such a position again."

It was by no means the flowery declaration she'd envisioned as a young lady, but Lily's breath caught in her chest at what Jack was admitting. He was at her mercy? That was not how she would have worded it, but that did not make it any less truthful. Nor apt.

In the weeks she'd known Jack, he'd become a fixture in her life. A few blissful moments in his company had the power to lighten her soul. And the mere hint of losing him was enough to shatter her heart. It was not as though she would cease to exist without him, but his presence affected her world.

And Jack felt the same.

There was no denying that the prospect was terrifying. To trust her heart to another took more courage than Lily had realized it would.

"Please, do not leave me," he begged again.

Jack's fear shone in his eyes, pleading with her to stay, and Lily knew it would take a heart of stone to turn aside from such naked need. Here was the Jack who'd touched her heart so many times. Though that confident, determined man was something to admire, it was seeing this glimpse into his fragile heart that bound her to him all the tighter.

Nudging him towards the sofa, Lily sat beside Jack, taking his hand in hers as gathered her thoughts. Having had plenty of time to ponder this moment while awaiting Jack's return, Lily knew what to say, but she still needed a moment to decide on the proper wording.

Of course, it was difficult to do so when she found herself staring at Jack's hand in hers; they fit so perfectly together. Her thumb brushed along the base of his palm, her heart warming with each delicate touch.

"I do not comprehend your logic, but the Jack I know may be stubborn and difficult at times but never cruel—at least, not to anyone undeserving. And I'm choosing to trust that your intentions were well-meaning." Lily paused and then added with a note of chagrin, "I certainly have a history of believing the worst of you, but I am willing to wait for an explanation before leaping to conclusions."

Though Jack did not relax, she felt the tension in his muscles easing. Unfortunately, it returned in force when she said, "But it wasn't the announcement that hurt me. It was your coldness in the park."

Taking a deep breath, Lily forged ahead. "I knew something was bothering you, and you turned away and refused to explain. Then you vanished. I sat here for hours as my only recourse was to lie in wait until you reappeared."

Jack opened his mouth as though to answer, and Lily squeezed his hand, but no words came out. His eyes darted away from her, and his free fingers began that rapid beat once more on his knee.

"I am not expecting grand orations on the subject," she said. "Even the simplest explanation would be preferable to silence."

Chapter 30

Never was there a greater fool than Jack Hatcher. Lily sat there, pleading for the simplest of words, and Jack could not give her even the smallest of them. She may think it no great thing, but she was blessed with an abundance of words.

There was a reason why Silas was entrusted with that side of the business. When it came to giving orders or making decisions, Jack did not struggle to get his point across, but when faced with explaining his feelings, he might as well be mute. Few people ever asked him such things, and even fewer cared about the answer, and such disuse had caused his tongue to atrophy.

"Jack, please," she said, and he wanted to. Truly, he did. But the words fled when he reached for them.

Lily made a move to stand again, but Jack seized her hand, holding her in place.

"I am no good with words. I never have been." That was a beginning, but far from enough. Sorting through his thoughts, Jack tried to explain it. "When I speak they come out wrong."

Lily cocked her head to the side with a huff. "Jack, that is simply not true. You've given me some of the sweetest compliments I've ever received."

Brows raised, Jack stared at her, recalling all the laughable attempts he'd made, and could not think of a single one that was worth repeating. "I thought them rather pathetic, and they certainly did not compare to DeVere's."

With a jerky laugh, Lily shook her head. "Not those. They were more than 'rather pathetic.' I am speaking of all the off-hand comments you made to me—telling me that you enjoy my conversation or saying that M. Chopin was a fool for not desiring my company."

Jack's lips curled, his brow scrunching. "Those are not compliments. They are facts."

Lily began that furious blinking of hers, and she turned her face away from him. With a tug of her hands, Jack drew her attention back to him. Tears gathered in her eyes, her cheeks blazing red as he gazed at her.

"Do you truly not understand how much that means to me?" asked Lily, her voice hitching. "I assure you that my company being desirable is not a fact to many people. I've been told I'm a bore, and that I am ugly and unwanted, yet you speak as though the opposite is a 'fact' that every rational human ought to accept."

Jack stared at her, his mind unable to move past the idea that someone could ever think such things about Lily, let alone say them directly to her.

"Your words are powerful because of what they signify," she explained. "They are simple, heartfelt signs of what you feel, and they mean far more than all the false sweetness that accompanies flattery. Your compliments are the truth as you see it, and it humbles me to know you view me in that light."

Her hands squeezed his, her fingers brushing along his skin, and Jack found it hard to focus on anything other than her touch and the sweet scent she carried with her. If not for the gravity of the situation, he would be quite content to never move from this place.

"I do not need poetry or flowery speeches," she said. "I simply need the truth—even if it is only the truth as you see it."

But the truth was rarely simple, and many of Jack's were filled with darkness that someone as bright as Lily should never experience.

"I do not want to make you cry," he said.

At that Lily gave a startled laugh. "Jack, I cry at anything. I once burst into tears over an advert I read in a magazine. It was ridiculous and not particularly sad, but it made me think of something sad, which was enough to make me a sobbing fool. Please, do not keep yourself closed off simply because you are afraid of hurting me."

Jack gave a hesitant nod.

"I struggle to trust in you and myself, but I am attempting to improve, and I am not demanding you tell me everything at present. All I need is a sign that you are willing to try as well." Leaning forward, Lily wrapped both of her hands around his, squeezing them tight. "Please, tell me what is going on in your head."

Instincts had saved Jack many a time. They'd helped him survive the navy and build his company into a success. Though Jack had thought they'd failed him of late, the truth was that they'd been buried beneath an avalanche of anxieties. The voice prodding him to greater and greater folly had been born from the fear of losing Lily, but with her grasping his hands, assuring him that all was not lost—yet—his instincts were finally free to speak their mind once more.

And Jack knew this was a pivotal moment.

Like that breath before an agreement was struck, this was that momentary pause between failure and fruition, and his action at this moment would determine which would come to pass. As much as his heart thumped at the thought of speaking out, the fear of losing Lily was far stronger. The time for equivocating was over, and the choice was either letting her go or letting her see his whole self.

Knowing it would taint her, his mouth remained firmly shut, but instinct came into play again, whispering to him that it was a mistake. Lily felt things deeply—far deeper than Jack had thought possible—but she was not weak. She was no stranger to heartache and hardship; others had tried to dull that light inside her, but it still shone brightly.

Lily was strong, and Jack had to trust in that.

"It's not easy for me to talk of such things," said Jack. The words came slowly, and each one was a battle, but he would not retreat once his course of action was set. "Captain Furton taught me many things, and chief among them was to bury the fury I felt whenever I saw his wretched face. If my control slipped for even a moment, I was punished, and when I'd grown immune to his beatings, he would punish my men in my stead. So, I learned to hold my tongue."

Lily fought against the tears. She knew it was pointless to do so, but she struggled all the same. In her mind, she could picture Jack as that poor lad, and her heart broke for the child and the hard man he became.

"You don't have to remain silent any longer," she said.

Jack gave a vague nod. "But it is not easy to undo a lifetime of habit."

With each touch of her hand, the tension eased from Jack, so Lily drew closer, sitting flush next to him. Though she doubted it was conscious, he let out a soft exhale, as though her proximity provided a balm for his soul. If that was what he needed, Lily was willing to give it.

"I know," she agreed. "But perhaps you can begin with an explanation as to why you announced our engagement in the papers."

Jack's gaze pulled away, but Lily nudged his chin, forcing his attention to her as he had done to her moments ago.

"I wanted to show you that I was in earnest," he murmured. Though she held his chin in place, his eyes drifted away, and Lily released her hold, her hand stroking along the edge of his jaw before dropping it to hold his hand once more. If it was easier for him not to look at her, then she would respect that. Instead, she chose to rest her head against his shoulder and give him the touch he seemed to need.

"You said DeVere made you feel wanted and admired and implied I was driven only by duty. I've tried so many ways to show you I am in earnest, but still, you doubt my intentions."

Lily's head rose to meet his gaze with wide eyes, her heart pausing between one beat and the next.

"I hurt you." Lily had known that her behavior with Mr. DeVere had led to this fracture between them, but she'd not realized just how much damage she'd truly done. She could see it there in his eyes, and phantom aches and pains played through her, making her heart shudder.

"Jack, I apologize and can only admit that my vanity and weakness are the culprits," said Lily. Her cheeks blazed as she turned her red face away from him. Withdrawing her hand from his, she pressed it to her stomach, as though that might calm the anxious flutter that sent a wave of nausea wafting through her. But Jack's hand was there, snatching hers again, as though it had been stolen away from its rightful owner, and something in that movement soothed the agony in her heart and loosened her tongue.

Lily clung to his hand, her fingers stroking the calloused skin. "The night we met I wasn't sneaking away for an assignation with some secret beau. I've never had one nor had any hope of gaining one. No man has ever shown the slightest interest in my company."

Jack gave a wordless objection that sounded more akin to a growl than anything human, and Lily squeezed his hand and amended, "No man other than you has ever shown the slightest interest in me. I was never courted. Never asked to dance by someone who was not pressed into service. Never told that I was pretty by anyone other than my family."

Lily's brow furrowed as she felt that rejection anew—as though it was happening at present and not merely a recalled memory.

"I was determined that if nothing else, I would know what it was like to be kissed," she said and began unraveling the whole tale. Once she started down that path, it was hard not to unveil it in its entirety. Speaking as she'd never done before, Lily gave every detail from the moment she'd written that silly letter to Mr. Farson.

"He never sent word that he was not going to come. He simply did not show." Lily paused before speaking the truth she had not admitted to anyone other than herself, and the words made her heart twist in her chest. "He chose to forego saying his farewells to people he'd known his entire life rather than see me. What does that say about his feelings towards my proposition? Can you call it anything other than revulsion? Disgust? Horror? Mr. Farson preferred to disappear to Canada rather than be in the same room as me."

Jack brushed a thumb across her cheek, wiping away the tears that had begun falling at some point. Then his lips were there, kissing the trails they'd made, but it only made Lily's eyes fill with more. As much as she despised leaning away, she knew she needed to finish.

"Then I was swept into a forced engagement to a gentleman who I thought did not care for me in the slightest, and Mr. DeVere strode in saying all these things I'd always longed to hear—"

But Lily found it impossible to continue because Jack pressed his thumb over her lips, silencing her. His eyes held hers, burning with that intensity only he could manage. It was palpable, filling Lily with such warmth and contentment; there could be no greater blessing than spending her life staring into those eyes.

There was a beauty all its own in receiving such a look. It spoke more than words could say, and in it, she saw his heart. Without filter or artifice. Without caveats. His heart belonged to her.

"You asked me several times why I was determined to go

through with this engagement, and I had hoped you would understand by now," he murmured. "But as you do not see the truth sitting right in front of your face, I will tell you in no uncertain terms."

He paused, that gentle thumb shifting so that it caressed the side of her lips. "I wanted to marry you from the very beginning. Our engagement was never a duty or obligation to me."

Tears threatened again, but Lily did not bother stemming them. Though no explicit declaration, she felt his meaning, and it set her heartbeat racing. For once, she had no words to give in reply, but even if she did, Lily suspected it would not have the same impact on the reticent Jack.

A thought leaped into her mind, but Lily shied away from it. A kiss would be too forward. Too bold. But even as she tried to think of any other possibility, Lily realized it was perfect. This was not the first time she'd stepped forward to grasp what she desired, and those stakes had been far lower than at present.

Without allowing herself another thought, Lily took his face in her hands and guided his lips to hers. With the exception of that first kiss of theirs, she had never initiated such a display, and that first time had meant nothing to either of them. But this kiss was a promise. A declaration. A wish for a lifetime more of this.

Jack was not a fellow to cry, but some part of him felt like doing so as Lily's love wrapped around his heart. Her kiss was sweetness and light, and he reined in the urge to take control and envelop her in the passion he felt. Holding this incredible lady in his arms, Jack felt awed that such a clumsy fool had stumbled into a lifetime with such a creature. Such perfection.

With slow, gentle touches, Lily released the kiss and stared into his eyes. Somewhere in the heat of the moment, she'd drawn close enough that she fairly sat on his lap, and Jack gave her a lazy smile which only grew as she gazed at him.

"Jack," she whispered as one of her hands caressed his

cheek, and his heart melted at the sound of his name on her lips.

"Can you forgive me?" he murmured.

"Only if you will do the same for me," came the quiet reply, her lips brushing against his. There was a hint of apprehension in her gaze, as though she feared the separation as much as he.

Words would never be Jack's strong suit, and though he would try for Lily's sake, in that moment, he knew there was a far better way to affirm his feelings. Closing the short distance, Jack captured her lips in another kiss, determined to make certain she felt just how deeply he loved her.

Epilogue

One Month Later

Weather was an uncooperative beast. Of course, anyone with sense knew better than to set store in British weather being cooperating, but love stripped away Jack's good sense. That said, he was certain that, like the rest of the deviations to his plans this Season, the rain was a blessing in disguise.

The raindrops thundered outside, crashing to the streets and soaking the world in gray, but the Ashbrooks' parlor was dry, warm, and comfortable. Jack and Lily's waylaid picnic had been altered, and though they were not blessed with a clear afternoon out in the park, they were surrounded by delicious food, and Lily was cuddled next to him in a manner she would not have employed had they been out in public.

Not an awful turn of events.

The food had been picked over, and Jack sat with a few bits of mending on his lap while Lily read aloud from the latest installment of *Vanity Fair*, and though Jack had grown to enjoy the story, he found her reading of it far more entertaining.

Lily was an abysmal narrator. Not that she was unable to read aloud, but rather, she was unable to do so in a consistent manner once the plot drew her in. Lily's voice dropped away into an incomprehensible whisper as her eyes scanned ahead. Then a gasp, and she grabbed at Jack's forearm. Casting a wide-eyed look at him, she turned her attention back to the page, reading the next sentences aloud at such a rapid pace that Jack was at a loss to follow, but he preferred watching the drama unfold for her than the tale itself.

Jack chuckled to himself, and his thoughts turned to their future. Mr. and Mrs. Kingsley were bound to arrive in London any day now, and the wedding would soon follow—the next morning, if Jack had any say in the matter. However, there were still plenty of details to settle before that blessed day.

"What is that look for?" she asked, as she was wont to do.

Putting another stitch in the shirt on his lap, Jack mentioned the last thing that had passed through his mind. "I was thinking about the townhouse."

Setting aside the serial, Lily rested her head against Jack's shoulder. Having her situated thus made it more difficult to sew, but he'd never say so; the pleasure outweighed the inconvenience.

"I am pleased with the property," said Lily, as she had many times before.

"But you prefer the country."

"I prefer being at your side, and until the waterworks project is complete, that is in London," said Lily. "Once it's finished, we can make other plans, but until then, I am quite happy with Chelsea."

Jack knew this was sensible, but a sliver of worry wriggled its way under his skin. Lily was used to much finer neighborhoods, and they had the money to secure better lodgings.

"No," she said, turning to face him fully. "I know that expression, and I will not allow you to doubt this a moment longer. I have been honest in my feelings on the matter, so there is no reason to fret. I couldn't give a fig if we live in a fashionable quarter. Besides, my parents will not stay in Town long, as they must return to Bristow to welcome their newest grandchild, and we'd be much happier settled next to our family."

Those words stirred up a torrent of feelings Jack hadn't expected to strike at that moment. Warmth settled into his chest that had nothing to do with the fire blazing in the hearth, and his heart felt as though it would expand right out past his ribs. Without Jack ever explaining his feelings for them, Lily simply understood that the Byrneses were family and had adopted them as her own, as they had done with her.

But more than that, the word "family" struck him in a manner it hadn't before. Perhaps it was talk of her brother's forthcoming child or the mention of "our" family, but Jack saw the future unfolding before them, and visions of them sitting thusly with *their* children climbing the furniture and cuddling into their arms filled his thoughts.

No man deserved such joy.

Jack's eyes weren't focused on her or the world around them, but Lily watched as the corners of his lips curled, growing into a grin.

"And what is going through your thoughts now, Mr. Hatcher?" asked Lily with a pert tone and a teasing smile.

Blinking, Jack's gaze moved to her, gazing into her eyes with a warm glow. Taking her left hand in his, he raised it to his lips, pressing a kiss to the ring he'd placed there two weeks prior. "I am very happy."

It was a simple statement, but Lily tucked it away in her heart, treasuring each syllable. There was much in her life that Lily was proud of, but she could not think of a thing that brought her as much joy as seeing this good man find peace.

Jack was not eloquent in such declarations, and Lily expected he never would be, but there were not words enough to match the glowing contentment radiating from him and the spark of pleasure that came to his eyes whenever he looked at her. In all those silent ways, he told her far better than any words how much he loved her, and Lily would not trade them for an endless supply of saccharine declarations.

Leaning closer, Lily paused a hair's breadth from his lips. "I love you."

The words were more for herself than for Jack, and he did not return them; he didn't need to. Day by day, he showed her by action and deed that he loved her as dearly as she did him. Closing the distance, Lily pressed her lips to his, showing Jack the happiness she'd found with him.

About the Author

Born and raised in Anchorage, M.A. Nichols is a lifelong Alaskan with a love of the outdoors. As a child she despised reading but through the love and persistence of her mother was taught the error of her ways and has had a deep, abiding relationship with it ever since.

She graduated with a bachelor's degree in landscape management from Brigham Young University and a master's in landscape architecture from Utah State University, neither of which has anything to do with why she became a writer, but is a fun little tidbit none-the-less. And no, she doesn't have any idea what type of plant you should put in that shady spot out by your deck. She's not that kind of landscape architect. Stop asking.

For more information about M.A. Nichols and her books visit her webpage at www.ma-nichols.com or check out her Goodreads page (www.goodreads.com/manichols). For up to date information and news, visit her Facebook page (www.facebook.com/manicholsauthor).

Exclusive Offer

Join the M.A. Nichols VIP Reader Club at

www.ma-nichols.com

to receive up-to-date information, exclusive offers, and the chance to get free Advance Reader Copies of future books!

Before You Go

Thank you for reading *A Stolen Kiss*!
If you enjoyed it, please write a review on Amazon and Goodreads and help us spread the word.

Printed in Great Britain
by Amazon